Baroness Orczy was t
of Baron Felix Orczy, a ......
composer and conductor. Orczy moved with her parents from
Budapest to Brussels and Paris, where she was educated. She
studied art in London and exhibited work in the Royal
Academy.

Orczy married Montagu Barstow and together they worked
as illustrators and jointly published an edition of Hungarian
folk tales. Orczy became famous in 1905 with the publication
of *The Scarlet Pimpernel* (originally a play co-written with her
husband). Its background of the French Revolution and
swashbuckling hero, Sir Percy Blakeney, was to prove
immensely popular. Sequel books followed and film and TV
versions were later made. Orczy also wrote detective stories.

She died in 1947.

BY THE SAME AUTHOR
ALL PUBLISHED BY HOUSE OF STRATUS

SIR PERCY LEADS THE BAND

Baroness Orczy

HOUSE OF
STRATUS

First published in 1936

Copyright © Sarah Orczy-Barstow Brown

This edition published in 2012 by House of Stratus, an imprint of Stratus Books Ltd., Lisandra House, Fore St., Looe, Cornwall, PL13 1AD, UK.

www.houseofstratus.com

Typeset, printed and bound by House of Stratus.

A catalogue record for this book is available from the British Library and the Library of Congress.

ISBN 0-7551-166-8-2

BOOK I

THE ABBÉ

CHAPTER ONE

The King on His Trial

THE HALL of the Pas Perdus, the precincts of the House of Justice, the corridors, the bureaux of the various officials, judges and advocates were all thronged that day as they had been during all the week, ever since Tuesday when the first question was put to the vote: "Is Louis Capet guilty of conspiring against liberty?" Louis Capet! Otherwise Louis XVI, descendant of a long line of kings of the Grand Monarque of Saint Louis, himself the anointed, the crowned King of France! And now! Arraigned at the bar before his fellow-men, before his one-time devoted subjects, or supposedly devoted, standing before them like any criminal, accused not of murder, or forgery or theft, but of conspiring against liberty.

A king on his trial! And for his life! Let there be no doubt about that. It is a matter of life or death for the King of France. There has been talk, endless talk and debate in the Hall of Justice ever since the eleventh day of December – over a month ago now when Louis first appeared before the bar of the Convention. Fifty-seven questions were put to the accused. "Louis Capet, didst thou do this, that or the other? Didst thou conspire against liberty?" Louis to all the questions gave the simple reply: "No! I did not do that, nor did I do the other. If I did, it was in accordance with the then existing laws of France."

A king on his trial! Heavens above, what a stupendous event! One that had only occurred once before in history – a hundred and fifty years ago when Charles I, King of England, stood at the bar before his people and Parliament, accused by them of conspiring against their liberty. The end of that was regicide. And now once again a king stood before his people accused of conspiring against their liberty. What the end would be, no one doubted for a moment. The paramount significance of the tragedy, the vital importance of what was at stake was reflected in the grave demeanour of the crowd that gathered day after day inside the precincts of the House of Justice. Men of all ages, of all creeds, of every kind of political opinion foregathered in the Salle des Pas Perdus, waited mostly in silence for scraps of news that came filtering through from the hall where a king – once their King – was standing his trial.

They waited for news, longing to see the end of this nerve-racking suspense, yet dreading to hear what the end would be.

On the Monday evening, one month after the opening of this momentous trial, the fifty-seven questions were finally disposed of. Advocate Barrère in a three hour speech, summed up the case and then invited Louis Capet to withdraw. And Louis the unfortunate, once Louis XVI, King of France, now just Louis Capet, was taken back to the Temple Prison where, separated from his wife and children, he could do nothing but await with patience and resignation the final issue of his judges' deliberations, and assist his legal counsels in the preparation of his defence.

And on Tuesday the 15th of January, 1793, the question of whether a King of France was guilty or not guilty of conspiracy was put to the vote. Not one question but three questions were put forward, each to be voted on separately and by every one of the seven hundred and forty-nine members of the National Convention. Is Louis Capet guilty of conspiring against liberty? Shall the sentence pronounced by the National Convention be final, or shall appeal be made to the people? If Louis Capet be found guilty what punishment should be meted out to him? The first two questions were disposed of on the Tuesday. By midday Louis Capet had been voted guilty by an immense majority. The second question took rather longer; the afternoon wore on, the shades of a midwinter evening blotted out the outside world and spread its gloomy mantle over this assembly of men, gathered here to indict their King and to pronounce sentence upon him. It was midnight before the voting on this second question was ended. By a majority of two to one the House decided that its verdict shall be final and that no appeal shall be made to the people. Such an appeal would mean civil war, cry the Extremists, the loud and turbulent Patriots, while the Moderates, the Girondins will have it that the people must not be ignored. But they are outvoted two to one and at the close of this memorable Tuesday, Louis Capet stands definitely guilty of conspiring against the liberty of the people and whatever sentence the National Convention may pronounce upon him shall be final, without appeal.

The loud and turbulent Patriots are full of hope. Marat, the people's friend, has apostrophied them from his bed of sickness, lashed them with his biting tongue: "O crowd of chatterers, can you not *act?*" And they are going to act. Let the third question be put to the vote, and the whole world shall see that Patriots can act as well as talk. So on this Wednesday, January 16th, 1793, they muster up in full force and swarm over the floors of the Salle des Pas Perdus, and of the corridors and committee rooms of the House of Justice. But somehow they are no longer turbulent now. Certain of triumph they appear almost overawed by the immensity of the tragedy which they have brought to a head.

Beyond the precincts of the Hall of Justice, the whole of Paris stands on the tiptoe of expectation. It is a raw midwinter day. The city is wrapped in a grey fog, through which every sound of voice or traffic comes muffled, as if emitted through cotton-wool. Like the noisy elements inside the hall, the people of Paris wait in silence, hushed into a kind of grim stupefaction at this stupendous thing which is going on inside there, and which they, in a measure, have brought about.

In the hall itself the seven hundred and forty-nine deputies are all at their posts. After some talk and orders of the day put forward by one Patriot or another, Danton's proposal that the Convention shall sit in permanent session till the whole business of Louis Capet is finished and done with, is passed by a substantial majority. After which the voting on the third question begins. It is close on eight o'clock in the evening. The ushers in loud shrill voices call up the deputies by name and constituency, one by one: summon each one to mount the tribune and say, on his soul and conscience, what punishment shall be meted out to the accused. And one by one, seven hundred and forty-nine men then mounted the tribune, said their say, justified their verdict and recorded their vote. The whole of that night and subsequent days and nights, from Wednesday evening until Friday afternoon, the procedure went on. Evening faded into night, night yielded to day and day to night again while a king's life hung in the balance. In the grey light of day, through the weary hours of the night, the three portentous words came muffled through the thin curtain of fog which pervaded the hall and dimmed the feeble flickering light of candles. Death! Banishment! Imprisonment till peace with the rest of Europe be signed. The word that came most often from the tribune was death, though often tempered with weak recommendations for mercy; but all day Thursday and most of Friday the balance trembled between banishment and death. Some of the votes were never in doubt, Robespierre's for instance, or that of Danton who disdained to justify his verdict; he stood only for one minute on the tribune, just long enough to say curtly: *"La Mort sans phrases!"* then resumed his seat, folded his arms and went quietly to sleep. "Death without so much talk!" Why talk? Louis Capet has got to die, so why argue?

Was there ever so strange a proceeding? Eye-witnesses, men like Sieyès and Roland have described the scene as one of the most remarkable ever witnessed in the history of the Revolution, and the moment when Philippe d'Orléans, now nicknamed Philippe Égalité, and own kinsman of the accused, boldly voted death on his soul and conscience, the most tense in any history. A strange proceeding indeed! Philippe d'Orléans the traitor, the profligate, casting his vote against his kinsman; and up in the galleries among a privileged crowd a number of smartly dressed ladies, flaunting their laces and tricolour cockades and munching chocolates, while the honourable deputies who had already recorded their votes came to entertain them with small talk and bring them ices and refreshments. Some have cards and pins and prick down the deaths or banishments or imprisonments as they occur, something like race-cards on which with many a giggle they record their bets. Here in the galleries there is quite an element of fashion. No gloom here, no sense of foreboding or impending tragedy. Smart ladies! The beautiful Téroigne de Méricourt, the austere Madame Roland, the youthful Teresia Cabarrus.

At dusk on Friday evening the voting was done. The secretaries sorted the papers and made the count. When this was over President Vergniaud demanded silence. And in a hush so profound that the rustle of a silk dress up in the gallery caused everyone to give a start, he made the solemn declaration: "In the name of the Convention I declare that the punishment it pronounces on Louis Capet is that of death."

CHAPTER TWO

Sentence

SCARCELY were the words out of the President's mouth than the King's advocates came running in. They lodged a protest in his name. They demanded delay and appeal to the people. The latter was promptly rejected – unanimously. Appeal to the people had been put to the vote last Tuesday, and been definitely settled then. Delay might be granted, but for the moment nothing more could be done. Everyone was sick to death of the whole thing. Nerve-racked. Tomorrow should decide.

And it did. Delay or no delay? Patriots said "No." Philippe d'Orléans, kinsman of the accused, said "No!" A few said "Yes!"

But finally, during the small hours of Sunday morning, that point – perhaps the grimmest of the lot – was also settled. "No delay! Death within twenty-four hours." The final count showed a majority of seventy.

The Minister of Justice was sent to the Temple to break the news to the accused. To his credit be it said that he did not like the errand. "What a horrible business!" he was heard to say. But Louis received the news calmly, as a king should. He asked for a delay of three days to prepare himself for death, also for a confessor. The latter request was granted on condition that the confessor should be a man of the Convention's own choosing: but not delay. The verdict had been: "Death within twenty-four hours." There could be no question of respite.

Paris that Sunday morning woke to the news and was appalled. It had been expected, but there are events in this world that are expected, that are known to be certain to come, and yet when they do come they cause stupefaction. And Paris was stupefied. The Extremists rejoiced: the rowdy elements went about shouting *"Vive la Liberté!"* waving tricolour flags, carrying spikes crowned with red caps, but Paris as a whole did not respond. It pondered over the verdict, and shuddered at the murder of Lepelletier the deputy who had put forward the proposal: "No delay! Death within twenty-four hours!" His proposal had been carried by a majority of seventy. It was then two o'clock in the morning, and he went on to Février's in the Palais Royal to get some supper. He had finished eating and was paying his bill, when he was suddenly attacked by an unknown man, said to have once belonged to the King's Guard, who plunged a dagger in the deputy's breast shouting: "Regicide! Take that!" and in the confusion that ensued made good his escape. And the six hundred and ninety-six deputies who had voted for death without a recommendation for mercy shut themselves up in the apartments, being in fear of their lives.

The cafés and restaurants on the other hand did a roaring trade all that day, Sunday Paris, though stupefied, had to be fed, and did feed too, and talked only in whispers – but talked nevertheless. Groups lingered over their coffee and *Fine*, and said the few things that were safe to say, in view of those turbulent Patriots who proclaimed every man, woman or child to be a traitor who showed any sympathy for the "conspirator" Louis Capet. There was also talk of war. England . . . Spain. Especially England, with Burke demanding sanctions against the regicide Republic. It could only be a matter of days now before she declared war. She had been itching to do so ever since Louis Capet had been deprived of his throne.

Ambassador Chauvelin was still in London, but soon he would be recalled and his papers handed courteously to him, for undoubtedly war was imminent. English families residing in France were preparing to leave the country.

But a good many stayed on: men in business, journalists or merely idlers. They mostly dined at Février's in the Palais Royal, the restaurant *à la mode*, where those deputies who were most in the public eye could always be met with on a Sunday. Robespierre and his friend Desmoulins, the elegant Saint-Just, President Vergniaud and others dined there regularly and foreign newspaper correspondents frequented the place in the hope of picking up bits of gossip for their journals. On this particular Sunday there were about a dozen strangers gathered round the large table in the centre, where a somewhat meagre dinner was being served in view of the existing shortage of provisions and the penury that already stalked the countryside and more particularly the cities. But in spite of the meagreness of the fare, good temper was not lacking round the board where the strangers were sitting. Most of them were English and they tackled the scraggy meat and thin wine put before them, with the happy-go-lucky tolerance that is so essentially English.

"What say you to beef with mustard?" one of the men quoted while he struggled with a tough piece of boiled pork garnished with haricot beans.

"I like it passing well," his neighbour completed the quotation, "but for the moment I have a fancy for a Lancashire hot-pot, such as my old lady makes at home."

"Well!" broke in a man obviously from the north, "Sunday at my home is the day for haggis, and with a wineglassful of good Scotch whisky poured over it, I tell you my friends . . ."

Two men were sitting together at a table close by. One of them said, speaking in French and with a contemptuous shrug: "These English! Their one subject of conversation is food."

The other, without commenting on this, merely remarked: "You understand English then, Monsieur le Baron?"

"Yes. Don't you?"

"I never had any lessons," the other replied vaguely.

The two men were a strange contrast both in appearance and in speech. The one who had been addressed as Monsieur le Baron – it was not yet a crime to use a title in Republican France – was short and broad-shouldered. He had a florid face, sensual lips and prominent eyes. He spoke French with a hardly perceptible guttural accent, which to a sensitive ear might have betrayed his German or Austrian origin. His manner and way of speaking were abrupt and fussy: his short, fat hands with the spatulated fingers were forever fidgeting with something, making bread pellets or drumming with obvious nervosity on the table. The other was tall, above the average at any rate in this country: his speech was deliberate, almost pedantic in its purity of expression like a professor delivering a lecture at the Sorbonne: his hands, though slender, betrayed unusual strength. He scarcely ever moved them. Both men were very simply dressed, in black coats and cloth breeches, but while Monsieur le Baron's coat fitted him where it touched, the other's complete suit was nothing short of a masterpiece of the tailor's art.

Just then there rose a general clatter in the room: chairs scraping against the tiled floor, calls for hats and coats, comprehensive leave- takings, and more or less noisy exodus through the swing-doors. Robespierre and Desmoulins as they went out passed the time of day with Monsieur le Baron.

"*Eh bien*, de Batz," Robespierre said to him with a laugh, "I have won my bet, haven't I? Louis Capet has got his desserts."

De Batz shrugged his fat shoulders.

"Not yet," he retorted dryly.

When those two had gone, and were immediately followed by Vergniaud and St. Just, he who was called de Batz leaned back in his chair and gave a deep sigh of relief.

"Ah!" he said, "the air is purer now that filthy crowd has gone."

"You appeared to be on quite friendly terms with Monsieur Robespierre anyway," the other remarked with a cool smile.

"Appearances are often deceptive, my dear Professor," De Batz retorted. "Ah?"

"Now take your case. I first met you at a meeting of the Jacobin Club, or was it the Feuillants? I forget which of those pestiferous gatherings you honoured with your presence; but anyway, had I only judged by appearances I would have avoided you like the plague, like I avoid that dirty crowd of assassins. . ."

"But you were there yourself, Monsieur le Baron," the Professor observed.

"I went out of curiosity, my friend, as you did and as a number of respectable-looking people did also. I sized up those respectable people very quickly. I had no use for them. They were just the sort of nincompoops whom Danton's oratory soon turns into potential regicides. But I accosted you that evening because I saw that you were different."

"Why different?"

"Your cultured speech and the cleanliness of your collar."

"You flatter me, sir."

"We talked of many things at first, if you remember. We touched on philosophy and on the poets, on English rhetoric and Italian art: and I went home that night convinced that I had met a kindred spirit, whom I hoped to meet again. When you entered this place an hour ago, and honoured me by allowing me to sit at your table, I felt that Chance had been benign to me."

"Again you flatter me, sir."

The room in the meanwhile had soon become deserted. There remained only de Batz and the Professor at one table, and in the farther corner a group of three men, two of whom were playing dominoes and the third reading a newspaper. De Batz's restless eyes took a quick survey of the room, then he leaned over the table and fixed his gaze on the other's placid face.

"I propose to flatter you still more, my friend," he said, sinking his voice to a whisper. "Nay! I may say to honour you . . ."

"Indeed?"

"By asking you to help me . . ."

"To do what?"

"To save the King."

"A heavy task, sir."

"But not impossible. Listen. I have five hundred friends who will be posted to-morrow in different houses along the route between the Temple and the Place de la Révolution. At a signal from me, they will rush the carriage in which only His Majesty and his confessor will be sitting, they will drag the King out of it, and in the melée smuggle him into a house close by, all the inhabitants of which are in my pay. You are silent, sir?" de Batz went on, his thick guttural voice hoarse with emotion. "Of what are you thinking?" he added impatiently, seeing that the other remained impassive, almost motionless.

"Of General Santerre," the Professor replied, "and his eighty thousand armed men. Are they also in your pay?"

"Eighty thousand?" de Batz rejoined with a sneer: "Bah!"

"Do you doubt the figure?"

"No! I do not. I know all about Santerre and his eighty thousand armed men, his bristling cannon that are already being set up on the Place de la Révolution, and his cannoneers who will stand by with match burning. But you must take surprise into consideration. The unexpected. The sudden panic. The men off their guard. As a matter of fact I could tell you of things that occurred before my very eyes when that daredevil Englishman whom they call the Scarlet Pimpernel snatched condemned prisoners from the very tumbrils that took them to execution. Surely you know about that?"

"I do," the Professor put in quietly, "but I don't suppose that those tumbrils were escorted by eighty thousand armed men. There is such a thing in this world as the impossible, you know, Monsieur le Baron: things that are beyond man's power to effect."

"Then you won't help me?"

"You have not yet told me what you want me to do."

"I am not going to ask you to risk your life," de Batz said, trying to keep the suspicion of a sneer out of his tone. "There are five hundred of us for that, and one more or less wouldn't make any difference to our chance of success. But there is one little matter in which you could render our cause a signal service, and incidentally help to save His Majesty the King."

"What may that be, sir?"

A pause, after which Batz resumed with seeming irrelevance: "There is an Irish priest, the Abbé Edgeworth, you have met him perhaps?"

"Yes! I know him."

"He is known by renown to the King. The Convention, as perhaps you are aware, has acceded to His Majesty's desire for a confessor, but those inhuman brutes have made it a condition that that confessor shall be of their own choosing. We know what that means. Some apostate priest whose presence would distress and perhaps unnerve His Majesty when he will have need of all his courage. You agree with me?"

"Of course."

"Equally, of course, we want someone to be by the side of His Majesty during that harrowing drive from the Temple, and to prepare and encourage him for the *coup* which we are contemplating.

"The Abbé Edgeworth is the man we want for this mission. His loyalty is unquestioned, so is his courage. Cléry, the King's devoted valet, has tried to get in touch with him, and so have His Majesty's advocates, but they failed to find him. He is hiding somewhere in Paris, that we know. Until fairly recently he was a lecturer at the Sorbonne. I understand that you too, Monsieur le Professeur, have graced that seat of learning. Anyway, I thought that you might make enquiries in that direction. If you succeed," de Batz concluded, his voice thick with excitement, "you will have done your share in saving our King."

There was a moment's pause while de Batz, taking out his handkerchief from his pocket, wiped his moist hands and his forehead which was streaming with perspiration. Seeing that the Professor still sat silent and impassive he said, with obvious impatience: "Surely you are not hesitating, Monsieur le Professeur! A little thing like that! And for such a cause! I would scour Paris myself, only that my hands are full. And my five hundred adherents—"

"You should apply to one of them, Monsieur le Baron," the other broke in quietly.

Monsieur le Baron gave a jump.

"You don't mean to say that you hesitate?" he uttered in a hoarse whisper.

"I do more than that, Monsieur le Baron. I refuse."

"Refuse? . . . ref—"

De Batz was choking. His passed his thick finger round the edge of his cravat.

"Refuse what?" he queried, trying to speak calmly.

"To lend a hand in dragging the Abbé Edgeworth into this affair."

De Batz was striving to control his temper: under his breath he muttered the words "Poltroon! Coward!" once or twice. Aloud he said:

"You are afraid?"

"I am a man of peace," the Professor replied.

"I don't believe it," de Batz protested. "No man with decent feeling in him would refuse to render this service. Good God, man! You are not risking your life, not like I and my friends are willing to do. You can help us, I know. You must have a reason – a valid reason – for refusing to do so. As I say, you wouldn't be risking your life . . ."

"Not mine, but that of an innocent and a good man."

"What the devil do you mean?"

"You are proposing to throw the Abbé Edgeworth to the wolves."

"I am not. I am proposing to give him the chance of doing his bit in the work of saving the life of his King. He will thank me on his knees for this."

"He probably would, for he is of the stuff that martyrs are made. But I will not help you to send him to his death."

With that he rose, ready to go, and reached for his hat and coat. They hung on a peg just above de Batz's head, and de Batz made no movement to get out of the way.

"Don't go, man," he said earnestly, "not yet. Listen to me. You don't understand. It is all perfectly easy. In less than an hour I shall blow who the apostate priest is whom the Convention are sending to His Majesty. I know all those fellows. Most of them are in my pay. They are useful, if distinctly dirty, tools. To substitute our abbé for the man chosen by the Convention will entail no risk, present no difficulties, and will cost me less than the price of a good dinner. Now what do you say?"

"What I said before," the other rejoined firmly. "Whoever accompanies Louis XVI to the guillotine, if he be other than the one chosen by the Convention, will be a marked man. His life will not be worth twelve hours' purchase!"

"The guillotine? The guillotine?" de Batz retorted hotly. "Who talks of the guillotine and of Louis XVI in one breath? I tell you, man, that our King will never mount the steps of the guillotine. There are five hundred of us worth a hundred thousand of Santerre's armed men who will drag him out of the clutches of those assassins."

"May I have my coat?" was the Professor's quiet rejoinder.

His calmness brought de Batz's temper to boiling point. He jumped to his feet, snatched down the Professor's coat from its peg and threw it down with a vicious snarl on the nearest chair. The Professor, seemingly quite unperturbed, picked it up, put it on and with a polite *"Au revoir,* Monsieur le Baron!" to which the latter did not deign to respond, he walked quietly out of the restaurant.

CHAPTER THREE

The League

IT was about an hour or two later. In a sparsely furnished room on the second floor of an apartment house in the Rue du Bac five men had met: four of them were sitting about on more or less rickety chairs, while the fifth stood by the window, gazing out into the dusk and on the gloomy outlook of the narrow street. He was tall above the average, was this individual, still dressed in the black, well-tailored suit which he had worn during his dinner in company with the Austrian Baron at Février's, and which suggested a professional man: a professor perhaps, at the university.

The outlook through the window was indeed gloomy. But outside depression did not apparently weigh on the spirits of the men. There was no look of despondency on their faces, rather the reverse, they looked eager and excited, and the back of the tall man in black with the broad shoulders and narrow hips suggested energy rather than dejection. After a time he turned away from the window and found a perch on the edge of a broken-down truckle bed that stood in a corner of the room.

"Well!" he began addressing the others collectively, "you heard what that madman said?"

"Most of it," one of them replied.

"He has a crack-brained scheme of stirring up five hundred madcaps into shouting and rushing the carriage in which the King will be driven from prison to the scaffold. Five hundred lunatics egged on by that candidate for Bedlam, trying to reach that carriage which will be escorted by eighty thousand armed men! It would be ludicrous if it were not so tragic."

"One wonders," remarked one of them, "who those wretched five hundred are."

"Young royalists," the other replied, "all of them known to the Committees. As a matter of fact I happen to know that most of them, if not all, will receive a visit from the police during the early hours of the morning, and will not be allowed to leave their apartments till after the execution of the King."

"Heavens, man!" the eldest of the four men exclaimed, "how did you know that?"

"It was quite simple, my dear fellow, and quite easy. The crowd filed out as you know directly the final verdict was proclaimed. It was three o'clock in the morning. Everybody there was almost delirious with excitement. No one took notice of anybody else. The President and the other judges went into the refreshment-room which is reserved for them. You know the one I mean. It is in the Tour de César, at the back of the Hall of Justice. It has no door, only an archway. There was still quite a crowd moving along the corridors. I got as near the archway as I could, and I heard Vergniaud give the order that every inhabitant of the city, known to have royalist or even moderate tendencies, must be under police surveillance in their own apartments until midday."

"Percy, you are wonderful!" the young man exclaimed fervently.

"Tony, you are an idiot!" the other retorted with a laugh.

"Then we may take it that our Austrian friend's scheme will just fizzle out like a damp squib?"

"You had never thought, had you, Blakeney, that we . . ."

"God forbid!" Sir Percy broke in emphatically. "I wouldn't risk your precious lives in what common sense tells me is an impossible scheme. It may be quixotic. I dare say it is; but what in Heaven's name does that megalomaniac hope to accomplish? To break through a cordon of troops ten deep? Folly, of course! But even supposing he and his five hundred did succeed in approaching the carriage, what do they hope to do *afterwards?* Do they propose to fight the entire garrison of the city which is a hundred and thirty thousand strong? Does he imagine for a moment that the entire population of Paris will rise as one man and suddenly take up the cause of kingship? Folly, of course! Folly of the worst type, because the first outcome of a hand-to-hand fight in the streets would be the murder of the King in the open street by some unknown hand. Isn't that so?"

They all agreed. Their chief was not in the habit of talking lengthily on any point. That he did so on this occasion was proof of how keenly he felt about the whole thing. Did he wish to justify before these devoted followers of his, his inaction with regard to the condemned King? I do not think so. He was accustomed to blind obedience – that was indeed the factor that held the League of the Scarlet Pimpernel so indissolubly together – and three of the four men who were here with him to-day, Lord Anthony Dewhurst, Sir Andrew Ffoulkes and Lord Hastings, were his most enthusiastic followers.

Be that as it may, he did speak lengthily on this occasion, and placed before his friends a clear expose of the situation on the morrow as far as any attempt at rescuing the King was concerned. But there was something more. The others knew there was something else coming, or their chief would not have given them the almost imperceptible signal when he left the restaurant to wait for him in this squalid apartment, which had for some time been their accustomed meeting place. They waited in silence and presently Sir Percy spoke again.

"Putting, therefore, aside the question of the King whose fate, of course, horrifies us all, the man we have got to think of now is that unfortunate priest whom de Batz wants to drag forcibly into this scheme, and who will surely lose his head if our League does not intervene."

"The Abbé Edgeworth?" one of them said.

"Exactly. Edgeworth is of Irish extraction, which adds to our interest in him. Still! That isn't the point. He is a very good man, who has worked unremittingly in the slums of Paris. Anyway, we are not going to throw him to the wolves, are we?"

They all nodded assent. And Ffoulkes added: "Of course not if you say so, Percy."

"I shall know towards morning whether de Batz has arranged to substitute him for the man whom the Convention has chosen as confessor for the King. As soon as I do get definite information about that I will get in touch with you. We will take our stand at seven o'clock on the Place de la Révolution, at the angle of the Rue Égalité which used to be the Rue Royale. That will be the nearest point we can get to the guillotine. After the King's head has fallen there will be an immense commotion in the crowd and a rush for those horrible souvenirs which the executioner will sell to the highest bidder. It makes one's gorge rise even to think of that. But it will be our opportunity. Between the five of us we'll soon get hold of Edgeworth and get him to safety."

"Where do you think of taking him?" Lord Tony asked.

"To Choisy. You remember the Levets?"

"Of course. I like old Levet. He is a sportsman."

"I like him too," Sir Andrew added, "and I am terribly sorry for the poor old mother. I don't mind the girl either, but I don't trust that sweetheart of hers."

"Which one?" Blakeney queried with a smile. "Pretty little Blanche Levet has quite a number."

"Ffoulkes means that doctor fellow," here interposed the youngest of the three men, Lord St. John Devinne, who had sat silently and obviously morose up to now, taking no part in the conversation between his chief and his other friends. He was a good-looking, tall young man of the usual high-bred English type, and could have been called decidedly handsome but for a certain look of obstinacy coupled with weakness, which lurked in his grey eyes and was accentuated by the somewhat effeminate curve of his lips.

"Pradel isn't a bad sort really," Sir Andrew responded. "Perhaps a little to fond of spouting about *Liberté*, *Égalité*, and all the rest of it."

"I can't stand the brute," Devinne muttered sullenly. "He is always talking and arguing and telling the unwashed crowds what fine fellows they really are, if only they knew it, and what good times they are going to have in the future."

He shrugged and added with bitter contempt:"*Liberté? Égalité?* What consummate rot!"

"Well!" Sir Percy interposed in his quiet, incisive voice, "isn't there just something to be said for it? The under-dog has had a pretty bad time in France. He is snarling now, and biting. But Pradel – I know him – is an intellectual, he will never be an assassin."

Devinne shrugged again and murmured: "I am not so sure about that." While Lord Tony broke in with his cheery laugh and said: "I'll tell you what's the matter with our friend Pradel."

"What?" Sir Andrew asked.

"He is in love."

"Of course. With little Blanche Levet."

"Not he. He is in love with Cécile de la Rodière."

This was received with derision and incredulity.

"What rubbish!" Sir Andrew said.

"Not really?" Hastings queried.

But Blakeney assented: "I am afraid it's true."

While Devinne broke in hotly: "He wouldn't dare!"

"There's nothing very daring in being in love, my dear fellow," Sir Percy remarked dryly.

"Then why did you say you were *afraid* it was true," the other retorted.

"Because that sort of thing invariably leads to trouble even in these days."

"Can you see Madame la Marquise," was Sir Andrew Ffoulkes' somewhat bitter comment on the situation, "and her son François, if they should happen to find out that the village doctor is in love with Mademoiselle de la Rodière?"

"I can," Devinne remarked spitefully. "There would be the good old story, which I must say has something to be said for it: a sound thrashing for Monsieur Pradel at the hands of Monsieur le Marquis, and . . ."

He paused, and a dark flush spread over his good-looking face. Chancing to look up he had met his chief's glance which rested upon him with an expression that was difficult to define. It was good- humoured, pitying, slightly sarcastic, and, anyway, reduced the obstinate young man to silence.

There was silence for a moment or two. Somehow Lord St. John Devinne's attitude, his curt argument with the chief, seemed to have thrown a kind of damper on the eagerness of the others. Blakeney after a time consulted his watch and then said very quietly: "It is time we got back to business."

At once they were ready to listen. The word "business" meant so much to them: excitement, adventure, the spice of their lives. Only Devinne remained silent and sullen, never once looking up in the direction of his chief.

"Listen, you fellows," Blakeney now resumed in his firm, most authoritative tone, "if you hear nothing from me between now and to-morrow morning, it will mean that they have roped in that unfortunate abbé. Well, we are not going to allow that. He is a splendid chap, who does a great deal of good work among the poor, and if he allows himself to be roped in, it will be from an exaggerated sense of duty. Anyway, if you don't hear from me, we'll meet, as I said, at seven o'clock sharp at the angle of the Rue Égalité and the Place de la Révolution. After that, all you'll have to do will be to stick to me as closely as you can, and if we get separated we meet again at Choisy. Make yourselves look as demmed a set of ruffians as you can. That shouldn't be difficult."

Again he paused before concluding: "If on the other hand, the King is not to be accompanied to the scaffold by the Abbé Edgeworth, I will bring or send word to you here, not later than five o'clock in the morning. Remember that my orders to you all for the night are: don't get yourselves caught. If you do, there will be trouble for us all."

The others smiled. He then nodded to them, said briefly: "That is all. Good night! Bless you!" and the next moment was gone. The others listened intently for a while, trying to catch the sound of his footsteps down the stone staircase, but none came, and they went over to the window, and looked out into the street. Through the fog and driving sleet they could just perceive the tall figure of their chief as he went across the road and then disappeared in the night.

With one accord three gallant English gentlemen murmured a fervent: "God guard him!" But Devinne still remained silent, and after a little while went out of the room.

Lord Tony said, speaking to both the others:

"Do you trust that fellow Devinne?" and then added emphatically: "I do not."

My Lord Hastings shook his head thoughtfully.

"I wonder what is the matter with him."

"I can tell you that," Lord Tony observed. "He is in love with Mademoiselle de la Rodière. He met her in Paris five years ago, before all this revolutionary trouble had begun. Her mother and, of course, her brother won't hear of her marrying a foreigner, any more than a village doctor, and Devinne, you know, is a queer-tempered fellow. He cannot really look on that fellow Pradel as a serious rival, and yet, as you could see just now, he absolutely hates him and vents his spleen upon him. His attitude to the chief I call unpardonable. That is why I do not trust him."

Whereupon Sir Andrew murmured under his breath: "If we have a traitor in the camp, then God help the lot of us."

21

CHAPTER FOUR

January Twenty-first

THE streets of Paris on that morning were silent as the grave: only at the gate of the Temple prison, when the King stepped out into the street, accompanied by the Abbé Edgeworth, and entered the carriage that was waiting for him, were there a few feeble cries of "Mercy! Mercy!" uttered mostly by women. No other sound came from the crowd that had assembled round the Temple gate. All along the route too, there was silence. No one dared speak or utter a cry of compassion, for every man was in terror of his neighbour, who might denounce him as a traitor to the Republic. The windows of all the houses were closed, and no face was to be seen at them, peering out into the street. Eighty thousand men at arms stood aligned, between the prison and the Place de la Revolution, where the guillotine awaited the royal victim of this glorious revolution. Through that cordon no man or body could break, and at every street corner cannons bristled and the cannoneers stood waiting with match burning, silent and motionless like stone statues rather than men. Nor was there sound of wheel traffic along the streets, only the rumble of one carriage, in which sat the descendant of sixteen kings about to die a shameful death by the sentence of his people. Louis sat in the carriage listening to Abbé Edgeworth who read out to him the Prayers for the Dying.

At the angle of the Boulevard Bonne Nouvelle and the Rue de la Lune on a hillock made up of debris from recent excavations, a short stout, florid man was standing, wrapped in a dark cape. It was the Baron de Batz. He had been standing here for the past three hours, trying vainly to keep himself warm by stamping his feet on the frozen ground. Two hours ago a couple of young men came down the narrow Rue de la Lune and joined the lonely watcher. There was some whispered conversation between the three of them, after which they all remained silent at their post, and from the height on which they stood, they scanned the crowd to right and left of them with ever increasing anxiety. But there was no sign of any of the five hundred accomplices who were to aid de Batz in his crazy scheme of saving the King. As a matter of fact de Batz didn't know that in the early hours of the morning most of those five hundred had been roused from sleep by peremptory knocks at their door. A couple of gendarmes had then entered their apartment with orders to keep them under observation, and not to allow them outside their houses until past midday. De Batz and the two friends who were with him now had spent the night talking and scheming in a tavern on the Boulevard and thus escaped this domiciliary visit. They could not understand what had happened, and as time went on they fell to cursing their fellow-conspirators for their treachery or cowardice. Time went on, leaden-footed but inexorable. From the direction of the Temple prison there had already come the ominous sound of the roll of drums, soon followed by the rumble of carriage wheels.

Fog and sleet blurred the distant outline of the Boulevard but soon through the vaporous mist de Batz and his friends could perceive the vanguard of the military cortege. First the mounted gendarmerie, barring the whole width of the street, then the grenadiers of the National Guard, then the artillery, followed by the drummers, and finally the carriage itself, hermetically closed with shutters against the windows, and round it and behind it more and more troops, more cannon and drummers and grenadiers. De Batz and his friends saw the march past. Luckily for them their five hundred adherents were not there to shout and wave their arms and attempt to break through a cordon of soldiery stronger than any that had ever marched through the streets of a city before. The three men were soon submerged in the crowd that moved and surged in the direction of the Place de la Révolution.

Here in front of the guillotine the carriage came to a halt. The Place de la Révolution behind the troops was crowded with idlers who were trying to get a view of the awe-inspiring spectacle. It was a great thing to see a king on trial for his life. It was a still greater thing to see him die.

The carriage door was opened. General Santerre commanded a general beating of drums as the King of France mounted the steps of the guillotine. The Abbé Edgeworth was close beside his King, still murmuring the Prayers for the Dying.

It was all over in a moment. Louis tried to say a few words to his people protesting his innocence, but Santerre cried *"Tambours!"* once more and the roll of drums drowned those last words of the dying monarch. The axe fell. There were shouts of *"Vive la République!"* there were caps raised on bayonets, hats were waved, and an excited crowd made a rush for the scaffold as the executioner, held up the dead monarch's head. Handkerchiefs were dipped in the blood. Locks of hair were cut off the head and sold by the executioner for pieces of silver. There followed half an hour of frantic excitement, during which men shrieked and women screamed, men tumbled over one another trying to rush up the steps of the guillotine, and were hurled down again by the executioner and his aides, while missiles of every kind flew over the heads of this singing, waving, tumultuous mob. The din was incessant and drowned the intermittent roll of drums and the shouts of command from the officers to the soldiery.

And throughout all this uproar the Abbé Edgeworth remained on his knees, on the spot where last he had had a sight of his King, and had urged this son of St. Louis to mount serenely up to heaven. He paid no attention to all the wild screaming and roaring, or to the occasional cries: *"À la lanterne le calotin!"* which were hurled threateningly at his calm kneeling figure.

"À moi le calotin!" came at one time with a roar like that of

an unchained bull, quite close to his ear.

"*Non, à moi!*"

"*À moi! À moi!*"

It just went through the Abbé's mind that some in the crowd were thirsting for his blood, that they would presently drag him to the guillotine, and that he would be sent to his death in just the same way as his King had been. But the thought did not frighten him. He went on mumbling his prayers, until suddenly he felt himself seized round the shoulders and lifted off his knees, while a frantic crowd still cried: "*À lanterne le calotin!*" in the intervals of roaring with laughter.

In the excitement of securing relics the tumultuous crowd forgot the *calotin*, so wild a rush was there for the platform of the guillotine, where the gruesome auction was about to take place. The Abbé by now was only half conscious. He felt the pushing and the jostling all round him, and then a heavy cloak or shawl was wrapped all round him, through which all the hideous sounds became more and more muffled and subdued, till they ceased altogether, and he finally completely lost consciousness.

On the Place de la Révolution, this half-hour of frantic excitement gradually passed away. Presently the troops departed and the crowd gradually dispersed. Men returned to their usual avocations, went to restaurants and to cafes, bought, sold and bartered, as if this 21st day of January, 1793 had not been one of the most stupendous ones in the whole course of history.

In the Hall of the Convention members of the Government rubbed their hands together, and deputies called to one another across the room: "*C'est fait, c'est fait!* It is done!" The great thing is done. A king has died on the scaffold like a common criminal for having conspired against the liberty of his people.

It was not until evening that the Convention in Committee decided that the priest who had received the last confession of Louis Capet had better be put out of the way. He was not the man whom the Government had chosen for the purpose. Who knows what strange and uncomfortable things Louis Capet may have confided to him at the last? Anyway he was better dead than alive, the committee decided, and the police was instructed to proceed at once with his arrest.

But somehow or other in the turmoil which immediately followed the execution of Louis Capet, the Abbé Edgeworth had disappeared.

CHAPTER FIVE

The Levets of Choisy

THE Levet family at this time was composed of four members. The old man Charles – he was actually not more than fifty but had always been known as "old Levet" as against his eldest son "young Levet," of whom more anon. The old man, then, was by profession a herbalist; his work took him out into the meadows and the mountains and along river banks to collect the medicinal herbs required by the druggists. This kind of life – lonely of necessity for the most part – had made him silent and introspective. He had lived with Nature and knew her every mood: nothing in her frightened him: frosts, snows, thunderstorms were his friends. He did not fear them: he communed with them. Outside nature, two loves had filled his life: his wife and his eldest son. Young Levet, who was a lieutenant in the Royal Guard, was killed while defending the Tuileries attacked by the mob in August '92. Old Levet was never the same man after that. Sparing of words before, he became taciturn and morose. His wife never recovered from the shock. She had a paralytic stroke and had hovered between life and death ever since, unable to speak, unable to move, her great dark eyes alone reflecting the mental anguish which news from Paris of the horrors of the Revolution caused to her enfeebled mind. Both she and her husband, like the beloved eldest son, were ardent royalists, and poor Henriette Levet had very nearly died when she heard other members of her family or friends speak of the trial of the King and the possibility of his death.

The second and now only son of the Levets, Augustin, was a priest, attached to Saint-Sulpice. Like his father he was sparing of words save in the exercise of his calling. Whatever time he was able to spare from his duties in the parish, he spent with his mother, reading to her from books of devotion or the *Lives of the Saints*, in a dull, dispassionate voice from which the poor sick woman did not seem to derive much comfort. On the other hand, Blanche, the daughter of the Levets, did her best to bring an atmosphere not exactly of cheerfulness, as that seemed impossible, but of distraction and of brightness into the Levet household. She was pretty, not yet twenty, and young men gathered round her like flies round a honey-pot. Her brother's constant admonitions that she should take life seriously had little effect on her mercurial temperament. In order not to come in conflict with her family and most of the friends who frequented her father's house, she professed enthusiasm for the royalist cause, and as she had a quick, inventive brain she knew how to exhibit loyalty for the King and horror at his misfortunes. But it was all very much on the surface; her political views, such as they were, did not interfere with her ready acceptance of the homage of young men of avowedly revolutionary opinions such, for instance, as Louis Maurin, the young lawyer who was very much in love with Blanche and very much in awe of her papa, two reasons which caused him to keep his way of thinking to himself. Old Levet did not actually forbid Louis Maurin the house, but he did not encourage the young man's visits; however, when he did come, which was as often as he dared, Louis was very discreet, and Blanche's provocative smile caused him to endure patiently the old man's wrathful glances, whenever politics cropped up as subject of conversation.

As a matter of fact Blanche did no more than flirt with young Maurin, as she did with anything that wore breeches and avowed admiration for her. The youth of Choisy mostly did. All except the local doctor, Simon Pradel of Provençal parentage, erudite, good-looking, athletic, and immensely popular in the commune where, with a small fortune left to him by an uncle whom he had never seen, he had founded and endowed a hospital for sick children. He came frequently to the house in his capacity as doctor to Madame Levet: the poor woman's large eyes spoke the welcome that her lips could not utter, and he was the only man with whom old Levet cared to have what he called a talk, which meant that he listened with sympathy and even an occasional smile to what the young doctor had to say.

Blanche did more than listen on those occasions, and both with smiles and glances she showed Pradel that his visits were welcome, although, as with all her admirers, she did no more than flirt with this one also. But strangely enough the young man remained impervious to the spoilt beauty's blandishments, and his manner towards her was no different to that which he displayed towards Marie Bachelier, the maid of all work. In Choisy itself Pradel was called by some a misanthrope and even a woman-hater, but there were others who declared that they had seen Dr. Pradel roaming o' nights in the purlieus of the Château de la Rodière, in the hope, so they said, of catching a glimpse of Mademoiselle Cécile. Some of this tittle-tattle did not fail to reach pretty Blanche Levet's ears, and it is an uncontrovertible axiom that pique will always enkindle love. Jealousy too played its part in this sudden wakening of Blanche's unsophisticated heart. Certain it is that what had been at first little else than warmhearted sympathy for the young doctor became something very like infatuation, almost in the turn of a hand.

CHAPTER SIX

News

THIS 21st day of January had been one of unmitigated terror and despair for the inmates of the Levets' house at Choisy. Old Levet had gone out quite early in the morning. With snow on the ground and a fog lying thick over the river and the meadows he could not gather herbs and simples and follow his usual avocation. What he wanted above all, however, was to be alone, and then to wander into the town in search of news. And he knew that he would have to break that news to his wife. If he didn't tell her, she would guess, and when she knew she would surely die.

And so the old man – really old now though he was no more than fifty – wandered out into the streets of Choisy alone, communing with himself, trying all in vain to steel himself against the awful blow that was sure to fall. All the morning he wandered aimlessly. But at ten o'clock he came to a halt. There was something in the air that told him that the awesome deed was accomplished: it was a distant rumbling that sounded like the roll of thunder; but Levet knew in his heart that it was the roll of drums, announcing to the world that the head of a King of France had fallen under the guillotine. And in his heart he felt acute physical pain, and a sudden intense hatred for the people all around him. Old Levet fled down the street. It led to the river and the bridge. At the bridge-head he stopped. There was a cornerstone there he sat down on it; and waited. He had risen very early in the morning, and when he opened the front door of his house, he saw a note weighted down with a stone lying on the doorstep. He stooped and picked it up and read it, well knowing where the note came from.

He had had several like it before, usually giving him instructions how to help in a deed of mercy. He had always been ready to help and to obey those instructions for they came from a man whom he only knew vaguely as a professor at some university, but whom he respected above all men he had ever come across. Charles Levet had always given what help he could, often at considerable risk to himself.

The note to-day also gave him instructions, very simple ones this time. All it said was: "Wait at the bridge-head from noon till dusk." It was only ten o'clock as yet, but old Levet didn't care. What were hours to him, now that such an awful calamity had sullied the fair name of France forever? He was numb with cold and fatigue, but he didn't care. He just sat there, waiting and watching, with lacklustre eyes, the stream of traffic go by over the bridge.

A distant church clock had struck four when out of the crowd of passers-by two figures detached themselves and made straight for the corner-stone where old Levet was sitting, waiting patiently. A tall figure and a short one: two men, both dressed in black and wrapped in heavy capes against the cold. Levet shook himself out of his torpor. The taller of the two men helped him to struggle to his feet, and then said: "This is the Abbé Edgeworth, Charles. He was with His Majesty until the last."

"We'll go straight home," Levet responded simply. "It is cold here, and Monsieur l'Abbé is welcome."

Without another word the three men started to walk back through the town. It was characteristic of Levet that he made no further comment, nor did he ask a question. He walked briskly, ahead of the other two, looking neither to right nor left. The priest appeared to be in a state of exhaustion; his tall friend held him tightly by the arm, to enable him to walk at all. At a distance of some hundred metres or so from his house old Levet came to a halt. He waited till the other two came close to him, then he said simply: "My wife is very ill. She knows nothing yet. Perhaps she guesses. But I must prepare her. Will you wait here?"

It was quite dark now, and the fog very dense. Levet's shrunken figure was quickly lost to view.

CHAPTER SEVEN

Monsieur le Professeur

THE Levet's house stood about four metres back from the road, behind a low wall which was surmounted by an iron railing. An iron grille gave access to a tiny front garden, intersected by a narrow brick path which led to the front door. Charles Levet went into the house, closing the door noiselessly. He took off his cloak, and went straight into the sitting-room. It adjoined his wife's bedroom. The double communicating doors were wide open, and he could see the invalid stretched out on her bed, with her thin arms spread outside the coverlet. Her great dark eyes looked agonisingly expectant. Her son Augustin was on his knees beside the bed, murmuring half-audible prayers. As soon as she caught sight of her husband, she guessed that all was over, and that the unforgivable crime had been committed. Old Levet knew that she guessed. He came quickly to the bedside. An ashen-grey hue spread over the dying woman's face and a film gathered over her eyes.

"The doctor," old Levet commanded, speaking to his son.

"Too late," Augustin responded without rising from his knees: "her soul has fled to God!" He turned over a page in his book of devotion and began reciting the Prayers for the Dead.

Levet stooped and kissed his dead wife's forehead. Then he reverently closed her eyes. The shock, even though she had expected it, had killed her. The death of her eldest son had stretched her on a bed of sickness, the death of her King had brought about the end. The horror of the deed the knowledge of the appalling sacrilege had snapped the attenuated thread that held her to life.

Levet broke in, with some impatience, on his son's orisons: "Where is your sister?" he asked.

"She went out a few moments ago to fetch Pradel. I could see that my mother was passing away, so I sent her."

"She shouldn't have gone out alone at night, in this fog, too . . ."

"She wasn't alone," the young priest rejoined, "Louis Maurin was with her."

At the mention of the name the old man flared up: "You don't mean to tell me that to-day of all days, that renegade was in my house?"

Augustin gave an indifferent shrug. His father went on with unabated vehemence: "With your mother lying on the point of death, Augustin, you should not have allowed this outrage."

"Communion with the dying," the priest retorted, "was of greater import than political quarrels. Maurin didn't stay long," he went on; "I had to send for Pradel, I wanted him to go. But Blanche insisted on going herself. But what does it all matter, father? In face of what happened today what does anything matter in this sinful world?"

Charles Levet remained standing, silent and almost motionless by the bedside of his dead wife. Then he turned abruptly and went through the sitting-room out into the street. Some two hundred metres up the road he came on Blakeney and the priest who were waiting for him. The latter by now was scarcely able to stand; he was leaning heavily against the Englishman's shoulder.

Levet said simply: "My wife is dead," and then added: "Come, Monsieur l'Abbé, you are welcome! And you too, Monsieur le Professeur."

Between them the two men supported the tottering footsteps of the Abbé, almost carried him, in fact, as far as the grille. Here the three men came to a halt, and Blakeney said: "I think Monsieur l'Abbé will be all right now. When he has had some food and a short rest, he will be able to come with me as far as the château. Monsieur le Marquis will look after him the rest of the night and," he added speaking to the priest, "we hope within the next twenty-four hours, Monsieur l'Abbé, to have you well on the way to permanent safety."

"I don't know," the Abbé murmured feebly, "how to show my gratitude to you, sir. You and your friends were heroic in dragging me away from that cruel mob. I don't even know who you are – yet you saved my life at risk of your own – why you did it I cannot guess—"

"Don't try, Monsieur l'Abbé," Blakeney broke in quietly, "and reserve your gratitude for my friend Charles Levet, without whose loyalty my friends and I would have been helpless."

He gave Levet's hand a friendly squeeze and opened the grille for the two men to pass through. He waited a moment or two till they reached the front door, and was on the point of turning to go when he was confronted by two figures which had just emerged out of the fog. One of them was Blanche Levet. Blakeney raised his hat and she exclaimed: "If it isn't Monsieur le Professeur? Why! What are you doing in Choisy, monsieur, at this time of night?"

She turned to her companion and went on still lightly and inconsequently:"Louis, don't you know Monsieur le Professeur—"

"D'Arblay," Blakeney put in, as Blanche had paused, not knowing the name of her father's friend, who had always been referred to in the house as *Monsieur le Professeur.* "No" he continued, turning to the young lawyer, "I have not yet had the honour of meeting Monsieur – I mean citizen—"

"Maurin," Blanche broke in, "Louis Maurin, and now you know each other's names, will you both come in and—"

"Not now, mademoiselle," Blakeney said, "Madame Levet is too ill to—"

"My mother is dead," Blanche rejoined quietly. "I went to fetch Docteur Pradel, because Augustin wished me to, but I knew then already that she was dead."

She spoke without any emotion, Evidently no great tie of

filial love bound her to her sick mother. She murmured a quick "Good night," however. Blakeney held the grille open for her, and she ran swiftly into the house.

The two men waited a moment or two until they heard the door of the house close behind the young girl. Then Maurin said: "Are you going back to Choisy, citizen?" When Blakeney replied with a curt "Yes!" the lawyer continued: "May I walk with you part of the way? I am going into the town myself."

On the way down the street, Louis Maurin did most of the talking, he spoke of the great event of the day, but did so in a sober, quiet manner. Evidently he did not belong to the Extremist Party, or at any rate did not wish to appear as anything but a moderate and patriotic Republican. Blakeney answered in monosyllables. He knew little, he said, about politics; science, he said, was a hard taskmaster who monopolised all his time. Arrived opposite the Café Tison on the Grand' Place, he was about to take his leave when Maurin insisted that they should drink a *Fine* together. Blakeney hesitated for a few seconds; then he suddenly made up his mind and he and the young lawyer went into the cafe together.

Louis Maurin had begun to interest him.

CHAPTER EIGHT

Maurin the Lawyer

THERE was quite a crowd in the café. A number of idlers and quidnuncs had drifted out by now from Paris bringing with them news of the great event, and of the minor happenings that clustered round it. Philipe d'Orléans, now known as Philipe Égalité, Louis Capet's own cousin, had driven in a smart cabriolet to the Place de la Révolution, and watched his kinsman's head fall under the guillotine. "A good patriot, what?" was the universal comment on his attitude. The priest who had been with Capet to the last had mysteriously disappeared at the very moment when, in the Hall of Justice, a decree had been promulgated ordering his arrest. He was, it seems, a dangerous conspirator whom traitors in the pay of Austria had sent to the Temple prison as a substitute for the priest chosen by the Convention to attend on Louis Capet. This news was received with execration. But the priest could not have gone far. The police would soon get him, and he would then pay his second visit to Madame la Guillotine with no chance of paying her a third.

That was the general trend of conversation in the Café Tison: the telling of news and the comments thereon. Louis Maurin and Blakeney had secured a table in a quiet corner of the room; they ordered coffee and *Fine*, and the lawyer told the waiter to bring him pen, ink and paper. These were set before him. He said a polite "Will you excuse me?" to his *vis-à-vis* before settling down to write. When he had finished what appeared to be a longish letter, he slipped it into an envelope, closed and addressed it, and then summoned the waiter back. He handed him the letter together with some small money, and said peremptorily:

"There is a commissionaire outside. Give him this and tell him to take it at once to the Town Hall."

The waiter said: "Yes, citizen!" and went out with the letter, after which short incident the two men sat on silently opposite one another for a time, sipping their coffee and *Fine*, watching the bustling crowd around them, and listening to the chatter and comments and expressions of approval and disapproval more or less earsplitting, as the news of the quidnuncs brought were welcome or the reverse. And suddenly Maurin came out with an abrupt question: "Who was that with old Levet just now, Monsieur le Professeur?" he asked. "Do you happen to know? He was dressed like a priest. I am sure I saw a cassock."

He blurted this out in a loud, rasping voice, almost as if he felt irritated by Monsieur le Professeur's composure and desired to upset it. He did not know, astute lawyer though he was, that he was sitting opposite a man whom no power on earth could ever ruffle or disturb. The man to him was just a black-coated worker like himself, a professor at some university or other, a Frenchman, of course, judging from his precise and highly cultured speech.

"I saw no one," Blakeney replied simply. "Perhaps it was a priest called in to attend Madame Levet. You heard Mademoiselle Blanche say that her mother was dying."

"Dead, I understood," Maurin commented dryly. "But Levet, anyhow, had no need to send for a priest. His own son is a *calotin*."

"Indeed? Then it must have been the doctor."

"The doctor? No, Blanche and I went to fetch Dr. Pradel but he was not in."

Maurin remained silent for a minute or two and then said decisively:

"I am sure, or nearly sure, that it was not Pradel. Of course

the fog was very dense and I may have been mistaken. But I
don't think I was. At any rate . . ."

He paused, and thoughtfully sipped his coffee over the rim of
his cup; he seemed to be watching his *vis-à-vis* very intently.

Suddenly he said: "I shall be going to the Town Hall presently.
Will you accompany me, Monsieur le Professeur?"

"To the Town Hall? I regret but I . . ."

"It won't take up much of your time," the young lawyer
insisted, "and your presence would be very helpful to me."

"How so?"

"As a witness."

"Would you mind explaining? I don't quite understand."

Maurin called for another *Fine*, drank it down at a gulp and
went on: "Should I be boring you, Monsieur le Professeur, if I
were to tell you something of my own sentimental history. You
are, I know, an intimate friend of the Levets, and my story is
closely connected with theirs. Shall I be boring you?" he
reiterated.

"Not in the least," Blakeney answered courteously.

The young man leaned across the table and lowering his voice
to a whisper he began: "I love Blanche Levet. My great desire is
to make her my wife. Unfortunately her father hates me like
poison. Though I am a moderate, if convinced Republican, he
classes me with all those whom he calls assassins and regicides."
He paused a moment, then once more insisted: "You are quite
sure that this does not bore you, Monsieur le Professeur?"

"Quite sure," Blakeney replied.

"You are very kind. I was hoping to enlist your sympathy,
perhaps your co-operation, because Blanche has often told me
that old Levet has a great regard for you."

"And I for him."

"Quite so. Now, my dear Professeur," the lawyer went on
confidentially, "when I saw just now old Levet introducing a
man surreptitiously into his house, a scheme suggested itself to
me which I fervently hope will bring about my union with the
woman of my choice. I cannot tell you what put it into my head

that Levet was acting surreptitiously, all I know is that the thought did occur to me, and that it gave rise in my mind to the scheme which, with your permission, I will now put before you, as I say, with a view to soliciting your kind co-operation. Will you allow me to proceed?"

"Please do," Blakeney responded. "You interest me enormously."

"You are very kind."

Once more the lawyer paused. The noise in the room made conversation difficult. He leaned further over the table, and went on still in a subdued tone of voice:

"Whether the man who was with Charles Levet just now, and whom he took into his house was a genuine priest or not, I neither know nor care. He may be the fugitive Abbé Edgeworth for aught it matters to me. I am practically certain that it wasn't the doctor, but anyway he is just a pawn in the close game which I propose to play, a game, the ultimate stakes of which are my future welfare and success in my career. Old Levet has more money than you would think," he added unblushingly, "and Blanche, besides being very attractive – I am really in love with her – will have a considerable *dot*, whilst I . . ."

He gave a significant shrug and added: "Well! We understand one another, do we not, Monsieur le Professeur? With us black-coated workers money is the only ladder to success."

"Quite so," Blakeney assented imperturbably.

"Anyway what I am going to do is this. I have just sent a letter to the Chief of Section at the Town Hall, denouncing the Levet family as harbouring a traitor in their house. I enjoy a great deal of prestige with our local authorities and they will take my word for it that the Levets' guest is a dangerous conspirator against the Republic. Now do you guess my purpose?"

"Not exactly."

"It is really quite simple. Just think for a moment how we shall all stand within the next few hours. Levet, his daughter, his son and his guest arrested. I, Louis Maurin, using my influence with the authorities to get the family liberated. Levet's gratitude expressed by granting me his daughter's hand in marriage.

40

Surely you can see how splendidly it will all work."

"Not quite," Blakeney remarked after a slight pause.

"Where's the hitch?"

"I was thinking of the guest. Will your influence be extended towards his liberation also?"

"Oh!" the lawyer replied airily, "I am not going to trouble myself about him. If nothing is proved against him, if he is really just a constitutional priest called in to administer the sacraments to a dying woman, he will get his release without interference on my part."

"He may not."

The lawyer shrugged. "Anyway he will have to take his chance. My dear friend," he went on with an affected sigh, "a great many heads will fall within the next few days, weeks, months perhaps; are we not on the eve of far bigger things than have occurred as yet? One head more or less . . . what does it matter?"

To this Blakeney made no immediate reply; and presently the young lawyer resumed, putting all the persuasiveness he could command into his tone: "You will not refuse me your co-operation, will you, Monsieur le Professeur."

"You will pardon me," Blakeney responded, "but you have not yet told me what you desire me to do."

"Just for the moment, only to come with me as far as the Town Hall, and bear witness to the fact that old Levet introduced a man surreptitiously into his house this afternoon."

"But I don't know that he did."

Maurin shrugged. "Does that matter?" he queried blandly, "between friends?"

Then as Monsieur le Professeur made no comment on this amazing suggestion, he continued glibly: "It is all perfectly simple, my dear Professeur, as you will see, and nothing that will happen need upset your over-sensitive conscience. I will merely call upon you to confirm with a word or two, my statement that Charles Levet introduced someone furtively into his house, at the very time when his wife was breathing her last. There will be no question of an oath or anything of the sort, just a few words. But we will both insist that Levet's actions were furtive. Won't we? I can reckon on you for this can I not, my dear friend? I may call you my friend, may I not?"

"If you like."

"You really are most kind. And you will plead my cause with old Levet when my marriage with Blanche comes on the *tapis* presently, won't you, my friend? Funnily enough I felt you were going to be my friend the moment I sat down at this table opposite to you. But then Blanche had often spoken to me about you, and in what high regard her father held you . . . well!" he concluded, after he had paused for breath for a few seconds, "what do you say?" and his eyes glowing and eager, fastened themselves on the other's face.

By way of answer Blakeney rose.

"That the doors of the Town Hall will be closed against us, unless we hurry," he replied with a smile.

Maurin drew a deep sigh of satisfaction.

"Then you really are coming with me?" he exclaimed, and jumped to his feet. He beckoned to the waiter, and there ensued a friendly little dispute as to who should pay the bill, a dispute from which the lawyer gracefully retired, leaving his newly-found friend to settle both the bill and the gratuity. While he reached for his hat and cloak he just went on talking, talking as if something in his brain had let loose a veritable flood-gate of eloquence. He talked and he talked, and never noticed that Monsieur le Professeur, in the interval of settling with the waiter had scribbled a few lines on the back of the bill, and kept the crumpled bit of paper in the hollow of his hand. He piloted the voluble talker through the shrieking and gesticulating crowd as far as the door.

The next moment the two men were out in the Place. The fog seemed more dense than ever. As the Town Hall was at some distance from the Cafe Tison they started to walk briskly across the wide-open space. It was almost deserted, everyone having taken refuge against the cold and the damp in the brilliantly-lighted restaurants and cafes: all except a group of three or four slouchy-looking fellows clad in the promiscuous garments affected by the irregular Republican Guard. They were standing outside the Café Tison, very much in the way of the customers who went in or out, and had to be jostled and pushed aside by Monsieur le Professeur before he and Louis Maurin could get past.

CHAPTER NINE

Orders from the Chief

MAURIN was walking on ahead while he and Monsieur le Professeur crossed the Grand' Place. In the centre of the open space there was at that time a monumental fountain to which a short flight of circular steps gave access. In addition to the fog, a sharp frost now made progress difficult. The ground covered with a thin layer of half-melted snow, was very slippery, especially around the fountain which, though not playing at this hour had been going all day, and had scattered spray all around, so that the steps and the pavement around it were covered with a sheet of ice.

Maurin was treading warily. He nearly slipped at one point, and was just in time to save himself from falling. He called out a quick "Take care!" to his companion. But the warning came, apparently, just a few seconds too late for in answer to his call there came a sudden cry accompanied by a few vigorous swear words, quite unlike the usual pedantic speech of Monsieur le Professeur. The lawyer turned round at once and saw that learned gentleman sprawling on the ground.

"Whatever has happened?" he queried with ill-disguised impatience.

It was pretty obvious. Monsieur le Professeur lay, groaning, across the steps.

"Can't you get up?" the lawyer asked tartly.

"I'll try," the other replied. Apparently he made a genuine effort to rise, but fell back again groaning piteously.

"But," Maurin insisted with distinct acerbity, "I have to be at the Town Hall before six. It is ten minutes to now, and it is a good step down the Rue Haute. Can't you make an effort?"

"I'm afraid not. I think I have broken my ankle. I couldn't walk, unless you supported me."

"Then we should get to the Town Hall too late," the other retorted. "What's to be done?"

"You go, my friend, and I will follow as soon as I can. I dare say I can enlist the assistance of a passer-by to find me a cabriolet, and you can keep the Chief of Section talking till I come."

"Well, if you don't mind being left . . ."

"No, no! You go! I'll come along as quickly as possible."

"There's a fellow coming this way now. Shall I call him?"

"Thank you. If you will."

He seemed in great pain, and unable to move. A man in blouse and tattered breeches, apparently one of the irregular Republican Guard who had been hanging round the cafe loomed out of the fog, and came slouching along towards the fountain. Maurin hailed him.

"My friend is hurt," he said quickly; "will you look after him and bring him to the Town Hall as soon as you can? He will pay you well."

The man came nearer. He mumbled something about a cabriolet.

"Yes, yes!" Maurin acquiesced eagerly. "Try and get one. Don't wait! Run!"

After which peremptory order he turned once more to Monsieur le Professeur.

"You will not fail me, will you?" he insisted.

"No, no! I'll be with you as soon as I can. I promise."

Whereupon the lawyer finally went his way. The fog soon wrapped him up, out of sight, for he crossed the Place now almost at a run. How surprised, not to say gravely disturbed, he would have been if he had been gifted with second sight, and seen Monsieur le Professeur rise at once and without any effort to his feet, apparently quite unhurt. The fellow in blouse and tattered breeches was quite close to him again, and asked anxiously: "You are not really hurt, are you, Percy?"

"Of course not, you idiot," Blakeney replied with a light laugh. "Tell me! Have the others gone?"

"Tony and Hastings went straight to the Levets, according to your orders. I suppose you scribbled the note while you were in the cafe."

"As best I could. You deciphered it all right?"

"Yes! Tony and Hastings will take charge of the Abbé. The three of us are dressed in these rags as Irregulars of the Republican Guard. Tony has actually got a tricolour scarf round his middle. He and Hastings will formally arrest the Abbé and take him at once to La Rodière. Devinne went first to headquarters to change into his own clothes and then will go on straight to the château in a cabriolet to prepare the Marquis and his family for the arrival of the priest. Hastings or Tony will try to get in a word with old man Levet to assure him that everything is by your orders. That is right, isn't it?"

"Quite all right. Now you go on to the château yourself, my good fellow, and wait for me there. Tell the others as soon as they have seen the Abbé safely in the bosom of the La Rodière family, to take up their stand with you just outside the château gates. I will be there too as soon as I possibly can."

"Right!"

"You know your way?" "I'll find it."

And so they parted: one going to the right, the other to the left. Both were soon swallowed up by the fog. A cabriolet came lumbering along presently. Blakeney hailed him, and ordered the driver to take him to the Town Hall.

CHAPTER TEN

The Abbé Edgeworth

CHANCE favoured the two members of the League of the Scarlet Pimpernel, my Lord Hastings and Lord Anthony Dewhurst. They had their orders from the chief and went straight to the Levets' house, and it was Levet himself who opened the door to them in answer to their ring at the outside bell. Briefly they told him who had sent them and what their orders were, and the old man went at once in search of his guest. The Abbé Edgeworth had in the meanwhile enjoyed Charles Levet's hospitality: he had had food, a little drink and a short rest, but he still appeared dazed and aghast, as if moonstruck and awed by everything that had happened to him since dawn.

And now this kind old man telling him that all was well: powerful friends would take him to La Rodière where he would be received with open arms, and where he could remain until such time as a more permanent refuge could be found for him. The Abbé was bewildered. Who, he asked, were those wonderful friends who had rescued him at peril of their own lives, and now continued their work of mercy? But Levet couldn't tell him. He spoke vaguely of a man who was professor at a university and seemed to have marvellous courage, and limitless resources. He himself had only known him a little while. Who he was, he couldn't say. He came and went mysteriously and equally mysteriously would invariably be on the spot when innocent men, women or children's lives were threatened. His dead wife had looked upon the man as a messenger from heaven. There was no time to say more just now. Old Levet urged the Abbé to hurry.

A moment or two later he was standing once again at the gate of his house, watching three figures move away up the road. They looked like shadows in the fog. One of them was the Abbé Edgeworth. Levet didn't know the others.

These two, who were emissaries of the Professeur, had spoken French with a foreign accent. Levet thought they must have been English. But then it seemed incredible that foreigners would take any interest in the sufferings of Frenchmen who were loyal to their King. Englishmen especially. Why should they care? This awful revolution over here had nothing to do with them. Some people went so far as to assert that the English would soon declare war against France – that is to say, not against France but against this abominable Republic which had established itself on a foundation of outrage and of murder. Anyway, it was all quite ununderstandable. Old Levet went indoors, very perplexed and shaking his head. He went straight into the room where his wife lay dead.

Augustin was still in the room when Levet entered. He was talking in a subdued tone to a tall young man who had a tablet in his hand on which he was apparently making notes with a point of black lead. He was dressed in black from head to foot, with plain white frills at throat and wrist: he wore high boots, and his own hair, innocent of wig, was tied at the nape of the neck with a black bow. Apparently Levet knew that he was there, for he took no notice of him when he entered the room.

The young man, however, at once put tablet and pencil into his pocket and turned as if to go.

"Don't go, Pradel," Levet said curtly; "supper will be ready directly."

"If you will pardon me, Monsieur Levet," the other responded, "I will just say good night to Mademoiselle Blanche. I have been summoned to the château, and am already rather late."

"Someone ill up there?" the old man queried.

"Seemingly."

"Who is it?"

"They didn't tell me. Monsieur le Marquis's pet dog perhaps," the young doctor added with stinging bitterness, "or his favourite horse."

Levet made no remark on this. He moved to his wife's bedside, and Simon Pradel, after bidding him and Augustin good night, went out of the room.

Blanche was in the sitting-room, apparently waiting for him.

"You are not going, Simon?" she asked eagerly as soon as he came through the door.

"I am afraid I must, mademoiselle."

"Can't you stay and have supper with us?" she insisted so earnestly this time, that her voice shook a little and a few tears gathered in her eyes.

"I am sorry," he replied gently, "but I really must go."

"Why?"

He gave a slight shrug. "Professional visit, mademoiselle," he said.

"You are going to the château," she retorted.

"What makes you say that?" he countered with a smile.

"You have your best clothes on, and your finest linen."

His smile broadened. It was a pleasant smile, which lent to his somewhat stern face a great deal of charm. He looked down ruefully at his well-worn suit of black.

"I have only this one," he said, "and I have great regard for clean linen."

Blanche said nothing for a moment or two. She was very obviously fighting a wave of emotion which caused her lips to quiver, and tears to gather thick and fast in her eyes. And all at once she moved up, close to him, and placed a hand on his arm.

"Don't go to the château, Simon," she entreated.

"My dear, I must. Madame la Marquise might be ill. Besides . . ."

"Besides what?" And as Simon didn't reply to this challenge, she went on vehemently: "You only go there because you hope to have a word or two with Cécile de la Rodière. You, a distinguished medical man, with medals and degrees from the great universities of Europe, you demean yourself by attending on these people's horses and dogs like any common veterinary lout. Have you no pride, Simon? And all the time you must know that that aristocrat's daughter can never be anything to you."

Pradel had remained silent during this vehement tirade. He appeared detached and indifferent, as if the girl's lashing words were not addressed to him. Only the smile had vanished from his face leaving it rather pale and stern. When Blanche had finished speaking, chiefly because the words were choked in her throat, she sank into a chair and dissolved in tears. She cried and sobbed in a veritable paroxysm of grief. Pradel waited in silence till the worst of that paroxysm had passed, then he said gently: "Mademoiselle Blanche, I am sure you meant kindly by me, when you struck at me with so much contempt and cruelty. I assure you that I bear you no ill-will for what you said just now. With your permission I will call in tonight on my way back from the château to see how your dear father is bearing up. Frankly I am a little anxious about him. He is no age, but he has a tired heart, and he has had a great deal to endure to-day. Good night, mademoiselle."

After he had gone, Blanche roused herself sufficiently to go into the kitchen and order supper to be brought in at once. They all sat down to table and the old man said grace before he served the soup. They had just begun to eat, when a cabriolet drove up to the grille. A vigorous pull at the outside bell caused old Levet to rise. The family only kept one maid of all work and she was busy dishing up, so he went himself to the door as he most usually did: before he had time to reach the grille, the bell was pulled again.

"I wonder who that can be," Blanche remarked.

"Whoever it is seems in a great hurry," observed her brother.

Old Levet opened the door. Louis Maurin stepped over the threshold. He appeared breathless with excitement. Before Levet could formulate a question he thrust the old man back into the vestibule, exclaiming: "Ah! My good friend! Such a calamity! Thank God I am just in time."

"In time for what?" Levet muttered. He had disliked the lawyer at all times, for he looked on him as a traitor and now a regicide, but never had he hated him so bitterly as he did to-day.

"I chanced to be at the Town Hall," Maurin went on, still breathlessly, "and heard that there is an order out for your arrest and I am afraid that the order includes your family – and your guest," he concluded significantly.

Levet appeared to take the news with complete indifference. The mock arrest of the Abbé Edgeworth by two emissaries of Monsieur le Professeur had assured him that the priest at any rate had nothing to fear. He gave a slight shrug and said quietly: "Let them arrest me and my family, if they want to. We are willing to share the fate of our King."

"Don't talk like that, my dear friend," the lawyer admonished earnestly, "such talk has become really dangerous now. And you have your son and daughter to think of."

"They are of one mind with me," Levet retorted gruffly, "and if that is all you have come to say . . ."

Instinct of hospitality, which with old Levet amounted to a virtue, did prevent his ordering this "traitor" summarily out of his house.

"I came from pure motives of friendship," the young man rejoined, in a tone of gentle reproach, "to warn you of what was impending. The matter is far more serious than you seem to realise."

"I needed no warning. Loyal people like ourselves must be prepared these days for any calamity."

"But there is your guest . . ." Maurin put in.

"My guest? What guest?"

"The man you brought to your house this afternoon. The authorities have got to know of this surreptitious visit. It has aroused their suspicion. Hence the order for your arrest – and his."

Old Levet gave another shrug.

"There's no one here," he said coolly, "except my son and daughter and the maid."

"Come, come, my dear friend," the lawyer retorted, and his tone became more reproachful, and more gentle like that of a father admonishing his obstinate child, "you must not incriminate yourself by denying indisputable facts. I myself saw you introducing a stranger into your house, and your friend the professor can also bear witness to this."

"I tell you there's no stranger here," old Levet reasserted harshly. "And now I pray you to excuse me. My family waits with supper for me."

The words were scarcely out of his mouth when the sound of a rumble of wheels accompanied by the tramping of measured footsteps was heard approaching the house. There was a cry of "Halt!" outside the grille and then the usual summons: "In the name of the Republic!" the grille was thrust open, there was more tramping of heavy feet over the stone path to the house, and loud banging on the massive front door.

"What did I tell you?" Maurin queried. He pushed past old Levet and strode quickly across the vestibule to the dining-room, where at the sound of that ominous call Blanche and Augustin had jumped to their feet. The lawyer put one finger to his lips and murmured rapidly: "Do not be afraid. I am watching over you all. You have nothing to fear. But tell me quickly, where is the stranger?"

"The stranger?" Augustin responded. "What stranger?"

"You know quite well," the other retorted. "Your father's guest, whom he brought here this afternoon."

"There has been no one here all day," Augustin rejoined quietly. "My mother died. Dr. Pradel was here to certify. There has been no one else."

Maurin turned sharply to the girl.

"Blanche," he said earnestly, "tell me the truth. Where is your father's guest?"

"Augustin has told you, Louis," she replied, "there is no one here but ourselves."

"They will search the house you know," he insisted.

"Let them."

"And question your maid."

"She can only tell them the truth."

The lawyer was decidedly nonplussed. Looking about him, he could not help noticing that only three places were laid round the table, and that there were only three half-empty soup plates there, while the tureen still stood on the sideboard.

Through the door, which was ajar, he could hear old Levet give categorical replies to the questions which the sergeant of the guard put to him.

"There is no one here."

"Only the doctor came this afternoon."

"He came to certify."

"My son and daughter are at supper. My wife is dead. You can question the maid."

Maurin spoke once more to Blanche.

"Mademoiselle," he entreated, "for your own sake, tell me the truth."

"I have told you," she reasserted, "there is no one here except ourselves."

The lawyer smothered the harsh word which came to his lips: he said nothing more, however, turned on his heel and went out of the room.

"What is all this?" he asked curtly of the sergeant.

"You know best, citizen lawyer," was the soldier's equally curt reply.

"I?" Maurin retorted unblushingly. "What the devil has it got to do with me?"

"Well, it was you, I understand, who denounced these people."

"That is a lie," the other protested hotly.

"Who did then?"

"A friend of the family, Professor d'Arblay."

"Where is he?"

"He had an accident in the road. Sprained his ankle. He had

to drive home."

"Where is his home?

"I don't know. I hardly know him."

"But you were with him in the Town Hall. You were seen coming out of the Chief Commissary's cabinet."

"I was there on professional business," the lawyer retorted tartly, "and you have no right to question me like that. I had nothing to do with this denunciation, as I have the honour of being on friendly terms with this family. And I may as well tell you that I shall use ail the influence I possess to clear the whole of this matter up. So you had better behave decently while you are in this house. It won't be good for you if you do not."

He raised his voice and spoke peremptorily like one accustomed to be listened to with deference. But the sergeant seemed unimpressed. All he said was: "Very well, citizen. You will act, no doubt, as you think best in your own interests. I have only my duty to perform."

He gave a quick order to two of his men, who immediately stepped forward and took up their stand one on each side of Charles Levet. The sergeant then crossed the vestibule, and taking no further notice of the lawyer, he went into the dining-room. Blanche and Augustin had resumed their seats at the table. Blanche sat with her chin cupped in her hand. Augustin, his eyes closed his fingers twined together, seemed absorbed in prayer. In the background Marie, the maid of all work, stood agape like a frightened hen.

The sergeant took a comprehensive survey of the room. He was a stolid-looking fellow, obviously a countryman and not over-endowed with intelligence, and he gave the impression that what he lacked in personality he strove to counterbalance by bluster: the sort of bumpkin in fact whom the Revolution had dragged out of obscurity and thrust into some measure of prominence, and who was determined to make the most of his unexpected rise to fortune. He took no further notice of the lawyer, cleared his throat, and announced with due pompousness: "In the name of the Republic!"

He then unfolded a paper which he had in his hand, and continued:

"I have here a list of all the inmates of this house, as given to the Chief of Section this afternoon, either by Citizen Maurin or his friend the Professeur with the sprained ankle, whose address is not known. I will read aloud the names on this list, and each one of you on hearing your name, say the one word, 'Present' and stand at attention. Now then!"

He then proceeded to read and to interpolate comments of his own after every name.

"Charles Levet, herbalist! We have got him safely already. Henriette his wife! She is dead, I understand. Augustin Levet, priest! . . . why don't you answer?" he interposed peremptorily as Augustin had not made the required reply, "and why don't you rise? Have you also got a sprained ankle?"

Augustin then rose obediently and spoke the word:

"Present."

"Blanche Levet, daughter of Charles," the solder continued.

"Present."

"Marie Bachelier, *aide ménage.*"

"Here I am, citizen sergeant," quoth Marie, nearly scared out of her wits."

"And a guest, identity unknown," the solder concluded; "where is he?" He rolled up the paper and thrust it into his belt.

"Where is the guest?" he reiterated gruffly, and still receiving no answer, he asked once more: "Where is he?"

He looked round from one to the other, rolling his eyes and clearing his throat in a manner destined to impress these "traitors."

Augustin thereupon said emphatically: "There is no one here." And Blanche shook her pretty head and declared: "No one has been here all day except Citizen Maurin and the citizen doctor."

By way of response to these declarations the sergeant of the Republican Guard turned on his heel and called to the small squad who were standing at attention, in the vestibule, some outside the front door. To Blanche and Augustin he merely remarked: "We'll soon see about that." And to old Levet, who was standing patiently between the two soldiers, seemingly quite unmoved by what was going on in his house, he said sternly: "I am about to order this house to be searched. So let me warn you, Citizen Levet, that if any stranger is found on your premises it will be a far more serious matter for you and your family than if you had given him up of your own accord."

Old Levet merely shook his head and reiterated simply: "There is no one here."

The sergeant then ordered his men to proceed with the search. It was thorough. The soldiers did not mince matters. They even invaded the room where Henriette Levet lay dead. They looked under her bed and lifted the sheet which covered her. Old Levet stood by, while this sacrilege was being committed, a silent figure as rigid as the dead. In the dining-room Augustin had once more taken refuge in prayer, while Blanche, half-dazed by all that she had gone through, sank back into a chair, her elbows resting on the table, and her eyes staring into vacancy.

Louis Maurin, as soon as the soldiers were out of the way, came and sat down opposite the young girl. He had remained silent and aloof while this last short episode was going on, but now he leaned over the table and began talking in an impressive whisper:

"Do not be afraid, Mademoiselle Blanche," he said. "I give you my word that nothing serious will happen to your father or to any of you, even if this meddlesome sergeant should discover your anonymous friend in this house. Please, please," he went on earnestly, as Blanche was obviously on the point of renewing her protest that there was no one here, "please say no more. I do firmly believe that you know nothing of what happened here this afternoon. I tell you I can, and will make the safety of those you care for a personal matter with the authorities. It might prove a little more difficult if your father has been sheltering someone surreptitiously instead of giving him up at once to the guard, but even so I can do it. My word on it, Mademoiselle

Blanche."

He was very persuasive and very earnest. The ghost of a smile flitted round Blanche's pretty mouth.

"You are very kind, Louis," she said.

"I would do anything for you, mademoiselle," the young man responded earnestly.

She sighed and murmured: "I cannot understand the whole thing."

"What can't you understand, mademoiselle?"

"Monsieur le Professeur. He seemed such a friend. Do you really think that it was he?"

"Who caused all this trouble, you mean?"

"Yes!"

"Well! I am not sure," Maurin replied vaguely. "One never knows. He may be a spy of the revolutionary government and he may have denounced your father. They are very clever, those fellows. They worm themselves into your confidence, and then betray you for a mere pittance. I wish your father had not made such a friend of him. But as I assured you just now, mademoiselle, you have no cause for worry. While I live, no possible harm shall come to you or to your family. You do trust me, don't you?"

She murmured a timid "Yes!" and gave him her hand, which he raised to his lips.

The soldiers in the meanwhile had continued their search on the floor above. Whilst this went on overhead, Maurin shot searching glances at the young girl to see if she betrayed any anxiety for the guest whom he firmly believed to be still in the house. But Blanche remained seemingly unmoved and, much to his chagrin, Maurice was forced to come to the conclusion that he had brought a squad of Republican Guards out on a fool's errand and that his well-laid plan would end in a manner not altogether to his credit and not in accordance with his hopes.

A few moments later the sergeant and his men came clattering downstairs again, all of them obviously ill-tempered at having been dragged out of barracks at this hour and in such abominable weather. The sergeant kicked the dining-room door open with his boot, and addressed the lawyer in a harsh, almost insulting tone: "I don't know what you were thinking of, citizen lawyer," he said, "when you stated before the Chief of Section that a suspicious stranger was lurking in this house. We have searched it from attic to cellar and there's no one in it except the family, one of whom is dead, and the others seemingly daft. At any rate I can't get anything out of them. I don't know if you can."

"It's no business of mine, as you well know, citizen sergeant," Maurin responded coolly, "to question these people any more than it is your business to question me. I attend to my duties, you had better attend to yours."

"My duty is to arrest the inmates of this house," the soldier countered, "and if they are wise they will come along quietly. Now then you," he added, addressing them all collectively: "Charles Levet, Augustin and Blanche Levet, and Marie Bachelier, I have a carriage waiting for you. Go and get ready quickly. I don't want to waste any more time."

Obediently and silently Blanche and Augustin made for the door. Blanche called to the maid who seemed by now more dead than alive.

"But this is an outrage," Maurin suddenly interposed vehemently, "you cannot leave the dead unguarded. Someone must remain in the house to prevent any sacrilege being committed."

The sergeant shrugged. "Sacrilege?" he put in with a sneer. "What is sacrilege? And why shouldn't the dead woman be alone in the house. She can't run away. Anyway if you feel like that, citizen lawyer, why don't you stay and look after her? Come on!" he concluded roughly, addressing the others, "didn't you hear me say I didn't want to waste any more time?"

He marshalled the three out of the room. As Blanche went past the lawyer, she threw him an appealing glance. He murmured under his breath: "I will look after her. I promise you."

Ten minutes later Charles Levet with his son and daughter

and the maid were seated in the chaise, and were driven under arrest to the Town Hall, there to be charged with treason – or intended treason – against the Republic.

CHAPTER ELEVEN

The Morning After

BUT the very next day all was well. Charles Levet with his daughter and son, and the maid, had certainly passed a very uncomfortable night in the cells of the municipal prison, and the next morning had been conducted before the Chief of Section, where they had to submit to a searching examination. And here things did not go any too well. Charles Levet was taciturn and obstinate, Blanche voluble and tearful, and Augustin detached, and Marie the maid was so scared that she said first one thing then another, and all things untrue. The Chief of Section was impatient. He was desirous of doing the right thing, but he was a local man and the Levets were people of his own class: nothing "aristocratic" about them and, therefore, not likely to plot against the Republic, or to favour fugitive *aristos*. Indeed, he was very much annoyed that Maurin the lawyer – a personal friend of his and also of his own class – should have taken it upon himself to make incriminating statements against the Levets. To have indicted the Levet family for treason would have been a very unpopular move in Choisy where the old herbalist was highly respected and his pretty daughter courted by half the youth of the commune.

After the interrogation of the accused, the worthy Chief of Section had an interview with Maurin. The latter, as supple as an eel, wriggled out of his awkward position with his usual skill, and in a few moments had succeeded in persuading his friend that he, individually, had nothing to do with the false accusation brought against the Levets. He had, he said, been foolish enough to listen to the insinuations brought against these good people by a man whom he had met casually that day. A professor, so he understood, at the University of Grenoble.

"But why," the chief asked with some acerbity, "did you allow yourself to be led by the nose, by a man whom you hardly knew at all?"

"I said," the lawyer responded, "that I had met him casually that day, but I had often heard old Levet speak about him. He seemed to be a friend of the family and so—"

"A friend?" the other broke in. "But you say that it was he who denounced these people."

"It was."

"How do you make that out?"

"Between you and me, my friend," the lawyer replied confidentially, "I have come to the conclusion that that so-called university professor was just an *agent provocateur*, in other words a spy of the government. There are a good many of those about, so I am told: the Convention makes use of them to ferret out obscure conspiracies, and treasonable associations. They get a small pittance for every plot they discover, and so much for every head that they bring to the guillotine."

"And so you think that this professor—"

"Was just such another. I do. I met him outside the Levet's house. He took me by the arm and led me to the Café Tison, where he began his long story of how he had seen old Levet bring a man surreptitiously into the house. I, of course, thought it my duty to let you know at once. You would have blamed me if I had not, wouldn't you?"

"Of course."

"One thing is very certain," Maurin now put in persuasively; "when your squad came to arrest the Levets there was no one in the house but themselves."

"They may have smuggled someone out."

"Where to, my friend?" the lawyer argued. And he added lightly: "Now you are crediting old Levet with more brains than he has got."

He paused a moment, then finally went on:

"I don't know what you feel about it all, my good man, but I am convinced in my own mind that Charles Levet had no other visitor in his house . . . except, of course, Dr. Pradel," he added as if in an afterthought.

"Ah, yes! Dr. *Pradel* . . . I hadn't thought about him."

"Nor had I—till just now . . ."

Maurin rose and stretched out his hand to his friend who shook it warmly.

"Well!" he said glibly, "will you allow me to convey the good news to the Levets?"

"What good news?"

"That you have gone into the matter and have decided that the charge of treason against them has not been proved."

"Yes!" the chief responded after a moment's hesitation, "you may go and tell them that if you wish. I won't follow up the matter just now – but, of course, I shall bear it in mind. In the meanwhile," he concluded as he saw his friend to the door, "I will just send for Dr. Pradel and have a talk with him."

Louis Maurin came away from that interview much elated. He had gained his point, and a very little clever wordy manipulation on his part would easily convince the Levets that they owed their freedom to him. The Professeur had fortunately kept out of the way. Maurin devoutly hoped that he really had broken his ankle and would be laid up for some days; by that time his own wooing of the lovely Blanche, with the consent of her irascible papa, would be well on the way to a happy issue. But there was another matter that added greatly to his elation, and this was that he had put a spoke in the wheel of Simon Pradel, the one man in Choisy who, in his opinion, might prove a serious rival in the affections of Blanche. He was far too astute not to have scented this rivalry before now, and Blanche herself had unwittingly given to his sharp eyes more than one indication of the state of her feelings towards the young doctor.

Everything then was for the best in the best possible world, and Louis Maurin made his way to the prison cells where the Levet family were still awaiting their fate, there to tell them that he and no one else had persuaded the Chief of Section to order their immediate liberation. Whether he quite succeeded in so persuading them, is somewhat doubtful, certainly as far as Charles Levet was concerned, for the old man remained as taciturn as ever in spite of the young man's eloquent protestations, whilst Augustin murmured something about good deeds being their own reward. But their lack of enthusiasm was countered by Blanche's outspoken gratitude. With tears in her eyes she thanked Louis again and again for all that he had done for them all.

"We all tried to be brave," she said, "but, frankly, I for one was very frightened; as for poor Marie, she spent the night lamenting and calling on all the saints to protect her."

Later, when they reached the portal of the prison-house she said to her father: "Let us drive home, father. I am so anxious to know if everything has been all right in the house, with *maman* lying there alone."

It was a bright, frosty morning, but a thin layer of snow still lay on the ground. In this outlying part of the town, there were few passers-by and no cabriolets in sight, but a poor wretch in thin blouse and tattered breeches stood shivering in the middle of the road. He was an old man, with arched back and wrinkled, grimy face; from under his shabby red cap wisps of white hair fluttered in the wind. His teeth were chattering as he murmured a prayer for charity. Maurin called to him: "See if you can find a cabriolet, citizen, and bring it along. You might get one in the Place Verte and there will be five sous for you. We'll wait for it at the tavern over the way."

The man raised a finger to his forelock and shuffled off in the direction of the Place Verte, his sabots made no sound on the thin carpet of snow.

"What misery, *mon Dieu*," Blanche sighed while she watched the old caitiff's retreating figure. "And this is what they call Equality and Fraternity. Can't anything be done for a poor wretch like that? He seems almost a cripple with that humped back."

"He could go to the *Assistance Publique*," Maurin replied dryly, "but some of these fellows seem to prefer begging in the streets. This one, I should say, has been a soldier in—"He was about to say "In Louis Capet's army," but with Charles Levet within hearing, he thought better of it. This was obviously not the moment to irritate the old man.

"Come and drink a mug of hot ale with me while we wait," he suggested cheerily to the whole party. They were all very cold, having only had a meagre prison breakfast in the early hours of the morning: a small tavern over the way, at a short distance looked inviting. Old Levet would have demurred: he wore his most obstinate expression: but Blanche was obviously both weary and cold and the maid looked ready to faint with inanition; even Augustin cast longing eyes across the road. Louis Maurin without another word led the way, Levet followed reluctantly, the others with alacrity, and presently they were all seated at a table in a small stuffy room that reeked of lamp-oil and stale food, but sipping with gusto the hot ale which the landlord, surly and out-at-elbows, had placed before them.

CHAPTER TWELVE

A False Move

It was after the first ten minutes of desultory conversation among the party, that Louis Maurin made what he called afterwards the greatest mistake of his life. Indeed he often cursed himself afterwards for that twinge of jealousy, coupled with boastfulness, which prompted him to speak of Simon Pradel at all. It was just one of those false moves which even an experienced chess-player might make with a view to protecting his queen, only to find himself check-mated in the end. Little did the astute lawyer guess that by a few words carelessly spoken he was actually precipitating the ruin of his cherished hopes and helping to bring about that extraordinary series of events which caused so many heartburnings, set all the quidnuncs of Choisy gossiping and remained the chief topic of conversation round local firesides for many weeks to come.

Blanche had drunk the ale, said a few pleasant words to Maurin, chaffed her brother and the maid, and relapsed into silence. Maurin, who was feeling at peace with all the world and very pleased with himself, queried after a time: "Thoughtful, mademoiselle?"

It seemed almost as if she had dropped to sleep for she gave no sign of response, and Maurin insisted.

"Of what are you thinking, mademoiselle?"

She roused herself, gave a shrug, a sigh, a feeble smile and replied: "Friends."

"Why friends?" he asked again.

"I was just wondering how many of our friends will have to suffer as we did last night – as innocently I mean – arrest . . . imprisonment . . . anxiety . . . these are terrible times, Louis!"

"And there are worse to come, mademoiselle," he declared ostentatiously; "happy are those who have powerful friends to save them from disaster."

This hint was obvious, but neither old Levet nor Augustin responded to it. It was left for Blanche to say: "You have been very kind, Louis."

Silence once more, until Augustin remarked:

"We were, of course, innocent."

"That helped a little, of course," Maurin was willing to admit, "but you have no idea how obstinate the Committee are, once there has been actual denunciation of treason. And we must always remember those poor wretches who for a miserable pittance will ferret out the secrets of some who have not been clever enough to keep their political opinions to themselves."

"I suppose it was one of those wretches who trumped up a charge against us," Blanche remarked.

"Undoubtedly. And I had all the difficulty in the world – in fact I had to pledge my good name – before I could persuade the Chief of Section that the charge was trumped up."

He paused a moment, then added self-complacently:

"I shall find it still more difficult in the case of Simon Pradel, I'm afraid."

Blanche gave a start.

"Simon?" she queried. "What about Simon?"

"Didn't you know?"

"Know what?"

Already Maurin realised that he had made a false move when he mentioned Pradel. Blanche all at once had become the living representation of eager, feverish anxiety. Her cheeks were aflame, her eyes glittered, her voice positively quavered when she insisted on getting an explanation from the lawyer.

"Why don't you answer, Louis? What is there to know about Simon?"

66

Why, oh, why had he brought the doctor's name on the *tapis*? He had done it primarily for his own glorification, and in order to stand better and better with the Levets because of his influence and his zeal. Never had he intended to rouse dormant passion in the girl by speaking of the danger which threatened Pradel. Women are queer, he commented with bitterness to himself. Let a man be sick or in any way in need of their help, and at once he becomes an object of interest, or, as in this case, simple friendship at once flames into love.

Old Levet, who had hardly opened his mouth all this while, and had seemed to be too deeply absorbed in his own thoughts to take notice what was said around him, now put in a word.

"Don't worry, my girl," he said; "Simon is no fool, and there is no one in Choisy who would dare touch him."

By this time, Maurin had succeeded in turning his thoughts in another direction. Self-reproach gave place to his usual self-complacency and self-exaltation. He had made a false move, but he thanked his stars that he was in a position to retrieve it.

"I am afraid you are wrong there, Monsieur Levet," he observed unctuously. "As a matter of fact I happen to know that the Section has its eye on Dr. Pradel. His mysterious comings and goings yesterday, and his constant visits at the Château de la Rodière, which often extend late into the night, have aroused suspicion, and, as you know, from suspicion to denunciation there is only one step – and that one sometimes leads as far as the guillotine. However, as I had the pleasure of telling you just now, I will do my best for the doctor, seeing that he is your friend."

"And that he is innocent," Blanche asserted vehemently. "There was nothing mysterious about Simon's comings and goings yesterday. He only goes to the château when he is sent for professionally, nor does he extend his visits late into the night."

Maurin shrugged.

"I can only repeat what I have been told, mademoiselle," he said, "I can assure you . . ."

He felt that he had made another false move by saying that which was sure to arouse the girl's jealousy. Indeed he was beginning to think that luck had not attended him in the manner he had hoped, and was quite relieved when the sound of shuffling sabots over the sanded floor cut this awkward conversation short. Maurin looked round to see the old beggar of a while ago standing in the middle of the room, waiting at a respectful distance till he was spoken to.

Maurin queried sharply: "What do you want?"

The man raised a hand stiff with cold to his white forelock.

"The cabriolet, citizen," he murmured.

The poor wretch seemed unable to say more than that. With trembling finger he pointed to the door behind him. A ramshackle vehicle drawn by a miserable nag was waiting outside. Levet paid for the drinks and the whole party made their way to the door. At the last, when the family had crowded into the cabriolet, old Levet pressed a piece of silver into the beggar's shaky hand.

Maurin remained in the road outside the tavern until the vehicle had disappeared at a turning of the street. He was not the man ever to admit, even to himself, that he was in the wrong, but in this case he had, perhaps, been somewhat injudicious, and he felt that he must take an early opportunity to retrieve whatever blunder he may have committed. Blanche was very young, he commented to himself; she scarcely knew her own mind, and Pradel was the man whom she met the most constantly. But after this, gratitude would be sure to play an important role in the girl's attitude towards the friend who had helped her and her family out of a very difficult situation. Maurin prided himself on the fact that he had persuaded the girl, if not the others, that it was his influence and his alone that had brought about their liberation after a few hours' detention. She was already inclined to be grateful and affectionate for that. It would be his task after this to work unceasingly on her emotions and to his own advantage.

And reflecting thus, lawyer Maurin made tracks for home.

BOOK II

The Doctor

CHAPTER THIRTEEN

The Château de la Rodière

It had always been a stately château ever since the day when Luc de la Rodière, returning from the war with Holland after the peace of Ryswick, received this quasi-regal residence at the hands of Louis XIV in recognition for his gallantry in the field. It was still stately in this year 1793, even though it bore the indelible marks of four years of neglect following the riots of 1789 when the populace of Choisy, carried away by the events up in Paris and the storming of the Bastille, and egged on by paid agitators, marched in a body up to the château, smashed a quantity of furniture and a few windows and mirrors, tore curtains down and carpets up, ransacked the larders and cellars, and then marched down again with lusty shouts of the new popular cry: *"À la lanterne les aristos!"*

When the young Marquis with Madame, his mother, and Mademoiselle Cécile returned to La Rodière three days later, they found the château in the state in which the riotous crowd had left it; the stately hall on the ground floor, the banqueting room, the monumental staircase, the cellars and larders, were a mass of wreckage. The terrified personnel of lackeys and female servants had run away, leaving the ballroom where their late master had lain dead, still a litter of dead flowers and linen clothes, of torn lace and stumps of wax candles. Only Paul Leroux and his wife Marie had remained. They were old people—very old—who had served *feu* Monsieur le Marquis and his father and mother before him, first as kitchen wench and scullion, then on through the hierarchy of maid and valet, to that of butler and housekeeper. They had never known any other home but La Rodière: if they left it, they would not have known where to go: they had no children, no family, no kindred. And so they stayed on, after the mob had cleared away, and one by one the château staff – young and old, indoors and out of doors, garden and stablemen – had packed up their belongings and betaken themselves to their own homes wherever these might be. Paul and Marie stayed on and did their best to feed the horses and dogs that had been left behind, and to get a few rooms tidy and warm for the occupation of Madame la Marquise. And thus the widow and the young Marquis and Mademoiselle Cécile found them and their devastated home.

Thanks to the goodwill of Paul and Marie some semblance of order had been brought into the devastated part of the château: broken window-panes were replaced and torn carpets and curtains put out of sight. In the stables most of the horses and valuable dogs were sold or destroyed: Monsieur le Marquis only kept a couple of sporting dogs and two or three horses for his own use. Then, as the winter grew severe and fuel and food became scarce and dear, three pairs of willing hands were recruited from Choisy to supplement the exiguous staff of the once luxurious household. These willing hands, two outdoor men to help in the garden and stables and a girl in the house were now called *aides-ménage*, the appellation servant or groom being thought derogatory to the dignity of free-born citizens of France. Even then, special permission for employing these *aides* had to be obtained from the government: and this was only granted in consideration of the fact that Paul and Marie Leroux were old and infirm, and that it was they and not the *ci-devants* who required help.

This, then, was the house to which the Abbé Edgeworth was conducted in the evening of that horrible day when he had seen his anointed King perish on the guillotine like a common criminal. Ever since that early hour in the morning when he had been called in to administer the sacraments to the man who had once been Louis XVI, King of France, he had lived in a constant state of nerve-strain, and as the afternoon and evening wore on he felt that strain more and more acutely. Towards seven o'clock two men who looked more like cut-throats than any voluntary revolutionary guards the Abbé had ever seen had conducted him to La Rodière. Before he started out with them old Levet had assured him that everything was being done to ensure his safety: the same powerful and generous friend who had rescued him from the hands of a howling mob had further engineered the final means for his escape out of France.

The old priest accepted this explanation in perfect faith and trust. He assured his kind host that he was not the least bit afraid. He had gone through such a terrible experience that nothing could occur now to frighten him. Nor did anything untoward happen on the way. He got very tired stumping up the rugged track which was a short cut to the château. The monumental gates, no longer closed against intruders, were wide open. The Abbé and his escort passed through unchallenged and walked up the stately avenue.

The front door of the mansion was opened to them by Paul, who stood by deferentially in his threadbare but immaculately brushed suit of black, whilst the old priest stepped over the threshold.

Tired though he was the Abbé did not fail to turn immediately in order to express his gratitude to the two enigmatic ruffians who had guided his footsteps so carefully, but they had gone. Their footsteps in the clumsy sabots echoed down the long avenue for a time but they themselves had already disappeared in the gloom.

But this is by the way. The priest who by now was on the verge of exhaustion both mentally and physically, sank into an armchair which Paul offered him, and here he waited patiently with eyes closed and lips murmuring a feeble prayer while his arrival was being announced to Monsieur le Marquis.

A few moments later a young man came running down the stairs with arms outstretched, shouting a welcome even before he had caught sight of the priest.

François de la Rodière was the only son of the late Marquis. He had inherited the title and estates four years ago on the death of his father; he was a well-set-up, athletic-looking youth, who might have been called handsome but for an arrogant, not to say cruel, expression round his thin-lipped mouth, and a distinctly receding chin. He was dressed with utmost elegance, in the mode that had prevailed before the present regime of Equality had made tattered breeches, threadbare coats and soiled linen, the fashion.

The abbé rose at once to greet him.

"We were expecting you, Monsieur l'Abbé," the young man said cheerily. "My mother and sister are upstairs. I hope you are not too tired."

The Abbé was certainly tired, but he contrived to smile and to ask with some surprise:

"You were expecting me? But how could you know—?"

"It is all a long story, Father," François de la Rodière replied thoughtfully; "we are all of us under its spell for the moment. But never mind about that now. We'll tell you all about it when you have had supper and a rest."

The welcome which Madame la Marquise extended to the priest was no less cordial than that of her son. The Abbé Edgeworth, by virtue of his holy office, and because he had been privileged to attend the royal martyr during the last hours of his life, stood on an altogether different plane in the eyes of Madame from the rest of the despicable bourgeoisie. Thus Mademoiselle Cécile, her daughter, was ceremoniously presented to Monsieur l'Abbé, and so was the young English gentlemen, my lord Devinne, a friend of the family, who had ridden over from Paris that afternoon, bringing news of the terrible doings there. He had, it seems, also brought tidings of the Abbé Edgeworth's early arrival at La Rodière.

It was while the family and their guest were seated round the supper-table that Mademoiselle Cécile related to the priest the mysterious occurrence which had puzzled them all since morning.

"It was all so wonderful!" she explained, "and I cannot tell you, Father, how excited I am, because the first intimation we had that you were coming was addressed to me."

"To you, mademoiselle?"

"Yes! To me," she replied, "and you shall judge for yourself whether the whole thing is not enough to excite the most placid person, and I am anything but placid. Early this morning," she continued, "when I took my usual walk in the park, I saw down the avenue a scrubby-looking man coming slowly towards me from the direction of the gate. He was at some distance from where I was so I didn't really see him well, but somehow I knew that he had nothing to do with our own small staff. We are accustomed nowadays," she added with a pathetic little sigh, "to all sorts of people invading our privacy. This man, however, was obviously doing no harm; he just walked along, quite slowly, with his hands in his pockets, looking neither to right nor left. I didn't take any more notice of him until he came to one of the stone seats in the avenue. Then I saw him take a paper out of his pocket and lay it down on the seat, after which he gave me a distinct sign, drawing my attention to the paper; he then turned and went back the way he came and I lost sight of him behind the shrubbery." She paused a moment, almost out of breath with excitement, then she went on: "You may imagine, Father, how I hurried to the seat and picked up the mysterious message. Here it is," she said, and drew from the folds of her fichu a crumpled piece of paper. "I have not parted from it since I picked it up and read its contents. Listen what it says: 'The Abbé Edgeworth, vicaire of St. Andre, who accompanied the King of France to the scaffold will claim your hospitality to-day for the night.' Look at it, Monsieur l'Abbé. Isn't it extraordinary? I have shown it to *maman,* of course, and to François. They couldn't understand at all where it came from, until milord Devinne threw a still more puzzling light on the whole thing."

She held the paper out to the priest who took it from her, put his spectacles on his nose and glanced down on the mysterious note.

"It certainly is very curious," he said, "and it is not signed."

"Only with a rough drawing of a small scarlet flower," the girl observed. The priest handed the paper back to her. She took it, folded it together almost reverently and replaced it in the folds of her fichu. The Abbé turned to the young Englishman.

"And you, milord," he asked, "can actually throw some light on the sender of this anonymous message?"

"Not exactly that," Devinne protested, "but I can tell you this: that small scarlet flower is a device adopted by the chief of a band of English gentlemen who have pledged themselves to save innocent men and women and children from the tragic fate that befell the King of France today."

The old priest hastily crossed himself.

"May God forgive the sacrilege," he murmured. Then he went on: "But what a high ideal, milord! Saving the innocent! And Englishmen, you say? Are you a member of that heroic band yourself?"

"I have that honour."

"And your chief? Who is he?"

"Ah!" Devinne replied, "that is our secret – and his."

"Your pardon, milord! I had not thought to be indiscreet. The whole thing simply amazes me. It is so wonderful to do such noble deeds, to risk one's life for the sake of others who may be nothing to you, and do it all unknown, probably unthanked! And to think that I owe my life to such men as you, milord, to your friends and to your chief! And that little red flower? It is a Scarlet Pimpernel, is it not?"

"Yes!"

"I seem to have heard something about it. But only vaguely. The police here speak of an anonymous English spying organisation."

"We do no spying, Monsieur l'Abbé. The League of the Scarlet Pimpernel has nothing to do with politics."

"I am sure it has not. But I understand that even the government is greatly disturbed by its activities, and has offered a large reward for the apprehension, milord, of your chief. But God will protect him, never fear."

It was after this that the old priest seemed to collapse. He gave a gasp and sank back in his chair in a faint. François de la Rodière hastily called to Paul, and together the two men carried the old man upstairs to the room which had been prepared for him and put him to bed. When they came back and explained that Monsieur l'Abbé appeared to be very ill, Madame la Marquise gave orders to Paul that Dr. Pradel be fetched at once.

"The doctor is in the house now, Madame la Marquise," Paul observed.

"Doing what?" Madame asked.

"I sent for him, *maman*," François put in; "Stella needed a purge, and César got a splinter in his paw. But I thought he would be gone by now."

"And why hasn't he gone?"

"Marie had one of her bad attacks of rheumatism, Madame la Marquise, and Berthe the kitchen girl had a poisoned finger. The doctor has been seeing to them."

"Tell him to go up to Monsieur l'Abbé at once," Franfois commanded.

When Paul had gone, he turned to Lord Devinne.

"This is very unfortunate," he said. "I do hope it won't be a long affair. I don't mind the Abbé being here, say, a day or two, but you didn't say anything about his being a sick man."

"I didn't know that he was," the Englishman observed.

"Your wonderful chief should have told you," the other retorted with obvious ill-humour. "It won't be over-safe either for *maman* or for the rest of us to be harbouring a man who is under the ban of this murdering government. Believe me, milord, I—"

75

He was interrupted by the opening of the door and the entrance of Simon Pradel. Madame la Marquise gave him a gracious nod, and Cécile a kindly glance. François, on the other hand, did not take the trouble to greet him.

"It is upstairs you have got to go," he said curtly; "a friend of ours who was here at supper was suddenly taken ill."

Simon took no notice of the insolence of the young man's tone. He only frowned slightly, took his professional tablet and pencil from his pocket and asked: "What is the name of your friend, Monsieur le Marquis?"

"His name has nothing to do with you," the other retorted tartly.

"I am afraid it has, Monsieur le Marquis. I am bound by law to report to the local Section every case I attend within this area."

Madame la Marquise sighed and turned her head away; the word "Section" or "law" invariably upset her. But François suffered contradiction badly, especially on the part of this fellow Pradel whom he knew to hold democratic if not revolutionary views.

"You can go and report to the devil," he said with growing exasperation. He was still in a fume over the affair of the Abbé's inconvenient sickness, and now, what he considered presumption on the part of this purveyor of pills and purges, turned his annoyance into fury.

"Either," he went on, not attempting to control his temper, "either you go and attend to my guest upstairs or you clear out of my house in double quick time."

There was not much meekness in Simon Pradel either. The arrogance of these aristocrats exasperated him just as much as his own attitude exasperated them. His face went very white, and he was on the point of making a retort which probably would have had unpleasant consequences for everyone concerned when he caught a glance, an appealing glance, levelled at him out of Cécile's beautiful eyes.

"Our friend is old, Monsieur le Docteur," she said gently, "and very ill. I am sure he will tell you his name himself, for he has no reason to hide it."

The glance and the words froze the sharp retort on Pradel's lips. He succeeded in keeping his rising temper under control and without another word, and just a slight inclination of the head he went out of the room. François on the other hand made no attempt to swallow his wrath: he turned on his sister and said acidly: "You were a fool, Cécile. What that fellow wanted was a sound thrashing: your amiability will only encourage him in his insolence. All his like ought to have tasted the whip-lash long ago. If they had, we shouldn't be in the plight we are in to-day. Don't you agree with me, *maman,*" he concluded, appealing to his stately mother.

But Madame la Marquise who was very much upset by the incident had already sailed out of the room.

CHAPTER FOURTEEN

An Outrage

It was at daybreak the following morning that Simon Pradel left the château. He had spent the whole night at the bedside of the Abbé Edgeworth, fighting a stubborn fight against a tired heart, which threatened any moment to cease beating. The old priest was hardly conscious during all those hours, only swallowing mechanically at intervals the cordials and restoratives which the doctor forced between his lips. Just before six he rallied a little. His first request was for a priest to hear his confession.

"You are no longer in danger now," Pradel said to him gently. But the Abbé insisted.

"I must see a priest," he said; "It is three days since I made confession."

"You have nothing on your conscience, I am sure, Monsieur l'Abbé, and I am afraid of too much mental effort for you."

"Concern at being deprived of a brother's ministrations will be worse for me than any effort," the old man declared with serene obstinacy.

There was nothing for it but to humour the sick man. Pradel immediately thought of Augustin Levet and decided to go and fetch him. He collected his impedimenta, left instructions with the woman who was in charge of the invalid, and made his way, with much relief, out of this inhospitable château. The morning was clear and cold, the sun just rising above the woods of Charenton, flooded the valley with its pale, wintry light. In the park one or two labourers were at work, and in the stableyard away to the left Pradel saw three men, one of whom, a groom, was holding a horse by the bridle with another, presumably Lord Devinne, was about to mount; the third had his back turned towards the avenue and Pradel couldn't see who it was. He was walking quickly now in the direction of the gate, and suddenly became aware of a woman's figure walking in the same direction as himself, some distance ahead of him. For the moment he came to a halt, and stood stockstill, hardly crediting his own eyes. It was not often that such a piece of good fortune came his way. The joy of meeting Mademoiselle Cécile, alone, of speaking with her unobserved, had only occurred twice during these last twelve months when first he had learned to love her.

Pradel was no fool. He knew well enough that his love was absolutely hopeless: that is to say he had known it until recently when the greatest social upheaval the world had ever seen, turned the whole fabric of society topsy-turvy. He would hardly have been human if he had not since then begun, not exactly to hope, but to wonder. Opposition on the part of these arrogant patricians who constituted Mademoiselle Cécile's family would probably continue, but there was no knowing what the next few months, even weeks, might bring in the way of drawing these aristocrats out of their fortresses of pride, and leaving them more completely at the mercy of the much-despised middle class.

Pradel, of course, didn't think of all this at the moment when he saw Cécile de la Rodière walking alone in the park. He only marvelled at his own good fortune and hastened to overtake her. She was wrapped in an ample cloak from neck to ankles, but its hood had fallen away from her head and that same wintry sun that glistened on the river, touched the loose curls above her ears and made them shine like tiny streaks of gold.

All down the length of the avenue there were stone seats at intervals; the last of these was not very far from the entrance gate. Cécile came to a halt beside it, looked all round her almost, Pradel thought, as if she was expecting someone, and then sat down. At sound of the young man's footsteps she turned, and seeing him she rose, obviously a little confused. He came near, took off his hat, bowed low and said smiling: "Up betimes, mademoiselle?"

"The sunrise looked so beautiful from my window," she murmured, "I was tempted."

"I don't wonder. This morning air puts life into one."

Cécile sat down again. Without waiting for permission Simon sat down beside her.

"I might echo your question, Monsieur le Docteur," the girl resumed with a smile: "Up betimes?"

"Not exactly, mademoiselle. As a matter of fact I am ready for bed now."

"You have been up all night?"

"With my patient."

"The dear old man! How is he?"

"Better now. But he has had a bad night."

"And you were with him all the time?"

"Of course."

"That was kind. And," the girl added with a smile, "did he confess to you?"

"No. But I guessed."

"Was he raving then, in delirium?"

"No. He was very weak, but quite conscious."

"Then how could you guess?"

"He is a priest, for he has a tonsure. He is a fugitive since his name is withheld. It was not very difficult."

"You won't . . ." she implored impulsively.

"Mademoiselle!" he retorted with gentle reproach.

"I know. I know," she rejoined quickly. "I ought not to have asked. You would not be capable of such a mean action. Everyone knows how noble and generous you always are, and you must try and forgive me."

She gave a quaint little sigh, and added with a curious strain of bitterness: "We all seem a little unhinged these days. Nothing seems the same as it was just a few years ago. Our poor country has gone mad and so have we, in a way. But," she resumed more evenly, "I must not keep you from your rest. You lead such a busy life, you must not overtire yourself."

"Rest?" he exclaimed involuntarily. "Overtire myself? As if there was anything in the world . . ."

He contrived to check himself in time. The torrent of words which were about to rise, from his heart to his lips would have had consequences, the seriousness of which it had been difficult to overestimate. Cécile de la Rodière was woman enough to realise this also, but womanlike too, she didn't want the interview to end abruptly like this. So she rose and turned to walk towards the gate. He followed, thinking the while how gladly he would have lingered on, how gladly he would have prolonged this *tête-à-tête* which to her probably was banal enough but which for him had been one of the happiest moments of his lonely life. Cécile, however, said nothing till they reached the postern gate. Here she came to a standstill, and while he was in the act of opening the gate, she stretched her hand out to him.

"Am I forgiven?" she asked, and gave him a glance that would have addled a stoic's brain. What could a man in love do, but bend the knee and kiss the little hand. It was a moment of serenity and of peace, with the wintry sun touching the bare branches of sycamore and chestnut with its silvery light. Out of the depths of the shrubbery close by there came the sound of pattering tiny feet, the scarce perceptible movements of small rodents on the prowl. Then the beating of a horse's hoof in the near distance on the frozen ground, and a man's voice saying: "A pleasant journey, my friend, and come and see us soon again," followed almost immediately by a loud curse and a shout.

"What is that lout doing there?"

Cécile snatched her hand away, and turned frightened eyes in the direction whence the shout had come. But before Simon Pradel could jump to his feet, before Cécile could intervene, the young doctor was felled to the ground by a stunning blow from a riding-crop on the top of his head. All he heard as his senses reeled was Cécile's cry of horror and distress and her brother's infuriated shouts of "How dare you? How dare you?"

81

The crop was raised again and another blow came down, this time on the unfortunate young doctor's shoulders. But Pradel was not quite conscious now: he felt dizzy and sick and utterly helpless. All he could do was to put up one arm to shield his head from being hit again. He could just see Cécile's little feet beneath her skirt, and the edge of her cloak: he heard her agonised cry for help and Lord Devinne's voice calling out: "François! For God's sake stop! You might kill him."

He tried to struggle to his feet, cursing himself for his helplessness, when suddenly a curious sound came from somewhere close by. Was it from the shrubbery, or from the road opposite? Or from the cypress trees that stood sentinel outside the park gates? Impossible to say: but it had a curious paralysing effect on everyone there, on that madman blind with fury as well as on his helpless victim. And yet the sound had nothing terrifying in it; it was just a prolonged, drawly, rather inane laugh; but the fact that it appeared to come from nowhere in particular and that there was no one in sight who could possibly have laughed at this moment, lent to the sound something peculiar and eerie. The age of superstition had not yet died away. François's curses froze on his lips, his cheeks became ashen grey, his arm brandishing the crop remained poised above his head as if suddenly turned to stone.

"What was that?" he continued to murmur.

"Some yokel in the road," Lord Devinne suggested, and then added lightly: "Anyway, my friend, it saved you from committing a murder."

The spell only lasted a few moments. Already François had recovered his senses, and with them, his rage.

"Committed a murder?" he retorted roughly. "I wish I had killed the brute."

He turned to his sister. "Come, Cécile!" he commanded.

She wouldn't come; she desired nothing else but to minister to the stricken man. He was lying huddled up on the ground and a gash across his forehead caused the blood to stream down his face; he had quite lost consciousness. François gave the prone helpless form a vicious kick.

"François," the girl cried, herself roused to fury by his cowardice, "I forbid you . . ."

"And I swear to you that I will kill him, unless you come away with me at once."

Cécile, horrified and indignant and afraid that the boy might do some greater mischief still, turned to Lord Devinne and said coolly: "Milord, my brother is not responsible for his actions, so I must look to you to act as a Christian and a gentleman. If you need help, please call to Antoine in the stables. He will attend to Docteur Pradel, until he is able to get home."

She gave him a curt nod. Indeed, she did not attempt to conceal the contempt which she felt for his attitude during the whole of this infamous episode, for with the exception of the one call to François: "For God's sake, that's enough! You might kill him!" he had stood there beside his horse, with the reins over his arm, seemingly quite detached and indifferent to the abominable outrage perpetrated on a defenceless man. Even now as François by sheer force succeeded in dragging his sister away, he made a movement as if to get to horse again, until he met a last look from Cécile and apparently thought it better to make some show of human feeling.

"I'll get Antoine to give me a hand," he said, and leading his horse, he turned in the direction of the stables.

Chance, however, intervened. Antoine did not happen to be in the stables at the moment. Devinne tethered his horse in the yard, and then, after a few seconds' hesitation, he seemed to make up his mind to a certain course, and made his way round the shrubbery back to the château. His train of thought during those few seconds had been: "If I don't see Cécile now, she will brood over the whole thing, and imagine all sorts of things that didn't really happen."

Paul opened the door to him. He asked to see Mademoiselle. Paul took the message upstairs, but returned with a word from Mademoiselle that she was not feeling well and couldn't see anybody. Devinne sent up again, and again was refused. He asked when he might have the privilege of calling and was told that Mademoiselle could not say definitely. It would depend on the state of her health.

Useless to insist further, Devinne, very much chagrined, went back the way he came, feeling anything but at peace with the world in general and in particular with Simon Pradel, who was the primary cause of all this trouble. Back in the stable yard he found Antoine at work there; but all he did was to mount his horse and ride away without saying a word about a man lying unconscious by the roadside. However, when he rode past the gate he noted, rather to his surprise, that there was no sign of Simon Pradel.

"That sort of riff-raff is very tough," was my Lord Devinne's mental comment, as he put his horse to a trot down the road.

CHAPTER FIFTEEN

Alarming News

When Simon Pradel came back to complete consciousness, he found himself sitting propped up against a willow tree by the side of the little stream that runs winding its turbulent way for three or four hundred metres parallel with the road. His cloak was wrapped round him and his hat was at the back of his head. His head ached furiously and it took him some time to collect his senses and to remember what had happened. He put his hand to his forehead: it encountered a handkerchief tied round it underneath his hat.

Then he remembered everything, and insane fury took possession of him, body and soul. Nothing would do but he must at once to wreak vengeance on the coward who had reduced him to such a humiliating pass. How he could best get a private interview with François de la Rodière at a spot where the young miscreant could not call anyone to his aid, was the puzzle that, for the moment, defied solution. The order had probably been given already that if he, Pradel, called at the château, the door should be slammed in his face. And he laughed aloud with rage and bitterness at the thought that the man whose worthless life he could squeeze out with his own powerful hands was so hemmed in, even in these days, that nothing but mere chance would deliver him up to his victim's just revenge.

It was his own outburst of laughter that brought back to the young doctor's mind the curious incident which, as a matter of fact, had probably saved his life. There was no knowing to what lengths that madman would have gone in his senseless rage, had not that eerie laughter roused the echoes of the dawn and paralysed his murderous arm. But Pradel had no more idea than the others whence that laugh had come; all he knew was that it had saved his life, and that it remained as mysterious, as unaccountable, as the fact that here he was, propped up against a willow tree by the side of the stream, with his forehead bandaged, his hands and face wiped clean of blood and his clothes carefully freed from dirt. He did remember, but only vaguely, that he had been lifted off the ground by arms that seemed to be very powerful, and that he was being carried along in those same arms, he supposed across the road. A few seconds, and he remembered Cécile, the beloved hand extended to him, the kindly glance, the delicious *tête-à-tête* in the avenue. And he also remembered the Abbé Edgeworth and the old man's earnest request for the ministrations of a brother priest and his own determination to fetch Augustin Levet for this task.

Vengeance, then, would have to wait for that mere chance which might never come. God Himself had said "Vengeance is mine. I will repay!" What then?

With a last shrug of bitter contempt at his own impotence, Pradel turned his back finally on that château of evil. He was on the point of wending his way down the rough track which is a short cut into Choisy, when he saw a shabbily dressed little man who seemed to be lurking desultorily at the angle of the road. He took no notice, however, not even when he became aware that as soon as he himself had started to follow the track, the man immediately turned and went leisurely down the other way.

Walking downhill on slippery frozen ground was a painful process, with every step a jar, and every movement a strain on aching limbs: but will-power is a sturdy crutch, and so many different thoughts were running riot in Simon Pradel's mind that they left no room in his brain for self-pity. Less than an hour later he was outside the Levets' house, ringing the front door bell. There was no answer. He rang again and again. It seemed strange, he thought, that there should be no one astir in the house to watch over the dead. Old Levet with his habit of wandering about the countryside was a very early riser, so was Marie the maid. Augustin, of course, might have gone to church, but there was Blanche also; surely the two women would not have left the dead unguarded.

Vaguely apprehensive, not knowing what to think, Simon thought he would go to the church close by where he knew the Levets worshipped, hoping to find Augustin there. As he turned out of the gate he met the Widow Dupont, a neighbour of the Levets, who, at sight of him, threw up her arms and exclaimed: "Ah, citizen doctor, what a calamity!"

Pradel frowned enquiringly.

"Calamity? What calamity?"

"Didn't you know?"

"Know what?"

"The poor Levets! And the citizeness lying there dead, all alone! I and my girl would have gone in and kept watch as is only fitting, but we didn't know about it all until afterwards; and then the house was shut up like you see it now."

She talked on with the volubility peculiar to her kind. It was some time before Simon could get in a word edgeways.

"But in God's name, what has happened?" he broke in at last.

"They were arrested last night."

"Arrested?"

"And they are all going to be guillotined," the worthy widow concluded, with that curious mixture of awe and complacency so characteristic of a certain type of countrywoman. "All of them! Poor old Levet, his saintly son, pretty little Blanche and Marie, the maid. Not that I would care about Marie as a maid. She is a good girl, but she is not thorough in her work, if you know what I mean—"

"I know, I know. But tell me, how do you know all this, about the Levets? Did you see it happen?"

"No, citizen, I did not. But I did see Citizen Maurin, the

lawyer, afterwards – after they had all gone, that is, in a carriage and pair and lots of soldiers. I asked Citizen Maurin if they were really going to be guillotined, one never knows what may happen these days: like that poor King now – I should say Louis Capet – one never knows. Does one?"

But Pradel had heard enough. With a hasty word of thanks to the voluble widow, he turned and walked rapidly up the street. It was no use trying to find Augustin now, but he went into the nearest church, saw the cure, asked him or his coadjutor to go at once to La Rodière to see a sick man, and then, anxious to get first-hand news, he went on to Maurin's office. There he was told by the servant that the citizen lawyer was out for the moment but was expected back for *déjeuner*. It was now close on ten o'clock and there would be two hours to kill; time enough to go back home, swallow a cup of coffee and get some rest before attending to his correspondence and professional work. As he walked away from Maurin's house, Simon happened to look back and saw the shabby little man of a while ago go up to the front door and ring the bell. The same servant opened the door, but the shabby little man was at once admitted.

CHAPTER SIXTEEN

Rumour and Counter-Rumour

There is nothing like a village or a small provincial town for disseminating news. Within a few hours of its occurrence it was known all over Choisy that a dastardly outrage had been committed on the person of the much-beloved and highly respected citizen,

Dr. Pradel, by the *ci-devant* Marquis de la Rodière up at the château. Some of these rumours went even so far as to assert that it was a case of murder: this, however, was later on automatically contradicted, when Dr. Pradel was seen crossing the Grand' Place, looking pale and severe but certainly not dead.

When and how the rumour originated nobody knew but by evening it was all over the place and the principal subject of conversation at street corners and in the cafes. Even the tragic event of the day before was relegated to the background while various versions of the story, more or less contradictory, went from mouth to mouth. Louis Maurin was one of the first to hear of it, and it made him very angry indeed. His *aide-ménage*, Henri, related to a crony afterwards that the citizen lawyer had had two visits from a seedy-looking individual, who often came to the office on business but whom he, Henri, didn't know by name. It was during this man's second visit that the citizen lawyer had flown into a rage. Henri had been quite frightened, and though he was not the least inquisitive by nature, he could not help overhearing what went on in the office.

"You consummate fool . . ." he heard his employer say.

And: "You told me to spread any rumours that were derogatory to him . . ."

Then again: "This is not derogatory, you idiot . . . it will just make a hero of him . . ."

All of which was very mysterious, as the crony was bound to admit. What a pity that the worthy *aide-ménage* could not hear more. It seems that the seedy-looking individual went away soon afterwards, looking very down in the mouth.

No wonder that Louis Maurin was furious. Everything he had planned recently for his wooing of Blanche Levet seemed to be going wrong. To spread rumours that were derogatory to Pradel's moral character was one thing. Blanche would be sure to hear of it, so would old Levet, and there was a good chance that the doctor would, in consequence, be forbidden the house. But to represent the man as the victim of aristocratic brutality and arrogance, to give, in fact, the whole incident a political significance, was to excite any young girl's imagination in favour of what she would call a martyr to his convictions. For that is the turn which rumour had now taken. Docteur Pradel, so said the gossips, had professed liberal views: the *ci-devants* up at the château, enraged at the execution of Louis Capet, had lost all sense of restraint, and had vented their fury on the first victim who came to their hand. In the cafés and at street corners there was talk among the hot-headed youths of Choisy to go up to La Rodière in a body and extract vengeance from those insolent *aristos* for the outrage committed on a respected member of the community. If this project was put into execution Simon Pradel would, of course, at once become the most important personage in Choisy. He would be elected mayor without doubt, even perhaps member of the Convention; a second Danton or Robespierre, there was no knowing. In spite of the cold on this frosty January evening, Maurin perspired profusely at the prospect of seeing Blanche dazzled by the doctor's glory, and old Levet thinking it prudent perhaps to have such a progressive politician for his son-in-law.

The thought was maddening. Maurin didn't feel that he

could endure it in solitude with only that fool of an *aide-ménage* for company. He saw the rosy future which he had mapped out for himself turning to darkly gathering clouds. It was now seven o'clock. The Levets would be at supper. He, Maurin, had every excuse for calling on them to enquire after their health after the trying ordeals of the past twenty-four hours, and to offer his services in connection with the funeral arrangements which could no longer be delayed.

Well wrapped up in a cosy mantle, the lawyer sallied forth. The Levets were at supper when he arrived. He was quite observant enough to note at once that there was an element of disturbance in the family circle. Blanche had evidently been crying: her eyes were heavy, and her cheeks aflame. She had pushed aside her plate of soup untasted. Augustin, serene and detached as usual, with his breviary propped up against a glass in front of him, was quietly finishing his, whilst Charles Levet's expression of face was inscrutable. Maurin had a shrewd suspicion, however, of what went on in the old royalist's mind. Pradel, in a sense, was his friend, and he was probably shocked at the story of the outrage, but deep down in his heart, the herbalist had kept a feeling of loyalty not only to his King, but to the *seigneur*. He had been born and bred in this loyalty, and in the belief that a *seigneur*, an aristocrat who was the prop and mainstay of the throne could do no wrong, or if he did, there was certainly a reason and an explanation for his misdoing. Augustin would look upon the outrage as the will of God, or a visitation of the devil, and would pray humbly and earnestly that Monsieur le Marquis de la Rodière be forgiven for his outburst of temper. Only Blanche would be indignant. Maurin's egoism merely attributed this to casual interest in a friend, the thought that the girl was seriously in love with the doctor, he dismissed as disturbing and certainly unlikely.

He had always prided himself on his tact. It was only his tact, so he believed, that enabled him ever to enter this house as a welcome guest, even though his political views were as abhorrent to old Levet as the plague. He entered the room now with hand outstretched and an air of debonnaire geniality, coupled with the solemnity due to a house wherein its mistress lay dead. He was asked to sit down and was offered a glass of wine. He talked of funeral arrangements, and volunteered to take upon himself all the trouble connected with legal formalities; he asked after everyone's health, professed to be the bearer of official apologies for the family's arrest and detention, and apparently was not aware that his volubility was countered by silence on the part of his three listeners. Blanche still looked very distressed, in fact, she seemed to have the greatest difficulty in restraining her tears. Maurin was on the point of broaching the subject of Pradel, when there was a ring at the bell.

"That'll be the citizen doctor," Marie remarked, and went waddling off like a duck to open the door.

"I'll see him outside," old Levet said, as he rose from the table. "Come, Augustin!" he called to his son.

To Maurin, who had been watching Blanche keenly, it seemed as if it had been at a sign from her that her father had called to Augustin and with him had gone out of the room. A moment or two later he could hear two of the men talking together in the passage, after which all three went into the sitting-room. There was no mistaking the expression in the girl's face now. It was all eagerness and excitement, and in her eyes there was just that look which only comes in a woman's eyes when the man she loves is near. Maurin cursed himself for his lack of judgement. He should have guessed which way the land lay and played his cards differently. It was not by involving Pradel in political imbroglios that he would succeed in turning Blanche against him. There were other means by which the budding love of a young and inexperienced girl could be changed first to pique and thence perhaps to hatred. And pique would surely throw Blanche into the arms of the man who knew how to play his cards well, that man, of course, being himself.

Fortunately Louis Maurin did, in his own estimation, hold the trump card now, and he made up his mind to play it at once. He nodded in the direction whence the sound of men talking came as a faint and confused murmur, and said blandly:

"Our young friend in there has got over his trouble of this morning quite quickly. He—"

"Don't speak of that outrage, Louis," Blanche broke in vehemently; "I can't bear it."

"My dear," he retorted suavely, "I was only going to say, that, like most men who are in love, he seems willing to endure both physical and moral humiliation, for the sake of the short glimpses he has of the lady of his choice. I don't blame him. We are all of us like that, you know, all of us who know what love is. I would endure anything for your sake, Blanche . . . even blows."

"And now you are talking nonsense," the girl rejoined dryly. "There was no question of love in the unprovoked insult which that abominable *aristo* put upon Simon."

The lawyer gave a light shrug and echoed with something of a sneer:

"Unprovoked? My dear Blanche!"

"Certainly it was unprovoked. Simon had been sitting up with a sick man all night. He was returning home in the small hours of the morning when that devil of a Marquis, coward as well as bully, fell on him from behind and knocked him senseless before he could defend himself."

Maurin gave a superior little smile.

"A very pretty story, my dear. May I ask from whom you had it?"

"Everyone in Choisy will tell you the same. Every detail is known—"

"No, dear, not every detail; nor will everyone in Choisy tell the pretty tale, for there is a man who stood by while the whole episode was going on, and who saw everything from the beginning."

"Some liar, I suppose," she retorted.

"No, not a liar. A man of integrity, of position, an official, in fact."

"And what did he tell you?"

Maurin smiled once more. Imperceptibly this time. Blanche plied him with questions. She wanted to know. She did not, as older women would have done, refuse to hear another word that might prove derogatory to the man she loved.

"Simon Pradel, my dear Blanche, was discovered by François de la Rodière making love to his sister, in the early dawn . . . after a night spent at the château, but not with a sick man. He was, in fact, kneeling at Mademoiselle's feet, kissing her hand in farewell. No wonder the *ci-devant* lost his temper."

"It's not true!" the girl cried, hot with indignation.

"I pledge you my word that it is," the lawyer responded calmly.

Already Blanche had jumped to her feet. She went to the door, threw it open, and pointed to it with a dramatic gesture.

"Out of the house, Citizen Louis Maurin," she said, speaking as calmly as he had done, "and never dare set foot into it again. You are a liar and a traducer and I hate you worse than anyone I have ever known in all my life."

She remained standing by the door, a forbidding, almost tragic figure. Maurin remained for a time where he was, his eyes fixed upon her, pondering within himself what he should do. The girl's sudden revulsion had struck him with dismay. It was so unexpected. Once again Fate, or a false move on his part perhaps, had upset all his plans.

For the moment, however, there was nothing for him to do but to obey. He rose slowly, picked up his hat and coat and went to the door. Striding past the girl he made her a low bow. As soon as he had gone through the door she slammed it to behind him.

CHAPTER SEVENTEEN

Timely Warning

It was in the early morning of the day following the outrage on Dr. Pradel that a cabriolet, more ramshackle perhaps than any that plied in Choisy, turned into the great gates of La Rodière and came to a halt at the front door of the château. A tall man, dressed in sober black, alighted from the vehicle and rang the outside bell. To Paul who opened the door to him, the tall man gave his name as d'Arblay, Professor at the University of Louvain in Belgium, and added that he desired to speak with Monsieur l'Abbé.

Paul was a little doubtful: one had to be so careful nowadays with so many spies of that murdering government about. The visitor looked respectable enough, but there was never any knowing, and Paul thought it wisest to shut the door in the Professor's face whilst he went to consult his better half. Marie too was doubtful. For months past now, no visitor had called at the château, and, of course, one never did know. In the end the two old people decided that the only thing to do was to report the whole matter to Monsieur le Marquis, and he would decide whether the *"Professeur"* was to be introduced into Monsieur l'Abbé's presence or not.

To their astonishment Monsieur le Marquis was overjoyed when he heard of the visit, and commanded that Monsieur le Professeur be shown at once into his own private room. Never had Monsieur le Marquis shown such condescension towards a member of the despised bourgeoisie, and Paul ushered in the visitor with as much deference as he would have shown to one who had a handle to his name.

François de la Rodière was indeed more than condescending. He greeted the tall Professor most cordially.

"Your visit is more than welcome, sir," he said. "I have been expecting it ever since yesterday at noon, when I received one of those mysterious messages signed with the device of a small red flower which have already puzzled us. You, I suppose, know all about it."

"All?" the Professor replied. "Not exactly, Monsieur le Marquis. But I have been asked to call here in a cabriolet for Monsieur l'Abbé Edgeworth, and to drive with him as far as Vitry, where friends of his who are of Belgian nationality and therefore safe from interference by the revolutionary government, will convey him safely to the frontier."

François could not help being impressed by the grave and dignified demeanour of this learned man, as well as by his exquisitely cut clothes and fine linen. To begin with he spoke French with a precision that amounted to pedantry, and this was strange in a Belgian: their French was usually execrable. He was tall and obviously powerful, and he had beautiful hands, one of which rested on the ivory knob of his cane. There was nothing Belgian about all that either, the Belgians being for the most part short and stocky and, with their Flemish ancestry, were of a very different fibre to the aristocracy of France. Puzzled, François remarked casually: "You are a Belgian, are you not, Professor?"

"Cosmopolitan would be a better word, Monsieur le Marquis," the other replied coolly. "I trust Monsieur l'Abbé is in a better state of health. The journey might be trying for an invalid."

"Oh! He is much better. Much, much better," François replied, then went on in a confidential manner: *"Entre nous,* my good Professor, his being ill here was somewhat inconvenient, not to say dangerous for the safety of Madame la Marquise and all of us. I shall be really thankful to have him out of the way."

"I am sure. Especially in view of the fact that the people down in Choisy are none too friendly towards your family."

"Oh! The riff-raff down in Choisy do not frighten me. Riff-raff! That is all they are. They shout and yell and break a window or two. No, no, I am not afraid of that rabble. Let them come. They will get their desserts."

"It is sometimes best to be prepared."

"I am prepared. With powder and shot. The first man who sets foot on the perron is a dead man, so are all who follow him."

"Retreat before a powerful enemy is sometimes more prudent and often more brave than assured resistance."

"You mean run away before that *canaille*. Not I. I'll see them all in hell first."

"I was thinking of Madame la Marquise and Mademoiselle Cécile."

"Then, pray," François retorted with supreme arrogance, "cease thinking of aught but your own business, which is to look after the welfare of Monsieur l'Abbé Edgeworth."

With that, he turned his back on his visitor and stalked out of the room, leaving the Professor standing there motionless, a thoughtful look in his deep blue eyes and a sarcastic curl round his firm lips. A moment or two later Paul came in.

"Monsieur l'Abbé is waiting to see Monsieur le Professeur," he said.

The latter gave a short, impatient sigh and followed Paul out of the room. His interview with the old priest was short. The Abbé with that patient acceptance of fate which he had shown since the one catastrophic event two days ago, was ready to follow this unknown friend as he had followed the two ruffianly guards the other day from the Levets' home to the château. He made his adieux to the family who had so generously sheltered him, expressed his thanks to them, as well as to Paul and Marie, who had looked after him, and finally stepped into the cabriolet which he understood would take him on to Vitry first, there to meet Belgian friends who would drive him by coach to the frontier. Monsieur le Professeur sat by his side and drove with him for about a kilometre or so; he then called to the driver to stop, alighted from the vehicle and bade the old priest farewell.

"The friends, Monsieur l'Abbé," he said finally, "who will take care of you at Vitry and convey you to the frontier, are kind and generous. The head of the family has held an official position in Paris for the Belgian Government. He has a safe-conduct for you. Try and think of no one but yourself until you are over the border. God guard you."

He then spoke a word or two to the driver which the Abbé failed to hear. There were two men on the box. One of them now got down and took his seat under the hood of the carriage. He looked something of a ruffian, but the Abbé did not mind his looks. He was used to friendly ruffians by now. He took a last look at the mysterious Professor, saw him standing bareheaded at the side of the road, his black cloak wrapped round his tall figure, one slender hand resting on the knob of his cane, his face a reflection of lofty thoughts within a noble soul.

It was a face and form the Abbé Edgeworth knew that he would never forget, even though he was destined never to see them again. As the driver whipped up his nag, the priest murmured a prayer to God to bless and guard this mysterious friend to whom he owed his safety and his life.

CHAPTER EIGHTEEN

Impending Trouble

Three days had gone by since the incident at La Rodière, and excitement in Choisy over the outrage on Dr. Pradel was working itself up to fever-pitch. In the evenings, men and women who had been at work in the government factories all day, would pour out in their hundreds and invade the cafes and restaurants, eager to hear further details of the abominable assault which by now had inflamed the passions of every adult in the commune. A devilish aristocrat had shown his hatred and contempt for the people by making a cowardly attack on one of the most respected citizens of Choisy, on a man who spent his life and fortune in ministering to the poor and doing good to every man, woman or child who called to him for help. Such an affront called aloud for vengeance. It was directed against the people, against the rights and privileges of every free-born citizen of France.

And paid agitators came down from Paris, and stood at street corners or on tables in cafés and restaurants and harangued the excited crowds that readily enough gathered round them to hear them speak.

The chief centre of this growing agitation was the Restaurant Tison adjoining the café of the same name on the Grand' Place; a great number of people, women as well as men, usually crowded in there in the evenings because it was known that the hero of the hour, Dr. Pradel, usually took his supper in the restaurant. People wanted to see him, to shake him by the hand

and to explain to him how ready everyone was in Choisy to avenge his wrongs on those arrogant *ci-devants* up at La Rodière.

Unfortunately Simon Pradel did not see eye to eye with that agitated crowd. He resented his own impotence bitterly enough, but he didn't want other people – certainly not a lot of rioters – to make trouble up at the château and God help them, strike perhaps at Mademoiselle Cécile whilst trying to punish her brother. Up to now he had succeeded in keeping the more aggressive hotheads within bounds. He had a great deal of influence with his fellow-citizens, was very highly respected and they did listen to him when he first begged, then commanded them to mind their own business and let him manage his own. In this, strangely enough, he had an ally in a man he detested, Louis Maurin, the lawyer, who appeared just as anxious as he was himself to put a stop to the insane project advocated by the agents of the government; this was to march in a body to La Rodière, there to loot or destroy the contents of the château as had already been done once, four years ago, and if not actually to murder the family of *aristos*, at any rate to give them a wholesome fright followed by exemplary punishment.

After Louis Maurin had been ignominiously turned out of the Levets' house by Blanche, he did not attempt to set foot in it again. He took to frequenting the Restaurant Tison more assiduously than ever before, there to use what influence he possessed to moderate the inflammatory harangues of the agitators, since he was hand in glove with most of these gentlemen. As a matter of fact the last thing in the world Maurin desired was an armed raid on La Rodière with Simon Pradel the centre of an admiring crowd, and the glorification of the one man who stood in the way of his cherished matrimonial schemes.

"You don't want to set the whole commune by the ears, Citizen Conty," he argued with the orator who had just ended an impassioned harangue amidst thunderous applause. "It is too soon for that sort of thing. The government wants you to incite the people to patriotism, to inflame their love for their country, not to work on this silly sentiment for one man, who, before you can put a stop to it, would become a sort of hero of the commune, be elected mayor and presently be sent to the Convention, there to become a dictator and rival to Robespierre or Danton, and what will you gain by that? Whereas if you will only bide your time . . ."

"Well, what should I gain by biding my time according to you, citizen lawyer?"

"Give those *aristos* up at the château enough rope, and presently you will be able to denounce them and get a big reward if they are condemned. I have known as much as twenty livres being paid for the apprehension of a *ci-devant* Marquis and thirty for his womenfolk. As for a prominent citizen like that fellow Pradel, I know that I can get you fifty livres the day he is brought to trial for treason."

The other man shrugged, spat and gave a coarse laugh.

"Do you hate him so much as all that, citizen lawyer?" he queried.

"I do not hate Docteur Pradel," Maurin replied loftily, "more than I do all traitors of the Republic, and I know that Pradel is a traitor."

"How do you know that?"

"He is constantly up at the château. He puts his professional pride in his pocket and gives purges to the *ci-devants'* horses and dogs. And do you know why he was thrashed the other morning? Because he had spent the night with the wench Cécile, and was bidding her a fond farewell in the early dawn, when they were both caught in a compromising position by her brother, who took the law in his own hands and broke his riding-crop over the shoulders of the amorous young doctor."

Conversation was difficult in this atmosphere of noisy excitement. In the farther corner of the crowded restaurant a small troupe of musicians were scraping the catgut, blowing down brass instruments and banging on drums to their own obvious satisfaction, for they made a great noise, wagged their heads and perspired profusely while they supplemented their ear-splitting attempts at a tune by singing lustily in accompaniment. They had struck up the opening bars of the old French ditty:

"*Il était une bergère,*
Et ron et ron petit pataplon."

"These cursed catgut scrapers," cried Conty in exasperation. "I'll have them turned out. One can't do anything with these fools while this row is going on."

The leader of the band was particularly active. Where he had got his fiddle from it was difficult to imagine: it gave forth sounds now creaking, now wheezing, anon screeching or howling and always discordant, provoking either laughter or the throwing of miscellaneous missiles at his head. They were all of them a scrubby lot, these musicians, unwashed, unshaven, in ragged breeches above their bare legs, shoes down-at-heel or else sabots, and grubby Phrygian caps adorned with tricolour cockades on their unkempt heads. They called themselves an itinerant orchestra whom the proprietor of the restaurant had enticed into the place under promise of a hot supper, and they were obviously doing their best to earn it:

"*Le chat qui la regarde,*
Et rem et roti petit pataplon."

"That rascal over there should be made to do honest work," Conty grunted, after he had made several vain attempts to shout the musicians down. "I call it an outrage on the country for a big hulking fellow like that to scrape a fiddle and ogle the girls when he should be training to fight the English."

"To fight the English?" Maurin interposed. "What do you mean, citizen?"

He and Conty had a tureen of hot soup on the table between them. Each dipped into it with a big ladle and filled up his plate to the rim. The soup was very hot and they blew on their spoons before conveying them to their mouths.

The musicians lifted up their cracked voices with a hoot and a cheer, whilst the chorus took up the lively tune:

"Le chat qui la regarde
D'un petit air fripon, pon, port,
D'un petit air fripon"

and the leader of the band, suiting the action to the word, cast side glances on the girls with an air as roguish as that of the cheese-maker's cat.

"What do you mean, Citizen Conty," the young lawyer reiterated, "by talking about fighting the English?"

"Just what I say," Conty replied. "We shall be at war with those barbarians before the month is out."

"Who told you that?"

"You'll hear of it, citizen lawyer. Ill news travels apace."

"But how did you know?" Maurin insisted.

"We government agents," Conty observed loftily, "know these things long before you ordinary people do."

"But . . ."

"As a matter of fact," the other now condescended to explain, "I was in Paris this morning. I met a number of deputies. There will be a debate about the whole affair in the Convention to-night. Citizen Chauvelin," he went on confidentially, "is back from London since the twenty-first. His work over there is finished, and he is travelling round the country on propaganda work for the government. Secret service, you know. I spoke with him. He told me he would be in Choisy tonight to have a look round. Now, you see," Conty concluded, as he attacked the savoury onion pie, "why I want to get all these fools into the right frame of mind. We want to show Paris what Choisy can do. What?"

"Chauvelin?" Maurin mused. "I've heard about him."

"And you'll see him presently. A clever fellow, but hard as steel. He was sent to England to represent our government, but he didn't stay long, and, name of a dog, how he does hate the English!"

The musicians had just led off with the last verse of the popular ditty:

"La bergère en colère,
Et ron, et ron, petit pataplon,"

when Conty jumped to his feet, and with a hasty: "There he is!" pushed his way through the crowd towards the door.

Arman Chauvelin, ex-envoy of the revolutionary government at the Court of St. James, had just returned from England, a sadder and wiser man: somewhat discredited perhaps, owing to his repeated failures in bringing the noted English spy, known as the Scarlet Pimpernel, to book, but nevertheless still standing high in the Councils of the various Committees, not only because of his great abilities, but because of his well-known hatred for the spy who had baffled him. He was still an important member of the Central Committee of Public Safety, and as such both respected and feared wherever he went.

Conty, the political agitator, was all obsequiousness when greeting this important personage. He conducted Citizen Chauvelin to the table where Louis Maurin had also finished eating, presented him to the lawyer, after which the two men pressed the newcomer to partake of supper as their guest. Chauvelin refused. He was not staying in Choisy this night, having other business to attend to, he said, in the Loiret district. He wouldn't even sit down. Despite his small, spare figure, he looked strangely impressive in his quietude, and, dressed as he was in sober black, amidst this noisy, excited crowd, many inquisitive glances were turned on him as he stood there. His thin white hands were clasped behind his back and he was listening to the answers which Conty and Maurin gave him in reply to his enquiries about the temper of the people in Choisy, and to their story of the outrage perpetrated on Docteur Pradel by the *ci-devant* Marquis up at La Rodière. This story interested him; he encouraged Conty in his efforts to keep the excitement of the populace at boiling point, and to inflame as far as possible the hatred of the people against the *aristos*. An armed raid on the château, he thought, would be a good move, if properly engineered, and as he intended to be back in Choisy in a couple of days, he desired the project to be put off until his return. He wouldn't listen to Maurin's objections to the raid.

"Those *aristos* at La Rodière interest me," he said. "There is an old woman, you say?"

"Yes," Conty informed him; "the *ci-devant* Marquise, the mother of the present young cub who thrashed Dr. Pradel."

"And there is a girl? A young girl?"

"Yes, citizen, and two old *aides-ménage*. But they are harmless enough."

"It would be so much better—" Maurin ventured to say.

"I was not asking your opinion, citizen lawyer," Chauvelin broke in haughtily. "What I've said, I've said. Prepare the way, Citizen Conty," he went on, "and as soon as I am back in Choisy I will let you know. If I mistake not," he added under his breath, almost as if he didn't wish the others to hear what he was saying, "we shall have some fun over that raid at La Rodière. An old woman, a young girl, two old servants! The very people to arouse the sympathy of our gallant English spies."

He nodded to the two men and turned to go. The crowd in the small restaurant was more dense than ever. People were sitting on the tables, the sideboards, and on the top of one another. The musicians had just played the last bar of the favoured tune, the chorus of which was bawled out by the enthusiastic crowd, to the accompaniment of thunderous handclaps and banging of miscellaneous tools on any surface that happened to be handy:

"La bergère en colère,
Tua son petit chaton, ton, ton,
Tua son petit chaton."

Chauvelin had real difficulty in pushing his way through this dense throng. He felt dazed, what with the noise and with the smell of stale food and of unwashed humanity; at any rate he put his curious experience down to an addled state of his brain, for while he was being pushed and jostled, and only saw individual faces through a kind of haze made of dust and fumes, he suddenly felt as if a pair of eyes, one pair only, was looking at him out of the hundred that were there. Of course, it was only a hallucination: he was sure it was, and yet for some reason or other he felt a cold shiver running down his spine. He tried to recapture the glance of those eyes, but no one now in the crowd seemed to be looking at him. The musicians had finished playing, or rather they tried to finish playing, but their audience wouldn't allow them to. Everyone was shouting at the top of his voice:

"Il était une bergere"

They wanted the whole of the six verses all over again.

Chauvelin got as far as the door, was on the point of opening it when a sound – the sound he hated more than any on earth – reached his ear above the din: it was a loud, prolonged, rather inane burst of laughter. Chauvelin did not swear, nor did he shiver again: his nerves were suddenly quite steady and if he could have translated his thoughts into words, he would have said with a chuckle: "I was right, then! And you are here, my gallant friend, at your old tricks again. Well, since you wish it, *à nous deux* once more, and I think I may promise you some fun, as you would call it, at La Rodière."

CHAPTER NINETEEN

The League

Although Choisy is only twelve or fifteen kilometres from Paris, it was in those days just a small provincial town with its Hotel de Ville and its Committee of Public Safety sitting there, its Grand' Place, its ancient castle then used as a prison, and its famous bridge across the Seine. To the South and West of the Grand' Place there were two or three residential streets with a few substantial, stone-built houses, the homes of professional men, or of tradespeople who had retired on a competence, and farther along a few isolated, poorer-looking houses, such a one as old Levet's, lying back from the road behind a small grille and a tiny from garden. But all these features only covered a small area, round which stretched fields and spinneys, with here and there a cottage for the most part roofless and derelict.

It was in one of these dilapidated cottages which stood in a meadow about half-way between Choisy and the height on which was perched the Château de La Rodière, that what looked like a troupe of itinerant musicians had sought shelter against the cold. They had made up a fire in the wide open hearth; the smoke curled up the chimney, and they sat round with their knees drawn up to their chins and their arms encircling their knees. There were four of them altogether inside the cottage, and one sat outside on a broken-down stool propped against the wall, apparently on the watch. In a corner of the room a number of musical instruments were piled up, a miscellaneous collection of violin, guitar, trumpet and drum.

Precariously perched on the top of this pile of rubbish sat Sir Percy Blakeney, Bart., the most fastidious dandy fashionable London had ever known, the arbiter of elegance, the friend of the Prince of Wales, the adored of every woman in England. He too was unwashed, unkempt, unshaved, his slender hands, those hands a queen had once termed exquisite, were covered with grime, his nails were in the deepest mourning. He wore a tattered blouse, on his head a Phrygian cap which had once been red. At the moment he was scraping a fiddle, drawing from it wailing sounds that provoked loud groans from his friends and an occasional missile hurled at his head.

"We are in for some fine sport, I imagine, what?" Lord Anthony Dewhurst remarked, and dug his teeth into a hard apple, which he had just extracted from his breeches' pocket.

"Tony," one of the others demanded – it was my Lord Hastings, "where did you get that apple?"

"My sweetheart gave it me. She stole it from her neighbour's garden . . ."

My Lord Tony got no further. He was attacked all at once from three sides. Three pairs of hands were stretched out to wrest the apple from him.

"We are in for some fine sport!" Lord Tony had declared before the attack on his apple was launched. He held it up at arm's length, trying to rescue it from his assailants who made grabs at it and invariably got in one another's way, until a firm hand finally seized it and Blakeney's pleasant drawly voice was raised to say:

"I'll toss you all for this precious thing . . . what there is left of it."

Sir Andrew Ffoulkes won the toss, and the apple, which had suffered wreckage during the fight, was finally hurled at the head of the revered chief, who had resumed his attempts at getting a tune out of his cracked fiddle. A distant church clock had struck eleven a few minutes ago. The man on the watch outside put his head in at the door and announced curtly: "Here he comes."

And presently Devinne came in. He was dressed in his ordinary clothes with dark coat, riding breeches and boots. His face wore a sullen look and he scarcely glanced either at his friends or at his chief, just flung himself on the ground in front of the fire and muttered between his teeth: "God! I'm tired!"

After a moment or two while no one else spoke he added as if grudgingly: "I'm sorry I'm late, Percy. I had to put up my horse and . . ."

"Listen to this, you fellows," Blakeney said with a chuckle as he scraped his fiddle and extracted from it a wailing version of the *Marseillaise*.

Young Devinne jumped to his feet, strode across the floor and snatched the fiddle out of Blakeney's hand.

"Percy!" he cried hoarsely.

"You don't like it, my dear fellow? Well, I don't blame you, but—"

"Percy," the young man rejoined, "you've got to be serious . . . you have got to help *me* ... it is all damnable . . . damnable ... I shall go mad if this goes on much longer . . . and if you don't help me."

He was obviously beside himself with excitement, strode up and down the place, his hand pressed tightly against his forehead. The words came tumbling out through his lips, whilst his voice was raucous with agitation.

Blakeney watched him for a moment or two without speaking. His face through all the grime and disfigurement wore that expression of infinite sympathy and understanding of which he, of all men, appeared to hold the secret, the understanding of other people's troubles and difficulties, and that wordless sympathy which so endeared him to his friends.

"Help you, my dear fellow," he now said. "Of course, we'll all help you, if you want us. What are we here for but to help each other, as well as those poor wretches who are in trouble through no fault of their own?"

Then, as Devinne said nothing for the moment, just continued to pace up and down, up and down like a trapped feline, he went on: "Tell us all about it, boy. It is this La Rodière business, isn't it?"

"It is. And a damnable business it will be, unless . . ."

"Unless what?"

"Unless you do something about it in double quick time. Those ruffians in Choisy are planning mischief. You knew that two days ago, and you have done nothing. I wanted to go up to La Rodière to warn them of what was in the wind. I could have done it yesterday, gone up there this morning. It wouldn't have interfered with any of your plans: and it would have meant all the world to me. But what did you do? You took me along with Stowmarries to drive that old abbé as far as Vitry, a job any fool could have done."

"But you did it so admirably, my dear fellow," Sir Percy put in quietly, when young Devinne paused for want of breath. He had come to a halt in front of his chief, glaring at him with eyes that held anything but deference; his face was flushed, beads of perspiration stood on his forehead and glued his matted hair to his temples.

"You did the fool's job, as you call it, as admirably as you have always done everything the League set you to do; and you did it because you happen to have been born a gentleman and the son of a very great gentleman who honoured me with his friendship, and because you have always remembered that you swore to me on your word of honour that, while we are all of us engaged on the business of the League, you would obey me in all things."

"An oath of that sort," the young man retorted vehemently, "does not bind a man when—"

"When he is in love, and the woman he loves is in danger . . ." Sir Percy broke in gently. "That is what you were going to say, was it not, lad?"

He rose and put a kindly hand on Devinne's shoulder.

"Don't think I don't understand, my dear fellow," he said earnestly. "I do. God knows I do. But you know that the word of honour of an English gentleman is a big thing. A very, very big thing and a very hard one sometimes. So hard that nothing on earth can break it: but if by the agency of some devil, that word should be broken, then honour is irretrievably shattered too.

"Now tell me," he resumed more lightly, "did you on your way back from Vitry call in on Charles Levet and tell him that the Abbé Edgeworth is by now safely on his way to the Belgian frontier?"

Devinne looked sullen.

"I forgot," he said curtly.

Blakeney gave a quaint little laugh:

"Gad! That is a pity," he said. "Fancy forgetting a little thing like that. But we have no control over our memory, have we? Well, dear lad, you have a long walk before you, so you'd best start right away now. Tell Charles Levet that the abbé is now with some Belgian friends who are looking after him. I promised the old man that I would let him know, he has been very good to us, and we must keep in touch with him. I have an idea that he and his family may have need of us one day."

Devinne still looked sulky.

"You want me to go to the Levets' house? Now?"

"Well, you did forget to call in on your way. Didn't you?"

"Then don't expect me back here – I shall go straight on to La Rodière."

There was a slight pause, during which no human sound disturbed the kind of awed hush that had fallen over this squalid derelict place. Blakeney had scarcely made a movement when young Devinne thus flung defiance in his face. Only Sir Andrew Ffoulkes, the man who perhaps among all the others knew every line around the mouth of his chief, and every expression in the deep-set lazy blue eyes, noted a certain stiffening of the massive figure, and a tightening of the firm lips. But this only lasted for a few seconds. The very next moment Blakeney threw back his head and his prolonged inimitable laugh raised the echo of the dilapidated walls. The humour of the situation had tickled his fancy. This boy!! . . . well! . . . it was absolutely priceless. Those flaming eyes, the obstinate mouth, the attitude of a schoolboy in the act of defying his schoolmaster, and half afraid of the cane in the dominie's hand seemed to him ludicrous in the extreme.

"My dear fellow," he said, and once again the friendly hand was laid on Devinne's shoulder, and the kindliest of lazy blue eyes looked down on this contumacious boy, "you really are a marvel. But don't let me keep you," he went on airily. "I don't suppose the Levets will invite you to dinner, and if they don't it will be hours before you are there and back and able to get something to eat. Anyway, you will meet us again in the restaurant, without fail, at one o'clock."

This, of course, was a command. Blakeney had been standing between Devinne and the direct access to the door. He now stepped a little to one side, leaving the way free for the young man to go out. There was an awkward moment. Devinne, half-ashamed but still half-defiant, would not meet the chief's gently ironical glance. The others said nothing, and after a minute or two, he finally strode out of the cottage. A thin layer of snow lay on the field and road, and deadened the sound of his footsteps. Glynde after a time put his head in at the door.

"He is out of sight," he announced.

Lord Hastings jumped to his feet.

"My turn to watch," he said. "Glynde is frozen stiff."

"Never mind about the watch now," Sir Percy interrupted. "We are fairly safe here, and there are one or two things I want to talk over with you fellows.

"We are agreed, are we not, that for the next day or two we must concentrate on those wretched people up at La Rodière? Monsieur le Marquis François we care nothing about, it is true, but there is the old lady, there is the young girl and there are the two old people who have been faithful servants and are, therefore, just as much in danger as their masters. We cannot leave François out of our calculations because neither his mother nor his sister would go away without him. So it will be five people – not to say six – whom we shall have to get over to England as soon as danger becomes really imminent. That might be even no later than this evening. We shall be up there with the riotous crowd during the afternoon, and we shall have our fiddle, our trumpets and our drums, not to mention our melodious voices with which we can always divert their thoughts from unprofitable mischiefs, to some equally boisterous but less dangerous channels. You all know the ropes now: we have played that game successfully before and can do it again, what?"

There was unanimous assent to the project.

"Yes, by gad!" came from one of them.

"It is a game I particularly affection," from another.

"Always makes me think of tally-ho!" – this from that keen sportsman, Lord Anthony Dewhurst.

And: "Go on, Percy! This is violently exciting," – from them all.

"We'll bide our time, of course," Blakeney now continued. "Our friends, the worst of the hotheads, once they have accomplished their purpose and asserted their rights and privileges to make themselves unpleasant to the *aristos*, will turn their backs on La Rodière, their spirits slightly damped perhaps. They will then crowd into the nearest cabaret, there is one close to the château, they will talk things over, eat and drink and allow those hellish agitators to talk their heads off, while we shall continue to addle their brains with strains of sentimental music. And all the time we'll be watching the opportunity for action. Of course, during the course of a long afternoon a number of incidents are certain to occur which we cannot foresee and which will either aid or hinder us. You know my favourite motto, to take Chance by the one hair on his head and force him to do my bidding. In a small place like this by far our best plan will be to proceed once more to La Rodière as soon as the crowd has made its way back to Choisy and we find the coast fairly clear. We'll go in the guise of a squad of Gendarmerie Nationale and there arrest Monsieur le Marquis, his mother, his sister and the two faithful old servants. With a little luck, those tactics are sure to succeed."

He paused a moment, striding up and down the narrow room, a set look on his face. His followers who watched him waited in silence, knowing that through that active brain the plan for the daring rescue of those innocents was gradually being elaborated and matured. After a time Blakeney resumed.

"I am not taking Devinne with us at any time this afternoon. The crowd up at the château is certain to deal harshly with the family, and if Mademoiselle Cécile is rough-handled he might do or say something rash which would compromise us all. So I shall send him to our headquarters outside Corbeil, to instruct Galveston and Holte to have horses ready and generally to be prepared for our arrival with a certain number of refugees, among whom there will be two ladies. Galveston is very expert in making all arrangements. I know I can trust him and Holte to do the necessary as far as lies in their power."

"At what time do you think you will carry the whole thing through, Percy?" one of the others asked. "The arrest, I mean, and the flight from La Rodière?"

"I cannot tell you that just yet. Sometime during the night, of course. I would prefer the early dawn for many reasons, if only for the sake of the light. The night might be very dark, bad for fast driving. But I will give you instructions about that later. It will only be by hearing the talk around us that I shall be able to decide finally. I shall also have to ascertain exactly how much help mine host of the cabaret will be willing to give us."

"You mean the cabaret on the Corbeil road, not far from La Rodière?"

"A matter of two or three hundred yards, yes. It boasts the poetic sign: 'The Dog Without a Tail.' I have been in touch with mine host and his Junoesque wife already."

"Percy, you are wonderful!"

"Glynde, you are an ass."

Laughter all round and then Blakeney resumed once more: "There will also be Pradel to consider."

"Pradel?" one of them asked. "Why?"

"If we leave him here, we'd only have to come back and get him later. They'll have him, you may be sure of that. He has one or two bitter enemies, as men of his outstanding worth always have, and there are always petty jealousies both male and female that make for mischief. Anyhow, he is too fine a fellow to be left for these wolves to devour. But I shall be better able to judge of all this after I have gauged the temper of the crowd both at La Rodière and afterwards."

"That young Marquis was a fool not to have got away before now."

"He wouldn't hear of it. You know their ways. They are all alike. Some of them quite fine fellows, but they have not yet learned to accept the inevitable, and the women, poor dears, have no influence over their menfolk."

"Then we are going up to La Rodière with the crowd, I take it," Lord Hastings observed.

"Certainly we are."

"You haven't forgotten, Percy, by any chance . . ?" Sir Andrew suggested.

"I think not. You mean, my dear friend Monsieur Chambertin, beg pardon, Chauvelin?" Blakeney rejoined gaily. "No, by gad, I had not forgotten him. I am pining for his agreeable society. I wonder now whether during his last stay in London he has learned how to tie his cravat as a gentleman should."

"Percy! Will you be . . ." Lord Tony hazarded.

"Careful, was the word you were going to say, eh, Tony? Of course, I *won't* be careful, but I give you my word that my friend Chambertin is not going to get me – not this time."

A soft look stole into his deep-set eyes. It seemed as if he had seen a vision of his exquisite wife Marguerite wandering lonely and anxious, in her garden at Richmond waiting for him, her husband and lover, who was her one absorbing thought, whilst he . . . she too was his absorbing thought, the great thought, that filled his mind and warmed his heart: but it was not all-absorbing. Foremost in his mind were all those innocents, little children, men and women, young and old who, unknown to themselves, seemed to call to him, to stretch out imploring arms towards him for comfort and for help: those were the moments when Marguerite's lovely face appeared blurred by the rain of tears shed in devastated homes and inside prison walls, and when he, the adoring husband and devoted lover, dismissed with a sigh of longing, all thoughts of holding her in his arms.

"And now," he said, his voice perfectly firm and incisive, "it is time that we collected our goods and saw whether our friends down at Choisy are ready for the fight."

They set to, to collect their musical instruments, their fiddles and drums and trumpets. Just for a moment the glamour of the coming adventure faded before one hideous fear of which not one of them had ever spoken yet, but which troubled them all.

Blakeney was humming the tune of the *Marseillaise*.

"I wish I could remember the words of the demmed thing," he said. "What comes after: *'Aux armes citoyens!'*? Ffoulkes, you ought to know."

Sir Andrew replied almost gruffly: "I don't," and Lord Tony called suddenly to his chief: "Percy."

"Yes! What is it?"

"That fellow, Devinne . . ."

"What about him?"

"You don't trust him, do you?"

"The son of old Gery Rudford, the straightest rider to hounds I ever knew? Of course I trust him."

"I wish you wouldn't," Hastings put in.

"The father may have been a sportsman," Glynde added; "the son certainly is not."

"Don't say that, my dear fellow," Blakeney rejoined; "it sounds like treason to the rest of us. The boy is all right. Just mad with jealousy, that's all. He has offended his lady love and she will have nothing more to do with him. I dare say he is sorry that he behaved quite so badly the other morning. I'll admit that he did behave like a cad. He is only a boy, and jealousy . . . well! We know what a bad counsellor jealousy can be. But between that and doing what you all have in your minds . . . egad! I'll not believe it!"

Hastings murmured savagely: "He'd better not."

Sir Phillip Glynde nearly punched a hole in the drum, trying to express his feelings, and Lord Tony muttered a murderous oath. Sir Andrew alone said nothing. He knew – they all did, in fact – that Blakeney was one of those men who are so absolutely loyal and straight, that they simply cannot conceive treachery in a friend. Not one of them trusted Devinne. It was all very well making allowances for a boy thwarted in love, but there had been an expression in this one's face which suggested something more sinister than petty jealousy, and though nothing more was said at the moment, they all registered a vow to keep a close eye on his movements until this adventure in Choisy, which promised to be so exciting, had come to a successful issue, and they were all back in England once more, when they hoped to enlist Lady Blakeney's support in persuading Percy not to rely on young Devinne again.

CHAPTER TWENTY

A Likely Ally

Heavy hearted and still sullen and rebellious, St. John Devinne, familiarly known as Johnny, made his way through the town to the Levets' house. All sorts of wild schemes chased one another through his brain, schemes which had the one main objective in view to see Cécile de la Rodière, and, by giving her and her family warning of the mischief contemplated against them by the rabble of Choisy, to worm himself once more into her good graces and regain the love which he had forfeited so foolishly.

Chance has a very funny way of shuffling the cards in the game of life. Here were two men, Louis Maurin, the French lawyer, and Lord St. John Devinne, son of an English Duke, both deadly enemies of Simon Pradel, the local doctor, who hardly knew either of them, but who was looked upon by both as a serious rival to their love, a rival who must incontinently be swept out of the way. Maurin desired his moral and physical downfall in order to find his way clear for the wooing of Blanche Levet, whilst Devinne had reluctantly come to the conclusion that Cécile de la Rodière had so far demeaned herself as to fall in love with the fellow. She certainly had turned her back on him, Devinne, ever since that fatal morning, and unless he now took strong measures on his own behalf, he might lose all chance of ever winning her.

Devinne hurried along, hoping to deliver his message at the Levets and be well on the way to La Rodière before the crowd had been stirred into an organised march on the château. He pulled the collar of his greatcoat up to his ears and his hat down to meet it, for the wind blowing right across the Grand' Place was cutting. At the angle of the Rue Verte he suddenly became aware of the man who at the moment was foremost in his thoughts. Simon Pradel was standing at the corner of the street, talking to a girl whose head was swathed in a shawl. Devinne thought that in her he recognised Levet's daughter, whom he had once seen at the château. She was talking heatedly and appeared distressed, for her voice shook as she spoke and she had one hand on Pradel's arm as if she were either entreating or restraining him. As he went past them, Devinne heard the girl say: "Don't go up there, Simon! Those *aristos* hate you. They will only think that you are fawning on them . . . don't go, Simon. . . you will regret it, and they will despise you for it . . . they will . . ."

She seemed to be working herself up into a state of excitement and kept on raising her voice until it sounded quite shrill.

Pradel tried to pacify her. "Hush, my dear," he said; "don't talk so loud: anyone might hear you."

But she was not to be pacified:

"I don't care who hears me," she retorted; "those *aristos* are devils who deserve all they will get. Why should you care what happens to them? . . . you only care because you are in love with Cécile . . ."

She burst into tears. Pradel put an arm round her shoulders.

"And now you talk like a foolish child. . . ."

Devinne had instinctively halted within earshot, but now he was in danger of being seen, and this he did not wish, so, rather reluctantly, he turned and went his way. It was too soon yet to gauge the importance of what he had heard, but already he felt that in this girl, who was obviously half crazy with jealousy, he might find a useful ally, should he fail to obtain an interview with Cécile on his own initiative. In any case, she must have the same desire that he had, namely, to keep Cécile and Pradel apart. This thought elated him, and it was with a more springy

119

step that he strode briskly down the Rue Verte and after a few minutes rang the outside bell of the Levets' house.

Charles Levet opened the door to him, received the message sent to him by his friend Professor d'Arblay, expressed his satisfaction at hearing that Monsieur l'Abbé Edgeworth was safely on his way to Belgium, asked his visitor to join the family at dinner, and on the latter's courteous refusal, bade him a friendly farewell. Back the other side of the gate, Devinne paused a moment to reconsider the whole situation. Should he continue his protest against an irksome discipline, which he felt was incompatible with his dignity as a man of action and of thought, or should he make a virtue of necessity, meet Blakeney and the others in the Restaurant Tison, hear their plans and then act in accordance with his own schemes and in his own interest?

On the whole he felt inclined to adopt the latter course. He didn't want to quarrel with Blakeney, not just yet, nor yet with the others who were all influential and popular men about town, who might, if the split came, make his position extremely uncomfortable in London. There was nothing he desired more at the moment than to extricate himself from the entanglement of the League, but he was wise enough to realise that if this was done at this juncture, he would, on his return to England, find the doors of more than one smart hostess closed against him. So for the moment there was nothing for it but to keep his appointment with Percy and the others in the Restaurant Tison, and in any case learn what plans were being evolved for this afternoon. If nothing was going to be done right away for the safety of Cécile, then he would act on his own. To this he had fully made up his mind. All this would mean going back now to that horrible cottage and getting once more into those filthy rags which he had come to hate, but he didn't really care now that he knew he could count on the co-operation of a jealous woman, whom he had heard cry out in a voice shrill with emotion: "You only care because you are in love with Cécile!"

BOOK III

MADEMOISELLE

CHAPTER TWENTY-ONE

Citizen Chauvelin

It must not be thought for a moment that authority as represented by the Gendarmerie Nationale, regular or volunteer, in any way approved, let alone aided and abetted, the insurrectionary movements that were such a feature of the first two years of the Revolution. Authority did not even wink at them, did its best, in fact, to put a stop to these marches and raids on neighbouring châteaux which only ended in a number of broken heads, in loot and unnecessary violence, and a severe remonstrance from the government who had its eye on all property owned by *ci-devants* and strongly disapproved of its wanton destruction at the hands of an irresponsible mob.

Thus it was that as soon as Simon Pradel became aware of the imminence of the mischief contemplated against the *aristos* up at La Rodière, and thinking only of Cécile and her safety, he went straight to the Hotel de Ville and drew the attention of the Chief Commissary of the Gendarmerie to what was in the wind.

"Citizen Conty," he explained, "has inflamed everyone's temper to such an extent that there is hardly a man or woman in Choisy to-day who will not march up to La Rodière, and even if they do not commit murder, will certainly destroy a great deal of property which rightly belongs to the nation."

He was clever enough to know that it was this argument that would prevail. The Chief Commissary looked grave. He was mindful of his own position, not to say his own head, and therefore took the one drastic course which was most likely to minimise the mischief. He gave it out through a proclamation blazoned by the town crier, that by order of the government there would be no Day of Rest this Sunday, and that the work in the factories would be carried on as usual. This meant that four-fifths of the male population of Choisy and one-third of its womenfolk would be kept at work until seven o'clock in the evening and that the plans for the afternoon's holiday would have to be considerably modified or abandoned altogether.

In the Restaurant Tison, which was to be the starting point for the march on La Rodière, turbulence had given place to gloom. Even the troupe of musicians who were working with a will to try and revive drooping spirits failed to bring about that state of excitement so essential to the success of the proposed plan. Citizen Conty, too, had received his orders. "Let the people simmer down," the Chief Commissary had commanded, "the government does not want a riot in Choisy just now." Conty didn't care one way or the other. He was paid to carry out government orders, and knew how to steer clear of trouble if these happened to be contradictory. It was close on two o'clock already. The factory bell calling the workers back would ring in half an hour, and Conty was getting anxious.

Once the workers had gone back to the factory it would be too late to carry out the original plan, which had been approved of by Chauvelin, and Conty didn't relish the idea of having to shoulder the responsibility of what might or might not occur in that case. He would have preferred to receive final orders from a member of an influential committee, one who alone could issue orders over the head of the Chief Commissary.

It was then with a feeling of intense relief that precisely at twenty minutes past two he saw the sable-clad figure of Chauvelin working his way towards him through the crowd.

"Well? And what have you done?" Chauvelin queried curtly, and refused the chair which Conty had obsequiously offered him.

"You have heard the proclamation, citizen?" Conty responded; "about work at the factory this afternoon?"

"I have. But I am asking you what you have done."

"Nothing, citizen. I was waiting for you."

"You didn't carry out my orders?"

"I hadn't any, citizen."

"Two days ago I gave you my commands to prepare the way for an armed raid on the château as soon as I was back in Choisy. Yesterday I sent you word that I would be back to-day. But I see no sign of a raid being organised either by you or anyone else."

"The decree was only promulgated a couple of hours ago. All the able-bodied men and women will have to go back to work in a few minutes; there was nothing to be done."

"How do you mean? There was nothing to be done? What about all these people here? I can see at least a hundred that do not work in the factory, more than enough for what I want."

Conty gave a contemptuous shrug.

"The halt and the maimed," he retorted acidly; "the weaklings and the women. I thought every moment you would come, Citizen Chauvelin, and issue a counter decree giving the workers their usual Day of Rest. As you didn't come, I didn't know what to do."

"So you let them all get into the doldrums."

"What could I do, citizen?" Conty reiterated sullenly. "I had no orders."

"You had no initiative, you mean? If you had you would have realised that if half the population of Choisy will in a moment or two go to work, the other half will still be here and ready for any mischief."

"Those bumpkins . . ."

"Yes, louts and muckworms and cinderwenches. And let me tell you, Citizen Conty, that it is not for you to sneer at such excellent material, rather see that you utilise it as I directed you

123

to do in the name of the government who know how to punish slackness as well as to reward energy."

Having said this, Chauvelin turned his back abruptly on the discomfited Conty and made for the door. Even as he did so an outside bell clanged out the summons for the workers to return to the factory. There was a general hubbub, chairs pushed aside and scraping against the stone floor, the tramp of feet all making for the door, voices shouting from one end of the room to the other. And right through the din, there came to Chauvelin's ears, at the very moment that he passed through the swing-doors, a sound that dominated every other, just a prolonged merry, irritatingly inane laugh.

Hardly had the last able-bodied man gone out of the place than Citizen Conty had climbed on the top of a table, and begun his harangue by apostrophising the musicians.

"What mean you, rascals," he cried lustily, "by scraping your fiddles to give us nothing but sentimental ballads fit only for weaklings to hear? Our fine men have gone to work for their country, and here you are trying to make us sing about shepherdesses and their cats. *Mordieu!* Have you never heard of the air that every patriotic Frenchman should know, an air that puts fire into our blood, not water: *'Allons enfants de la patrie! Le jour de gloire est arrivé!'*"

At first the people did not take much notice of Conty; the men had gone and there was nothing much to do but go back to one's own hovels and mope there till they returned. But when presently the musicians, in response to the speaker's challenge, took up the strains of the revolutionary song, they straightened out their backs, turned about the better to hear the impassioned oratory which now poured from Citizen Conty's lips.

He was in his element. He held all these poor, half-starved people in a fever by the magic of his oratory, and he would not allow their fever to cool down again. From an abstract reference to any château to the actual mention of La Rodière did not take him long. Now he was speaking of Docteur Pradel, the respected citizen of Choisy, the friend of the poor, who had dared to express his political opinions in the presence of those arrogant *ci-devants*, and what had happened? He had been insulted, outraged, thrashed like a dog!

"And you, citizens," he once more bellowed, "though the government has not called upon you to fashion bayonets and sabres, are you going to sit still and allow your sworn enemies, the enemies of France, to ride rough-shod over you now that our glorious revolution has levelled all ranks and brought the most exalted heads down under the guillotine? You have no sabres or bayonets, it is true, but you have your scythes and your axes and you have your fists. Are you going to sit still, I say, and not show those traitors up there on the hill that there is only one sovereignty in the world that counts and which they must obey, the sovereignty of the people?"

The magic words had their usual effect. A perfect storm of applause greeted them, and all at once they began to sing: *"Allons enfants de la patrie!"* and the musicians blew their trumpets and banged their drums and soon there reigned in the restaurant the sort of mighty row beloved by agitators.

CHAPTER TWENTY-TWO

At the Château

It did not take Conty long after that to persuade a couple of hundred people who were down in the dumps and saw no prospect of getting out of them that it was their duty to go at once to the Château de la Rodière and show those arrogant *ci-devants* that when the sovereignty of the people was questioned, it would know how to turn the tables on those who dared to flout it. So most of what was left of the population of Choisy assembled on the Grand' Place, there formed itself into a compact body and started to march through the town, and thence up the hill, headed by a band of musicians who had sprung up from nowhere a few days ago and had since then greatly contributed to the gaiety inside the cafe and restaurants by their spirited performance of popular airs. On this great occasion they headed the march with their fiddles and trumpets and drum. There were five of them altogether and their leader, a great hulking fellow who should have been fighting for his country instead of scraping the catgut, was soon very popular with the crowd. His rendering of the "Marseillaise" might be somewhat faulty, but he was such a lively kind of vagabond that he put everyone into good humour long before they reached the château.

And they remained in rare good humour. For them this march, this proposed baiting of the *aristos* was just an afternoon's holiday, something to take them out of themselves, to help them to forget their misery, their squalor, the ever-present fear that conditions of life would get worse rather than better. Above all, it lured them into the belief that this glorious revolution had done something stupendous for them – they didn't quite know what, poor things, but there it was: the millennium, so the men from Paris kept on assuring them.

Actually a mob – an angry mob – say in England, in Russia or Germany, is usually just a mass of dull, tenacious and probably vindictive humanity; but in France, even during the fiercest days of revolution, there was always an element of inventiveness, almost of genius, in the crowd of men and women that went hammering at the gates of châteaux, insisted on seeing its owners, even when, as in Versailles, these were still their King and Queen, and devised a score of ways of humiliating and baiting them without necessarily resorting to violence. Thus, a French mob is unlike any other in the world.

And so it was in this instance with the hundred or two of women and derelicts who marched up the hill to La Rodière in the wake of an unwashed, out-at-elbows, raffish troupe of musicians. They stumped along, those, at any rate who were able-bodied, shouting and singing snatches of the Marseillaise, not feeling the cold, which was bitter, nor the fatigue of breasting the incline up to the château, on a road slippery with ice and snow. They were as lively as they could be, not knowing exactly what they were going to do once they got up there and came face to face with the *ci-devant* Marquis and Marquise, for whom they had worked in the past and from whom they had received alternately many kindnesses and many blows.

And right in the rear of them all there walked two men. One of them was Citizen Conty, the paid agent of the government; the other was small and spare, was dressed from head to foot in sober black, his voluminous black cloak effectually concealing the tricolour scarf which he wore round his waist. He never spoke to his companion while they both trudged up the road in the wake of the crowd, but now and then he would throw quick, searching glances on the surrounding landscape and up at the cloud-covered sky, almost as if he were seeking to wrest from the heavens or the earth some secret which Nature alone could reveal. This was Citizen Chauvelin, at one time representative of the revolutionary government at the English Court, now a member of the newly constituted Committee of Public Safety, the most powerful organisation in the country, created for the suppression of treason and the unmasking of traitors and of spies.

At the top of the hill there, where the narrow footpath abuts on the main road, the two men came to a halt. Chauvelin said curtly to his companion: "You may go back now, Citizen Conty."

Conty was only too thankful to obey; he turned down the path and was soon out of sight and out of earshot.

Chauvelin walked on in the direction of the château. The crowd was a long way ahead now, even the stragglers had caught up with them, and there was lusty cheering when the gates of La Rodière first came into view.

Chauvelin came to a halt once more. There was no one in sight, and the perfect quietude of the place was only disturbed by the sound of revellings gradually dying away in the distance. Chauvelin now gave a soft, prolonged whistle, and, a minute or two later a man in the uniform of the Gendarmerie Nationale, but wrapped in a huge cloak from head to foot so that his accoutrements could not be seen, came out cautiously from the thicket close by. Chauvelin beckoned to him to approa"Well, citizen sergeant," he demanded, "did you notice any man who might be that damnable English spy?"

"No, citizen, I can't say that I did. I was well placed, too, and could see the whole crowd file past me, but I couldn't spot any man who appeared abnormally tall or who looked like an Englishman."

"I expect you were too dense to notice," Chauvelin retorted dryly. "But, anyway, it makes no matter. I will spot him soon enough. As soon as I do I will give the signal we agreed on. You remember it?"

"Yes, citizen. A long whistle twice and then one short one."

"How many men have you got?"

"Thirty, citizen, and three corporals."

"Where are they?"

"Twenty, with two corporals, in the stables. Ten with one corporal in the coach-house."

"Any outdoor workers about? Grooms or gardeners?"

"Two gardeners, citizen, and one in the stables."

"They understand?"

"Yes, citizen. I have promised them fifty livres each if they keep their eyes and mouth shut, and certain arrest and death if they do not. They are terrified and quite safe to hold their tongue."

"My orders, citizen sergeant, are that the men remain where they are till they hear the signal, two prolonged whistles, followed by one short one. Like this" – and he took a toy whistle out of his waistcoat pocket and blew softly into it, twice and once again, in the manner which he had described.

"As soon as they hear the whistle, but not before, they are to come out of their hiding-place and make their way in double quick time to the house. Ten men with one corporal will then take up their stand outside each of the three entrances of the château. You know where these are?"

"Quite well, citizen."

"No one must be allowed to go out of the château until I give the order."

"I quite understand, citizen."

"It will be the worse for you if you do not. I suppose the men know that we are after that damnable English spy who calls himself the Scarlet Pimpernel?"

"They know it, citizen."

"And that there is a government reward of fifty livres for every soldier of the Republic who aids in his capture?"

"The men are not likely to shirk their duty, citizen."

"Very well, then. And now about the *aristos* up there. There is the *ci-devant* Marquis with his mother and sister, also two *aides-ménage* who are not ashamed to serve those traitors to their country. Those five, then, will be under arrest, but remain in the château till we are ready for them. I will give you further orders as to them. We shall convey them under escort to Choisy some time between the later afternoon, after we have packed the rabble off, and early dawn to-morrow; I have not decided which, but will let you know later. You have a coach handy?"

"Yes, citizen. There is a cabaret close by here, farther up the road. We put up the coach there in the yard, and left two of our men in charge. The place is quiet and quite handy."

"That is all, citizen sergeant. You may go and transmit my orders to your corporals. As soon as you have done that, go as unobtrusively as you can into the house. No one will notice you. They will be too busy baiting the *aristos* by then. Keep as near as you can to the room where the crowd is at its thickest – the noise will guide you – and wait for me there."

Chauvelin, of the Committee of Public Safety, was not the man one could ever argue or plead with. The sergeant, resigned and submissive, saluted and turned on his heel. He walked away in the direction of the stables. Chauvelin remained for quite a long while standing there alone, his thoughts running riot in his brain. Twice the Scarlet Pimpernel had slipped through his fingers since that memorable night four months ago at Lord Grenville's ball in London when he, Chauvelin, had first realised that that daring and adventurous spy was none other than Sir Percy Blakeney, the arbiter of fashion, the seemingly inane fop who kept London society in a perpetual ripple of laughter at his foolish antics, the most fastidious exquisite in sybaritic England.

"You were part of that unwashed crowd in the Restaurant Tison, my fine friend," he murmured to himself, "for I heard you laugh and felt your eyes daring to mock me again. Mock me? Aye! But not for long, my gallant fellow. The trap is laid and you won't escape me this time, let me assure you of that, and it will be your 'dear Monsieur Chambertin' who will mock you when you are brought down and gagged and trussed like a fowl ready for roasting."

CHAPTER TWENTY-THREE

The Rigaudon

Now then *"allons enfants de la patri-i-i-e."* The crowd in a high
state of excitement had pushed open the great gates of La
Rodière – these were never bolted these days – and marched up
the stately avenue bordered by a double row of gigantic elms
which seemed to be waving and nodding their majestic crowns
at sight of the motley throng. Ahead of them all marched the
musicians, blowing with renewed gusto into their brass trumpets
or sending forth into the frosty atmosphere prolonged rolls of
drums. Only the fiddler was not in his usual place. He had
dropped back on the other side of the gate in order to fit a fresh
length of catgut on his violin to replace a broken one. But he was
not missed at this juncture, for the other musicians appeared
bent on proving the fact that a fiddle was not of much value as
a noise-maker when there were trumpets and drums in the
orchestra.

Up the crowd marched and mounted the perron steps to the
front door of the mansion. They pulled the chain and the bell
responded with a loud clang – once, twice and three times. They
were themselves making such a noise, shouting and singing, that
probably poor old Paul, rather scared but trying to be brave, did
not actually hear the bell. However, he did hear it after a time
and with shaking knees and trembling voice went to get his
orders from Monsieur le Marquis. By this time those in the
forefront of the crowd had tugged so hard at the bell-pull that
it snapped and came down with a clatter on the marble floor of

the perron; whereupon they set to with their fists and nearly brought the solid front door down with their hammerings and their kicks. They didn't hear Paul's shuffling footsteps coming down the great staircase, nor yet his drawing of the bolts, so that when after a minute or two, while they were still hammering and kicking, the door was opened abruptly, the foremost in the ranks tumbled over one another into the hall. This caused great hilarity. Hurrah! Hurrah! This was going to be a wonderful afternoon's holiday! Onward children of *la patrie*, the day of glory has certainly arrived. Striving, pushing, laughing, singing, waving arms and stamping feet the bulk of the crowd made its way up the grand staircase. Poor old Paul! As well attempt to stem the course of an avalanche as to stop this merry jostling crowd from going where it listed. Some of them indeed wandered into the reception-rooms to right and left of the hall, the larger and smaller dining-rooms, the library, the long gallery and so on, but they found nothing worth destroying.

Upstairs the rest of the merry party, after wandering from room to room, arrived in the grand *salon* where close on four years ago now the remains of the late Marquis de la Rodière had rested for three days before being removed for interment in Paris. On that occasion they had all come to a halt, awed in spite of themselves, by the somewhat eerie atmosphere of the place, the dead flowers, the torn laces, the smell of guttering candles and of stale incense. The crowd to-day, more jaunty than they were then, had also come to a halt, but only for a few moments. They stared wide-eyed at the objects ranged against the walls, the gilded consols, the mirrors, the crystal sconces and the chairs, and presently they spied the platform whereon in the happy olden days the musicians used to stand playing dance music for Monsieur le Marquis and his guests. The spinet was still there and the desk of the conductor, and a number of stands in gilded wood which were used for holding the pieces of music.

Amid much excitement and laughter the musicians were called up to mount the platform. This they were quite willing to do, but where was the leader, the fiddler with the grimy face and toothless mouth whose stentorian voice would have raised the dead? A small group who had wandered up to the window saw him stumping up the avenue. They gave a warning shout, the window was thrown open, and cries of *"Allons!* Hurry up!" soon galvanised him into activity. He was lame, and dragged his left leg, but the infirmity did not appear to worry him. As soon as he had reached the perron he started scraping his fiddle. He was met at the foot of the staircase by an enthusiastic throng who carried him shoulder high, and dropped him down all of a heap on the musicians' platform. And a queer sight did this vagabond orchestra look up there in their rags and tatters, unwashed, unkempt, wielding their ramshackle fiddles and trumpets and drumsticks.

The musicians struck up *"Sur le Pont d'Avignon"* the only dance tune they knew, and that one none too well.

> *"Sur le pont d'Avignon,*
> *On y danse, on y danse,*
> *Sur le pont d'Avignon,*
> *On y danse tout en rond."*

It was at this point that the outburst of laughter rose to such a high pitch that the thrifty housewives down below were tempted to abandon their loot. What had caused the uproar was the sudden appearance of the *ci-devant* Marquis through what seemed to be a hole in the wall. As a matter of fact this was a door masked by tapestry which gave first on a vestibule and thence on a small boudoir where Madame la Marquise had been sitting with François and Cécile, and with poor Marie huddled up in a corner like a frightened rabbit, all fully expecting that the tumultuous crowd would soon tire, and content itself as it had done four years ago with breaking a few windows, carrying off what portable furniture there was left in the *salon,* and ending its unpleasant visitation in the cellar and the larder, where there was little enough to tempt its greed.

François de la Rodière was for facing the rabble with a riding-

whip. For a time his sister was able to restrain him from such a
palpable act of folly, but presently the sound of ribald laughter
coming from the grand *salon* where his father had once lain in
state, surrounded by flowers and ecclesiastical appurtenances, so
outraged him that he lost all control over himself and all sense
of prudence. He shook off Cécile's detaining hand, and strode
out of the room. Madame la Marquise had offered no protest or
advice, she was one of those women, the product of generations
of French highborn ladies who, entrenched as it were in their
own dignity, never gave a single thought to such a matter as a
social upheaval. "It will all pass away," was their dictum, "God
will punish them all in His own time!" So she turned a deaf ear
to the rioting of the rabble, and went on with her crochet work
with perfect serenity.

Cécile, on the other hand, was all for conciliation. She knew
her brother's violent temper and genuinely feared for his safety
should he provoke the crowd, who at present seemed good-
tempered enough, either by word or gesture. She followed him
into the vestibule, and saw him take a riding-whip off the wall
and throw open the narrow door which gave on the grand *salon*.
The moment he did that the uproar in the *salon* which had been
deafening up to now suddenly died down. Complete silence
ensued, but only for a few seconds; the next moment François
had closed the door behind him and at once the hubbub in the
next room rose louder than ever and there came a terrific
outburst of hilarious shouting and laughter and vigorous
clapping of hands. Cécile stood there listening, terrified and
undecided, longing to go to her brother's assistance, yet feeling
the futility of any intervention on her part should the crowd
turn ugly. For a moment they appeared distinctly amused, for
the laughter went on louder than ever, and it was accompanied
by the measured stamping of feet, the clapping of hands and the
strains of dance music. What was going on in there? Cécile,
terrified at first, felt a little more reassured. She couldn't hear
her brother's voice, and apparently the people were enjoying
themselves, for they were dancing and laughing and the music

never ceased. At last anxiety got the better of prudence. Tentatively she in her turn opened the communicating door, and exactly the same thing happened that had greeted François de la Rodière's appearance in the crowded *salon*. Absolute silence for a few seconds, and then a terrific, uproarious shout.

What Cécile saw did indeed turn her almost sick with horror, for there was her brother in the middle of the room, dishevelled, with his necktie awry and his cheeks the colour of ashes, in the centre of a ring made up of the worst type of ragamuffins and cinderwenches she had ever seen, all holding hands and twirling round and round him to the tune of a wild *rigaudon*. His riding-whip was lying broken in half across the threshold at Cécile's feet. The crowd had seized upon him directly they were aware of his presence, torn the whip out of his hand, broken it and thrown it on the floor. They had dragged him and pushed him to the centre of the room, formed a ring round him, shouted injurious epithets and made rude gestures at him; and the more pale he got with rage, the more helpless he found himself, the louder was their laughter and the wilder their dance.

Cécile felt as if she were paralysed. She couldn't move, her knees were shaking under her, and before she could recover herself two women had seized her, one by each hand, and dragged her across the room, where she was thrust into the centre of another ring of uproarious females who danced and capered round her, holding hands and laughing at her obvious terror. It was all like a terrible nightmare. Cécile, trying in vain to control herself, could only put her hands up to her face so as to hide from the mocking crowd the blush of indignation and shame that flooded her cheeks at the sound of the obscene words that men and women, apparently all in right good-humour, flung at her, while they danced what seemed to the poor girl like a saraband of witches. Suddenly she heard a cry: "Make her dance, Jacques! Make the *aristo* step it with you! I'll warrant she has never danced the *rigaudon* with such a handsome partner before."

And Cécile was conscious first of a whiff of garlic, then of a

135

clammy hand seizing her own, and finally of a shoulder pressed against her side and of an arm around her waist. With a shudder she looked down and saw the grinning, puckish face and misshapen, dwarfish body of Jacques, the son of the local butcher, whom she had often befriended when he was baited by boys bigger and stronger than himself. He was leering up at her and clinging to her waist, trying to make her foot a measure with him. Now unlike her brother, Cécile de la Rodière was possessed of a good deal of sound common sense. She knew well enough that to try and run one's head against a stone wall could only result in bruises, if not worse. Here they were both of them, she and François, not to mention *maman*, at the mercy of a couple of hundred people who, though fairly good-tempered at the moment, might soon turn ugly if provoked. She rather felt as if she had been thrust into a cage full of wild beasts and that to humour them was the only chance of safety. She looked about her helplessly, hoping against hope that she might encounter a face that was neither cruel nor mocking, and in her heart prayed, prayed to God to deliver her from this nightmare.

And then suddenly the miracle happened. It was a miracle in very truth, for there in the wide-open doorway was the one man in the world, her world, on whom she could rely, the man who alone next to God could save her from this awful humiliation. Pradel! Simon Pradel! He looked flushed and anxious; he was panting as if he had been running hard for goodness knows how long. His dark, deep-set eyes roamed rapidly round the room till they encountered hers. Thank God! Thank God, that he was here! The scar across his forehead where François had hit him still showed crimson across the pale, damp skin, but his eyes were kind and reassuring. Hers were fastened on him with a look of appeal, and in a moment he was half across the room pushing his way towards her through the crowd.

All at once the crowd saw him. Docteur Pradel! Simon! Their Simon! The hero of the hour! A lusty cheer roused the echo of the vast hall at sight of him. Now indeed would the fun be fast and furious! Pradel, in the meanwhile, had reached the centre of

136

the room, he broke through the cordon that surrounded Cécile quite good-naturedly but very firmly he thrust Jacques the butcher's son to one side, took hold of the girl's trembling hand and put his strong arms round her waist.

"*Allons,*" he shouted to the musicians, "put some verve into your playing. 'Tis I will dance the *rigaudon* with the *aristo!*"

Nothing loth, the musicians blew their trumpets and beat their drums with renewed vigour:

"Sur le pont d'Avignon,
On y danse, on y danse,
Sur le pont d'Avignon,
On y danse tout en rond!"

A hundred couples were formed and soon they were all of them dancing and singing, not hoarsely or stridently, but just with immense gusto, as if they desired nothing but to enjoy a real jollity.

"Try to smile," Pradel whispered in Cécile's ear. "Be brave! Don't show that you are afraid!"

Cécile said: "I am not afraid." And indeed, with her hand in his, she tripped the *rigaudon* step by step and was no longer afraid. It seemed to her as if with Pradel's nearness the nightmare had become just a dream. Everything now was gay, almost happy. Cruelly and mockery, the desire to humiliate had faded from the faces of the crowd. Everyone was smiling at everybody else. One woman called out loudly across the room to Cécile: "Well chosen, my pretty! Our Simon will make you a fine husband! And you will give France some splendid sons!"

"Smile!" Pradel commanded. "Smile to them and nod! For God's sake, smile!"

And Cécile smiled and nodded while the cry was taken up. "Our Simon and the *aristo!* And a quiverful of handsome sons! Hurrah! Hurrah!"

In this wild saturnalia even François de la Rodière was forgotten.

It was he who suddenly became aware of a curiously incongruous figure of a man who at this point was working his way unobtrusively through the throng. Short, spare, dressed in sober black from head to foot, he had the tricolour scarf round his waist. No one in the crowd took any notice of him. Only François saw him, and in spite of the tell-tale tricolour scarf which proclaimed the man to be in the service of the revolutionary government, he felt that some sort of rescue from this devil's carnival could be effected through one who at any rate looked as if he had washed and brushed his clothes. François tried to attract his attention, but the man walked quietly on, till he was quite close to the spot where Cécile de la Rodière was still dancing with Simon Pradel. She and her partner had become mere units in the twirling, twisting, whirling crowd. Cécile was trying bravely to keep up the role of good-humour and even gaiety which Pradel had enjoined her to assume. She continued to step it, wondering how all this would end. She saw the little man in black wind his way in and out among the dancers, and she saw the leader of the musicians, the unkept, unshaved, toothless fiddler step down from the platform and, always playing his fiddle, follow on the heels of the little man in black. She was so fascinated by the sight of those two figures in such strange contrast, one to the other, one so spruce and trim, the other so grimy, one so stern and the other grinning all over his face, that she lost step and had to cling with both hands to her partner's arm.

Then it was that there occurred the strangest of all the strange events of this memorable day. The little man in black was now quite close to her, and the fiddler was immediately behind him and Cécile watched them both, fascinated. All of a sudden the fiddler threw back his head and laughed. Such curious laughter it was, quite merry, but somehow it suggested the merriment of a fool. Cécile stared at the man, for there was something almost eerie about him now, and Pradel too stared at him as amazed, as fascinated as was the girl herself, for the fiddler had thrown down his fiddle. He straightened his back and stretched out his arms till he appeared preternaturally tall, like a Titan or like a Samson about to shatter the marble pillars of the old château and to hurl them down with a thunderous crash in the midst of the revellers.

The little man in black also stared at the fiddler, and very slowly the whole expression of his face underwent a change, from surprise to horror and thence to triumph mixed with a kind of awe. His thin lips curled into a mocking smile and through them there came words spoken in English, a language which Cécile understood. What he said was: "So, my valiant Scarlet Pimpernel, we meet again at last!" and at the same time he put his hand in his waistcoat pocket and drew out what looked like an ordinary whistle which he was about to put to his mouth when the fiddler, with another outburst of inane laughter, knocked it out of his hand.

"A spy! A spy!" the fiddler cried in a stentorian voice. "We are betrayed. We shall be massacred! *Sauve qui peut!*"

And with a sudden stretch of his powerful arms he picked up the little man in black and threw him over his shoulder as if he were a bale of goods and ran with his struggling and kicking burden across the room towards the door. And all the time he continued to shout: "A spy! A spy! We shall all be massacred! Remember Paris last September!" And the crowd took up the cry as a crowd will, for are not one hundred humans the counterpart of one hundred sheep? They took up the cry and shouted: "A spy! A spy!" and ran in a body helter-skelter on the heels of the fiddler and his sable-clad load, out of the room across the marble vestibule, down the grand staircase and down below that, through the servants' old quarters, through the kitchen and the pantry, the wash- house and the buttery, and down by the winding staircase which led to the cellar. And behind him there was the crowd, no longer good-tempered now, or intent on holiday-making, but a real rabble this time, and a frightened crowd at that, jostling, pushing, tumbling over one another. An angry crowd is fearsome, but a frightened crowd is worse, for it is ready for anything – bloodshed, carnage, butchery.

Chauvelin felt himself carried in through the cellar door and then thrown none too gently down on a heap of dank straw. The next moment he heard that horrible, hideous, hated laugh, the mocking words: *"A bientôt*, my dear Monsieur Chambertin!" Then the banging to of a heavy door, the pushing of bolts, the clang of a chain and the grating of a rusty key in the lock, and nothing more. He was crouching on a heap of damp straw, in almost total darkness, sore in body, humiliated to the very depths of his soul, burning with rage and the bitterness of his disappointment.

He heard the talking and the laughter growing more and more indistinct and finally dying away altogether. The rabble had gone, but what was to become of him now? Would he be left to die of inanition, shut up in a cellar like a savage dog or cat? No! He felt quite sure that he need not fear that kind of revenge at the hands of the man whom he had pursued with such relentless hate. Instinctively he did pay this tribute to the most gallant foe he had ever pitted his wits against.

What then? He was left wondering. For how long he did not know. Was it for a few minutes or several hours? When presently he heard the rusty key grate once more in the lock, and once more the drawing of bolts, the clanking of a chain, instinctively he dragged himself away from the door. A shaft of yellow light from a lantern cut through the gloom of his prison, the door was opened, and that hateful mocking voice said: "Company for you, my dear Monsieur Chambertin!" And a bundle which turned out to be a man wrapped in a cloak and wearing the uniform of the Gendarmerie Nationale was thrust into the cellar, and landed on the damp straw beside him. The humble sergeant of gendarmerie had fared no better than the powerful and influential member of the Committee of Public Safety.

CHAPTER TWENTY-FOUR

A Strange Proposal

After a time Cécile gradually felt as if she had suddenly wakened from an ugly dream, during which every one of her senses had been put to torture. Her eyes, her ears, her nostrils had been outraged by evil smells and ribald words, and the wild antics of King Mob. Then all at once silence, almost peace. The sound of those unruly masses, shouting, singing, stumping, was gradually dying away. A few stragglers, yielding to curiosity, were even now going out of the room. In another remote corner François was struggling to his feet. He appeared dazed and like a man broken in body and spirit. He staggered as far as the tapestried door which led to vestibule and boudoir.

Pradel and Cécile were alone.

They were both silent. Constrained. She wanted to say something to him, but somehow the words would not come. She knew so little about this man who had, as a matter of fact, saved her reason. At one moment during this wild sarabande she had felt as if she were going mad. Then he had come and a sense of security had descended into her soul. But why she should have felt comforted, she couldn't say. She knew that he loved her, at any rate had loved her until that awful hour when he had suffered a terrible outrage at her brother's hands. He couldn't continue to love her after that. Could not. He must hate her and all her family. But if he did, why had he come running all the way from Choisy and stopped this hysterical multitude from doing her bodily harm? There was no ignoring the fact that he

had come running along all the way from Choisy, and that he
had saved her and *maman* and François from disaster. Then why
did he look so aloof, so entirely indifferent? Of course, he
belonged to the party that deposed the King, and proclaimed
the Republic; that, in fact, was François's chief grievance against
him. She had never heard him discuss politics, and she and
maman lived such a secluded life she didn't know much of what
went on. She hated all murderers and regicides—oh, regicides
above all!—but somehow she didn't believe that Pradel was one
of these. Even before the beginnings of this awful revolution he
had always spent most of his time – and people said half his
private fortune – in doing good to the needy and keeping up the
children's hospital in Choisy. Cécile knew all that. She had even
done her best in a small way in the past to help him with some
of his charitable work when knowledge of it came her way. No,
no, a man of that type was no murderer, no regicide. But it was
all very puzzling, Especially as he neither spoke nor moved,
apparently leaving the initiative to her.

At last she was able to take it. She mastered her absurd
diffidence and steadied her voice as best she could.

"I wish I knew how to thank you, Monsieur le Docteur," she
said. "You have saved my reason. I think if you had not interfered
when you did I should have gone mad."

"Not so bad as that, citizeness, I think," he responded with the
ghost of a smile.

Cécile liked his smile. It was kind. But she hated his calling
her "citizeness." She stiffened at the word and went on more
coolly: "You have remarkable influence over the people here.
They love you."

"They are not a bad crowd really," he said and then added
after a second's pause: "Not yet."

"It is strange how they followed that fiddler. Did you see
him?"

"Yes!"

"To me he did not seem human. More like a giant out of a
fairytale. Did you hear what that funny little man in black said

142

to him?"

"I heard, citizeness. But unfortunately, I did not understand. He spoke in English, I think."

"Yes! And he called the fiddler 'my valiant Scarlet Pimpernel.'"

"What is that?"

"You have never heard of the Scarlet Pimpernel?"

"Only as a mythical personage."

"He really does exist though. It was he, who—"

She paused abruptly, for she had been on the point of naming the Abbé Edgeworth and his escape from La Rodière. No news of the safety of the old priest had as yet been received and until it was definitely known that he was safe in Belgium, the secret of the escape must on no account be revealed. To Cécile's astonishment, however, Pradel himself alluded to it.

"Who engineered the escape of our mutual friend, Abbé Edgeworth you mean?"

"You knew?"

"I only guessed."

"And I can tell you definitely that it was the English spy whom they call the Scarlet Pimpernel who made every arrangement for the Abbé's safety."

"Then why do you call him a spy? An ugly word, meseems, for the noble work which he does."

"You are right there, Monsieur le Docteur. It is always fine to serve your country, or to serve humanity in whichever way seems to you best. I only used the word 'spy' because the Scarlet Pimpernel, so I have heard said, is never seen as himself, but always in disguise. That is why I thought that the fiddler—"

"Yes, citizeness?"

She shook her head.

"No, no," she said, "it can't be. He made no attempt to save me from those awful women. I suppose he does not think that we up here are in immediate danger. Do you think that we are?" she added abruptly and raised eyes shining with sudden fear up at Pradel.

He made no reply. What could he say? As a matter of fact it

was all over Choisy that the arrest of the *aristos* up at La Rodière was only a question of hours. That was why he had come running up to the château, not so much in terror for her of a boisterous crowd, as of the decree of the Committee of Public Safety, and the inevitable Gendarmerie Nationale.

"I don't mind for myself," Cécile went on after a moment or two, "but *maman* and—and . . . François . . . I know you hate him, and I dare say he deserves your hatred. But he is my brother . . . and *maman* . . . You don't think they would dare do anything to *maman* ...do you?"

She couldn't go on for the tears were choking her. She turned away, half ashamed that he should see those tears, and walked across to the window. She stood in the embrasure for a time looking out at first into vacancy, then gradually becoming aware of what was going on down below. The perron and the long avenue were all thronged with that same abominable multitude who had insulted and humiliated her before the advent of Pradel. They were all going away in a body now, quite good-tempered, rather noisy, still singing and shouting. The shades of evening were drawing in fast. It was close on five o'clock, and they were all going home ready to tell of their many adventures to the workers when they came out of the factories, and to the few who had not been fortunate enough to join in the revels of this memorable afternoon. Five o'clock and it was half-past three when first that unruly mass of humanity had invaded the château. One hour and a half of mental torture. To C6cile it seemed an eternity. And now they were going away. Silence would once more reign in the ancestral home of the La Rodières, silence but not peace, for terror of death would from this hour be always present within its walls, the nameless dread which holds its greatest sway o' nights, banishes sleep, and rears its head at every chance word spoken by careless lips: arrest, denunciation, imprisonment, the guillotine.

"Citizeness!"

Citizeness! Another of those chance words that brought the nameless dread striking at one's heart. It roused Cécile de la

Rodière out of her sombre mood. The noise of the crowd below was growing fainter and fainter. Most of the rioters were out of sight already. They had gone quietly enough, and now only a few laggards, men who were lame and women who were feeble, could be seen making their way down the avenue in the fast gathering gloom.

"Citizeness!"

The voice was kindly, rather hoarse, perhaps, and authoritative, but kindly nevertheless. Pradel had come up close to her. He it was who had spoken the chance word. Cécile turned to him.

"Yes, Monsieur le Docteur?"

"You asked me a straight question just now, and I ought to have answered it at once, knowing you to be proud and brave. But I wanted you to collect yourself a little. You are young and have gone through a great deal. Naturally enough, you are slightly unnerved. At the same time I feel that it is best for you and for you all that you should know the truth."

"The truth?"

"The authorities at Choisy have decided on the arrest of your mother, your brother, yourself and your two servants. Directly I learned their decision I ran up here to see what I, as a single individual, could do to save you. I was on my way up already, because I knew that I could do a great deal to prevent a lot of irresponsible women and weaklings from doing more than, perhaps, frightening you, and I would have been here earlier only I could not leave the hospital, where I was attending a really serious case. I thank Heaven that I could not leave sooner, and that I was obliged to call in at the Town Hall, where I learned, by the merest chance, that the Committee of Public Safety had ordered your arrest at the instance of one of its members, the order to be executed within the next twenty-four hours."

Cécile had listened to all this without making any movement or any sign that she understood the meaning of what Pradel had just told her. She had turned to face him and while he talked, her glance never wavered. She looked him straight in the eyes.

It was quite dark in the room now, only here in the window embrasure the last lingering evening light sent its dying shaft on the slim figure of Docteur Pradel. Never for one second did Cécile de la Rodière doubt that he spoke the truth. She could not have explained even to herself how it was she knew, but she was absolutely convinced that when he spoke of this awful danger of death to those she cared for, he was speaking the truth.

For some time after Pradel had finished speaking Cécile said nothing and made no movement. Slowly the purport of what he said penetrated into her brain. Arrest! Within twenty-four hours! It meant death, of course. The guillotine for them all. For *maman* and François and for Paul and Marie. The guillotine! The horrible thing that happened to others, even to the King. And now to oneself!

"Docteur Pradel," she murmured appealingly, "can nothing be done?"

"Yes, citizeness," he replied coldly; "something can be done, and it rests with you, I have told you the worst, but I earnestly believe that it is in my power to get you and your family and your two servants out of this trouble. If I am right in this belief, then I shall thank God on my knees for the privilege of being of service to you. May I proceed?"

"If you please, monsieur."

"I am afraid that what I am about to say will shock you, wound you, perhaps in your most cherished prejudices. Believe me, if I could see any other way of averting this terrible calamity, I would take it. I have, as perhaps you know, a certain amount of influence in the commune, not great enough, alas! to obtain a safe conduct for you and those you care for now that an order for your arrest has been issued by an actual member of the Committee for Public Safety, but I could demand one for my wife."

Cécile could not smother a gasp nor smother a cry: "Your wife, monsieur?"

"I pray you do not misunderstand me," Pradel rejoined calmly, even though at the sound of that cry of protest a shadow had spread over his face, leaving it more wan, more stern, too, than it had been before. "By a recent decree of the existing government marriage between citizens of this country only means going before the Mayor of the Commune and there reciting certain formulas which will bind them in matrimony for as long or as short a time as they desire. Should you decide to go through this ceremony with me, I swear to you that never through any fault of mine will you have cause to regret it. Once you are nominally my wife, I, as an important member of this commune, can protect you, your family and your servants until such time as I find it expedient and safe to convey you all out of this unfortunate country into Switzerland or Belgium, where you could remain until these troublesome times are past. Until then you will all live under my roof as honoured guests. I am a busy man, hardly ever at home. You will hardly ever see me; you need never speak to me unless you wish. And now, with your permission, I will leave you to think it all over quietly and perhaps, to consult with your family. Tomorrow at ten o'clock I will be back to receive your answer. We will then either go at once to the *Mairie* or I will offer you and the citizeness, your mother, my respectful adieux."

And he was gone. Cécile never heard him cross the room to go downstairs. All she heard were the strains of that ramshackle fiddle and the soft, wordless humming of the old, old tune:

"Ma chandelle est morte,
Je n'ai phis de feu,
Ouvre moi ta porte,
Pour l'amour de Dieu!"

Well! The door was open for her to pass through from the fear of death to promised security for all those whom she loved. Oh! If it had only been a question of herself, she would not have wasted a moment's reflection on that outrageous proposition.

Outrageous? Was it really outrageous? A proposition couched

in terms of dignified respect, and one calculated to safeguard the lives of all those she cared for, could not in all fairness be stigmatised as outrageous. Bold, perhaps, unique certainly: no girl, she supposed, had ever had such a remarkable proposal of marriage. But then the man who made it was nothing if not bold, and the situation was, of course, unique. Nor did she doubt him for an instant. From the first there had been something in his attitude and in the way he spoke that bore the imprint of absolute truth. No, she assuredly did not doubt him. The danger, she knew, was real enough; the way out of it she was convinced, was the only one possible. She was quite sorry now that Pradel had gone so quickly. There were so many things she would have liked to have asked him. The decision which she would have to make was one that should be made on the spur of the moment. The delay would give her a long, sleepless night and a great deal of nerve strain. And then there was the great question. Should she consult with *maman* or confront her with the accomplished fact? And there was François, too. He, with the impulse of youth and prejudice, would say: "Better death than dishonour," and would continue to look on the transaction as a perpetual blot on the escutcheon of the La Rodières.

She thought, anyhow, that she had best go back to *maman* now. As a matter of fact, she ought not to have left *maman* alone quite so long. But *maman* had François with her, as well as Marie and Paul too, probably. Whereas she, Cécile, was alone. She had no one to advise her, no one to help her analyse that strange mixture inside of her, of doubt and fear and, yes, elation, which was so unaccountable, so strange, so different to anything she had ever felt before. And why had Pradel made such a proposition to her? He loved her. She was woman enough to know that, then why—? Why not—? Again she sighed, longed somehow to be older, more experienced in the ways of men . . . or the ways of lovers.

And what in God's name was she going to say to *maman* and to François?

BOOK IV

THE TRAITOR

CHAPTER TWENTY-FIVE

Mutiny

In the meanwhile the cabaret up the road was doing a roaring trade. A goodly number of revellers, not satisfied with the excitement of the afternoon, had turned in there for a drink and a gossip. There was such a lot to talk about, and the company quickly formed itself into groups round separate tables, some talking over one thing, some another. Jacques the butcher's boy was there; he was baited for having allowed his partner, the *aristo*, to be taken from him by the citizen doctor.

"He was handsomer than you, Jacques," he was told; "that's what it was."

And Jacques, full of vanity, as many undersized boys and girls often are, declared most emphatically that he would bring the *aristo* to her knees, and that within the next three days.

"How wilt thou do that, thou ugly young moke?" he was asked, all in good humour.

"I shall make her marry me," he replied, puffing out his chest like a small turkey-cock.

Laughter all round, then someone queried:

"Thou'll make love to the *aristo?*"

"I will."

"And ask her in marriage?"

"Yes!"

"And if she says 'No!'"

"If she does, I'll warn her that I will go straight to the Chief Commissary and denounce her and her family as traitors, which will mean the guillotine for the lot of them. So what now?" he concluded with a ludicrous air of triumph.

"A splendid idea, Jacques," a lusty voice cried gaily, and a non-too-gentle hand gave the boy a vigorous slap on the back. "And we'll play a march at thy wedding."

It was the fiddler who had just come in with the other musicians.

It seems they had accompanied the bulk of the crowd part of the way down to Choisy, and then felt woefully thirsty, and came to the *"Chien sans Queue,"* which was so much nearer for a drink than the first cabaret down the other way. They certainly looked very weary, very grubby and very dry, which was small wonder, seeing that they had been on the go, marching with the crowd and blowing their trumpets, since before noon. Apparently, poor things, they had no money, for though they professed to have mouths as dry as lime-kilns, they did not order drinks, but took their stand in a corner of the room and proceeded to tune up their instruments, which means that they made the kind of noise one usually associates in concert halls with tuning-up, but when they had finished the process and started to play what might be called a tune, the sounds which their instruments emitted had no relation whatever to correct harmony. But when the woes of the shepherdess and her cat had been proclaimed in song from beginning to end once, twice and three times and the musicians, more weary and thirsty than ever, deputed their fiddler to go round and hold out his Phrygian cap in a mute appeal for sous wherewith to pay for drinks, the whole crowd suddenly discovered that it was getting late and that wives and mothers were waiting for them at home.

And one by one, or in groups of threes and fours they all filed out of the *"Chien sans Queue."* Only six sous had been thrown into the Phrygian cap. Polycarpe the landlord stood at his own front door for some time exchanging a few last words with his departing customers. His wife, the Junoesque Victoria, was clearing away the empty mugs in the tap-room. The fiddler put his long arm round her capacious waist and drew her, giggling and smirking, on his knee. She smacked his face with elephantine playfulness.

"You couldn't run about with me on your shoulder," she said, "as you did with that poor little man this afternoon."

"He was just a dirty spy," the fiddler retorted, "but if you will challenge me, my Juno, I will have a try with you also."

"Take me upstairs, then, to my room," she said, with a simper. "I am dog-tired after all that dancing and Polycarpe can finish clearing away."

"What will you give me if I do?"

"Free drinks, my beauty," she replied, and pinched his cheeks with her plump fingers, "if you do not drop me on the way."

To her great amazement, and no less to her delight, the fiddler did heave her up, not as if she were a feather or even a bale of goods certainly, but he did hold her in his arms and carry her not only to the door, but up the narrow staircase, whence she directed him to her bedroom, where she demanded to be deposited on the bed, which gave a loud creak under her goodly weight. She laughed when she saw him give a loud puff of exhaustion.

"Give the musicians free drinks all round," she commanded her husband.

Thus it was that presently five tired musicians were seated round one of the tables in a corner of the tap-room of the cabaret *Le Chien sans Queue* With them was Citizen Polycarpe the landlord who, for the moment, was sprawling across the table, his head buried in his arms and snoring like a grampus. The fiddler bent over him, turned his head over and with delicate, if very grimy finger, lifted the lid of one of his eyes.

"As drunk as a lord," he declared; "that stuff is very potent."

He had a smallish bottle in his hand which he now slipped

151

back into his pocket.

"And the gargantuan lady upstairs," he went on, "is sleeping the sleep of the just. So as soon as Devinne is here we can get on with business."

"He is here," one of the others said, "I am sure I heard his footsteps outside."

He rose and went to the door, called out softly into the night: "Devinne! All serene!"

A minute or two later St. John Devinne came in. He was dressed in ordinary clothes, had clean face and hands, but though normally he would not by his appearance have attracted any attention, here in this squalid tap-room in the midst of his friends all grimy and clad in nothing but rags, he looked strangely conspicuous and, as it were, out of key. A pair of lazy eyes, slightly sarcastic in expression, looked him up and down. Devinne caught the glance and something of a blush mounted to his cheeks, nor did he after that meet the eyes of his chief. He took his seat at the table, edging away as far as he could from the sprawling form of Polycarpe the landlord.

"May I know what has happened this afternoon?" he asked curtly.

"Of course you may, my dear fellow," Blakeney replied. "Here," he added, and pushed a mug and jug of wine nearer to St. John, "have a drink."

"No thanks."

Sir Andrew Ffoulkes, that young dandy, was busy polishing a tin trumpet. He looked up from his work, glanced up at the chief who gave him a slight nod, whereupon he proceeded to give a short succinct account of the stirring events at the château.

"I thought something of the sort was in the wind," Devinne said with dry sarcasm, "or I should not have been sent up to Paris on that futile errand."

There was complete silence for a moment or two after that. Lord Tony's fist clenched until the knuckles shone smooth and white. Glynde was seen to swallow hard as if to choke words that had risen to his throat. They all looked up at their chief who had not moved a muscle, had not even frowned. Now he gave a light little laugh.

"Do have a drink, Johnny," he said; "it will do you good."

Sir Andrew blew a subdued blast in his tin trumpet and Tony, Glynde and Hastings only swore under their breath. But the tension was eased for the moment, and Blakeney presently resumed:

"The errand, lad," he rejoined simply, "was not futile. One of us had to let Galveston and Holte know that they will have to meet us at headquarters on the St. Gif-Le Perrey Road any time within the next twenty-four hours. You would have been wiser, I think, for their sakes as well as your own, to have assumed some inconspicuous disguise, but you got through all right, I take it, so we won't say any more about that."

"Yes! I got through all right," Devinne mumbled sulkily. "I am not a fool."

"I am sure you are not, dear lad," Blakeney responded still very quietly, though to anyone who knew him as intimately as did Sir Andrew Ffoulkes or Lord Tony, there was just a *soupçon* of hardness now in the tone of his usually pleasant voice. "You were spared, at any rate, the painful sight of seeing your friends up at La Rodière baited by that unruly crowd."

"Yes! Damn them!"

"And then you know, Johnny, you are nothing of a musician really. Now you should have heard Ffoulkes on his trumpet, or Hastings who played second fiddle; they were demmed marvellous, I tell you. If I were not afraid of waking my Juno upstairs, I would give you a specimen of our performance, right up to the time when our friend Monsieur Chambertin appeared upon the scene."

"By the way," Lord Tony now put in, "what did you do ultimately with that worthy man?"

"I locked him and his sergeant up in the cellar. It won't hurt them to starve for a bit. We'll arrange for them to be let out as soon as we feel that they cannot do us any harm."

"I suppose I shall be told off to do that," Devinne muttered peevishly.

"That's an idea, Johnny," Blakeney responded with imperturbable good humour. "Splendid! But cheer up, lad. We have splendid work before us. When dawn breaks over the hills yonder, we will be out for sport which is fit for the gods. Sport which you all love. Breakneck rides across country, with those poor innocents to save from the wolves who will be howling at us close to our heels. By gad! You will all feel like gods yourselves. You will have lived, all of you. Lived, I tell you! My God! I thank Thee for the chance! That is what you will say."

Sir Percy now stood in his favourite attitude leaning against the wall, facing the five glowing pairs of eyes, his own fixed on something that he alone saw, something beyond these four squalid walls, the open country perhaps, the breakneck ride that lay ahead of him and his followers, or was it the flower-garden at Richmond, the banks of the Thames, the blue eyes of Marguerite calling to him, asking him to come back to her arms?

"You remember," he began after a few moments during which he seemed to be collecting his thoughts, "that there came a time when I allowed the crowd to get ahead of me and I remained behind ostensibly to put a new string to my fiddle. I hid in the dense shrubbery just inside the gates, and, after a few minutes, five, perhaps, I heard the welcome voice of our dear Monsieur Chauvelin. He gave that egregious agitator Conty the go-by, then he called to a soldier who had evidently been waiting for him, and gave him instructions for his well-conceived damnable plot which embraced the arrest of the whole La Rodière family and their two faithful servants, as well as the capture of mine humble self. I could hear every word he said. I learned that a squad of gendarmerie, thirty in number, was posted in the stables, and that at a certain signal given by my engaging friend, the men were to make their way up to the château and there to await further orders. As soon as this pair of blackguards had parted company, Chauvelin to go straight to the château, and the sergeant to transmit his orders, I slipped out of the gate and came on here.

"Worthy landlord Polycarpe is, of course, an old friend of ours. The place was deserted for the moment. I got him to open a couple of jorums of wine, into which I poured a good measure of this potent stuff, which that splendid fellow Barstow of York gave me recently. Look at old Polycarpe. You can see what a wonderful sleep it induces. With a jorum in each hand, my fiddle and a bunch of tin mugs, slung over my shoulder, I made my way to the stables, where, as you may well suppose, I was made extremely welcome. I stayed just long enough to see the wine poured out and handed round, then out I slipped, locking the stable and coach-house doors after me. Then back I went to join the merry throng in the château. The rest you know, and so much for the past. Now for the future. Give me some of this abominable vinegar to drink and I'll go on.

"Just before dawn we'll go up to La Rodière. I have the key of the stables in my pocket, and I want to give those nice soldiers another drink. That will keep them quiet till far into the morning. By that time we shall be well away. We'll divest some of them of their accoutrements, which will save us the trouble of going all the way to headquarters to get our own. I have thought the matter well over and, as I said this morning, I am quite positive that in this part of the country, and far from a large city, a mock arrest is by far our best plan. Fortune has favoured us, let me tell you, for there is a coach and pair here in the yard. I learned this also while I was eavesdropping. It was designed to accommodate the five prisoners. Now it will serve the same purpose for us with two of us on the box and the others freezing on the top, for it will be cold, I tell you. As soon as we have effected the arrest, we'll make for the St. Gif-Le Perrey Road. At St. Gif, Galveston and Holte will be at our usual quarters, ready with fresh horses to continue the journey to the coast."

"Then we don't start till dawn?" one of them asked.

"Just before dawn. The night will, I am afraid, be very dark, except at rare intervals, for there is a heavy bank of clouds coming over the mountains. We want the light, as we shall have to drive like the devil until well past Le Perrey."

"And we make for the coast?"

"For that little hole Trouville, this side of the Loire. You remember it, Ffoulkes? But we'll talk all that over before I leave you."

"You are not coming all the way?"

"No, only as far as St. Gif. Directly I have seen you all safely on the road I shall have to turn my attention to one other prisoner, and that will be a difficult task. I don't mean that it will be so materially, but Pradel, I feel, will be obstinate. He has his hospital here, and his poor patients. How am I going to persuade him that anyhow when those murderers have done away with him, his hospital and his poor patients will still have to exist somehow?"

While the chief spoke and the others hung as usual breathless on his lips, Devinne's expression of face became more and more glowering. A dark frown deepened between his eyes. Once or twice he tried to speak, but it was not until Blakeney paused that he suddenly banged his fist on the table.

"Pradel?" he cried. "What the devil do you mean?"

"Just what I said, my dear fellow," Sir Percy replied, with just the slightest possible lifting of his eyebrows. "The others understood. Why not you?"

"The others? The others? I don't care about the others. All I know is that that insolent brute Pradel—"

Up went Blakeney's slender, commanding hand.

"Do not call that man a brute, my lad. He is a fine fellow, and his life is in immediate danger, though he does not know it. He has a bitter and very influential enemy in the lawyer Maurin, who has put up a trumpery charge against him. I learned as lately as last night that his arrest has been finally decided on by the Chief Commissary and is only a matter of a couple of days, till enough false evidence, I suppose, has been collected against him."

"Well! And why not?" Devinne retorted hotly.

"There is no time to go into that now, my dear fellow," Blakeney replied with unruffled patience.

"Why not?"

At sound of this curt challenge to their chief, at the defiant tone of the boy's voice, the others lost all patience, and there was a chorus which should have been a warning to Devinne, that though Blakeney himself was as usual extraordinarily patient and understanding, they in a body, Ffoulkes, Tony, Hastings, Glynde, would not tolerate effrontery, let alone insubordination.

"You young cub!"

"Insolent worm! Wait till you feel my glove on your face."

"By gad! I'll wring his neck!" were some of the threats and epithets they hurled at Devinne. But the latter was now in one of those obstinate moods that opposition soon turns into open revolt, and this, in spite of the fact that Percy now put a firm, but still friendly, hand on his shoulder.

"If I didn't know, lad, what is at the back of your mind," he said gently, "I might remind you once again that you promised me obedience, just like the others, in all matters connected with our League. We should never accomplish the good work which we have all of us undertaken if there was mutiny in our small camp."

Devinne shook the kindly hand off his shoulder.

"Oh, you'll never understand," he muttered glumly.

"What? That you are in love with Cécile de la Rodière and jealous of Simon Pradel?"

"Don't talk of love, Blakeney. You don't know what it means."

A slight pause. Only a second or two, while a curious shadow seemed to flit over those deep-set eyes that held such a wealth of suppressed emotion in their glance, of sorrow and of doubt and of visions of ecstasy that mayhap the daring adventurer would never taste again. He gave a quick sigh and said simply: "Perhaps not, dear lad. You may be right. But we are not here to discuss matters of sentiment, and the knife which I am now about to wield will cut into your wounded vanity, and, I fear me, will hurt terribly. Cécile de la Rodière," he went on, and now his tone was very firm and he spoke very slowly, letting every word sink into the boy's consciousness, "is not and never will be in love with you. She is half in love with Pradel already—"

Devinne jumped to his feet.

"And that's a lie—" he cried hoarsely, and would have said more only that Glynde struck him full on the mouth.

The others, too, were beside themselves with fury. They laid rough hands on his shoulders. Lord Tony flung an insult in his face, and Hastings called out: "On your knees, you—"

Blakeney alone remained quite undisturbed. He only spoke when Hastings and Tony between them had nearly forced Devinne down on his knees; then he said with a light laugh: "Leave the boy alone, Hastings. You, too, Tony. Four against one is not a sporting proposition, is it?"

He took Devinne firmly under the arm, helped him to raise himself, and said quietly: "You are not quite yourself just now, are you, Johnny? Come out into the fresh air a bit. It will do you good."

Devinne tried to shake himself free, but held in Percy's iron grip, he was compelled to move with him across the room. The others naturally did not interfere. They were nursing their indignation, while they watched their chief lead the recalcitrant Johnny out of the room.

Now and then they cast anxious looks in the direction of the door, whenever St. John Devinne's rasping voice reached their ears.

CHAPTER TWENTY-SIX

Open Revolt

Outside, in the cold frosty night, a strange clash of wills was taking place with the issue never for a moment in doubt. Devinne, goaded by jealousy, had lost all sense of proportion and all sense of loyalty and honour. It was not only a question of a lover's hatred for a rival whom he still affected to despise, it was also jealousy of the power and influence of his chief, against whose orders he was determined to rebel.

St. John Devinne was an only son. His father, the old Duke of Rudford, a fine old sportsman as everyone acknowledged, had been inordinately proud of a boy born to him when he was past middle age. His mother did her best to spoil the child. She gave in to every one of his many caprices. When presently he went to school she loaded him with presents both of money and of "tuck," with the result that he became a little king among his schoolmates. The boy came down from Harrow rather more spoilt and certainly more arrogant than he was when he went up.

There followed, however, a rather better time for him morally, when he came under the direct influence of his father. He became quite a good sportsman, rode straight to hounds, was a fine boxer and fencer. During the fashionable seasons in London and in Bath he was a great favourite with the ladies, for he was an amusing talker and an elegant partner in the minuet. When in '90 Sir Percy Blakeney, Bart., accompanied by his beautiful young wife, made his dazzling entry in English society after a long sojourn in France, he became St. John Devinne's beau ideal. The boy's one aim in life was to emulate that perfect gentleman in all things. And when, after a time, he was actually admitted into the intimate circle of young exquisites of whom Sir Percy was the acknowledged leader, he felt that life could hold no greater happiness for him.

Then the League of the Scarlet Pimpernel was formed and in August '91 St. John Devinne was enrolled as a member and swore the prescribed oath of allegiance, secrecy and obedience to the chief. From certain correspondence that came to light subsequently, it has been established that Blakeney first spoke of his scheme for the establishment of the League with the old Duke, for there is a letter still extant written by the latter to his friend Percy, in which he says:

"Alas, that my two enemies old age and rheumatism prevent my becoming a member of that glorious League which you are contemplating. Gladly would I have sworn allegiance and obedience to you, my dear Percy, whom I love and respect more than any man I have ever known. If you on the other hand do really bear me the affection which you have expressed so beautifully in your letter to me, then allow my boy St. John to be one of your followers and to take what should have been my place by your side, proud to obey you in all things and swearing allegiance to you, second only to that which he owes to his King."

That, then, was the man who in these early days of '93 had gradually allowed his boyish vices to get the better of his finer nature. The devils of arrogance, obstinacy and rebellion against authority had been the overlords that presided over his development from youth to manhood. They were held in check during the first few months of an adventurous life, fuller and more glorious than he had ever dreamed of, but those three devils in him had got the upper hand over him again.

"You may talk as much as you like, Percy," he said, when he

found himself alone with his chief, "you will never induce me to lend a hand in that wild scheme of yours."

"What wild scheme do you mean, Johnny?"

"Risking all our lives to save that upstart from getting his deserts." "You are still alluding to Simon Pradel?"

"Of course I am. You don't know him as I do. You weren't there when he thrust his attentions on Cécile de la Rodière and was soundly thrashed by François for his pains."

"As it happens, my dear fellow, I was there and I saw and heard everything that went on. You gave me the lie just now when I told you what I know to be a fact, that Cécile de la Rodière is half in love with Simon Pradel. Hers is a simple, thoroughly fine nature which could not help being touched by the man's silent devotion to her. He has a scheme for saving her and her family from disaster, very much, in my opinion, at risk of his own life."

"A scheme?" Devinne retorted with a sneer. "He has a scheme, too, has he?"

"A scheme," Blakeney rejoined earnestly, "which has for its keystone his marriage with Mademoiselle Cécile."

"The devil!"

"No, not the devil, my dear fellow, only the little pagan god who has had a shot at you, too, with his arrow, but has not, me-thinks, wounded you very deeply."

"Anyhow, Cécile would not marry without her family's consent and they would never allow such a damnable *mésalliance.*"

"The word has not much meaning with us in England these days when foreign princes and dukes earn their living as best they can. And as I have already told you, our League has taken Simon Pradel under its protection along with the La Rodière family."

"You mean that *you* have taken him under *your* protection."

"Put it that way if you like."

"And that . . . in England—?"

"In England, too, of course. Don't we always look after our protegés once we have them over there?"

161

"Then let me tell you this, Blakeney," Devinne retorted, emboldened probably by the patient way in which his chief continued to speak with him. He was being treated like a child, certainly, but like a child of whom the stern schoolmaster was half afraid. "Let me tell you this, now that we are alone and those bullies in there are not here to interfere, that I resent your hectoring me in the manner you have done these last few days. You talk a lot about honour and obedience and all that sort of thing, but I am not a child and you are not a schoolmaster. I will do all I can to help you save Cécile de la Rodière and her mother, and even her brother, though I care less for him than for a brass farthing. But help save Pradel I will not, and that is my last word."

Blakeney had let him talk on without interruption. He tried with all the patience at his command to understand and to sympathise or, at any rate, to find some sort of an explanation for what seemed to him an inconceivable situation. He said very quietly: "Look here, Johnny, you tell me that you will not lend a hand in saving Pradel, that you intend, in fact, to go against my orders, which means going back on your word of honour. Now that is a very big thing to do, as I told you once before. I won't qualify it any other way, I'll just say that it is a big thing. Will you then tell me why you think of doing it? What is your excuse? Or explanation? You'll want a cast-iron one, my dear fellow, you know, to make me understand it."

Devinne shrugged.

"Excuse? I might refuse to give you one, for I don't admit your right to question me like this. But I will try and remember that we were friends once, and, as far as I am concerned, we can go on being friends. I have two cast-iron reasons why I refuse to risk my life in order to save Pradel, who is my enemy. He has tried to alienate Cécile's love from me. Thank Heaven, he has not succeeded, but he has tried and will go on trying, once he is out of this country, in safety in England. And you expect me to help him in that? You must think I am a fool. My second reason is that in my opinion we must concentrate on saving Madame la

Marquise and Mademoiselle Cécile, François, too, if you insist, but to hamper ourselves with those two old servants, not to mention that damned doctor fellow, is sheer madness to my mind, and I contend that I can make better use of my life than lose it perhaps in the pursuit of such folly."

Now that Devinne had paused for lack of breath and still panting with excitement, Blakeney gave him answer, with utmost calm, never once raising his voice.

"I thank you, my good fellow, for this explanation. I am beginning to understand now. As to your last remark, that is as may be. A man must judge for himself what his own life is worth, and to what use he can put it. It is impossible for any members of the League to arrange for you to return to England for at least another day or two. I am taking it that you would prefer to travel alone rather than in the company of those whom we are going to do our utmost to save from death. If I can possibly arrange it, I will get in touch with Everingham and Aincourt, who know nothing of your treachery—"

"Percy!" the other cried in angry protest.

"Who know nothing of your treachery," Blakeney reiterated with deliberate emphasis. "If they did," he added, with a short laugh, "they would possibly wring your neck."

"You needn't worry about me," Devinne retorted sullenly. "I can look after myself."

"Then do, my good fellow. It is the best thing you can do. Good night."

Did some feeling akin to shame assail St. John Devinne then? It is impossible to say. Certain it is that without another word or backward glance he started to walk away down the hill. And Blakeney with a bitter sigh went to rejoin his comrades in the tap-room. They asked him no questions, for they guessed, if only vaguely, what had happened, and that after this they would have to face that most deadly of all dangers, a traitor in the camp.

"If we have a traitor in the camp," Sir Andrew Ffoulkes had once said, "then God help the lot of us."

CHAPTER TWENTY-SEVEN

Treachery

It is a little difficult to analyse the feelings of a man like St. John Devinne, for he was not really by nature an out and out blackguard. Vanity more than anything else was at the root of his present dishonourable actions. He imagined himself more deeply in love with Cécile de la Rodière than he had ever been before, and more deeply than he actually was. Love in a man of Devinne's type does not really mean much, except the satisfaction of vanity, and, looking back on the pages of history in every civilised land, one cannot help but admit that vanity in men and women has caused more mischief, more misery and greater disasters than any other frailty to which humanity is heir.

He had formed a plan, of course, and all the way between the heights of La Rodière and the outskirts of Choisy, running when he could, stumbling often, falling more than once, he elaborated this plan. He covered the ground quickly enough, for the way was downhill all the time and it was no longer very dark, now that a pale moon shed its cold silvery light on the carpet of snow. Somewhere in the far distance a church clock struck the half-hour. Half-past eight it must be, reckoned Devinne, and the Levets would have finished supper. There was their house just in sight. Now for a lucky chance to find the girl alone, the girl who in an access of jealousy as great as his own had cried out: "You only care because you are in love with Cécile!" He paused a moment outside the grille in order to shake the snow and dirt off his clothes, to straighten his hat and adjust his cravat. Then he walked up to the front door and rang the bell. It was old man Levet who opened the door. Devinne raised his hat and said: "I have come with a message from Professeur d'Arblay. May I enter?"

"Certainly, monsieur," the old man replied, and as soon as Devinne stood beside him in the vestibule he added: "What can I do for Professeur d'Arblay?"

"The message is actually for your daughter, Monsieur Levet. But if you wish, I will deliver it to you."

"I will call my daughter," was Levet's simple response. He called to Blanche, who came out from the kitchen, a dishcloth still in her hand. Seeing a stranger, she quickly put the dishcloth down and wiped her hands on her apron.

"What is it, father?" she asked.

"A message for you from Professeur d'Arblay. If you want me, you can call. Monsieur," he added, with a slight bow to Devinne, "at your service."

He went into the sitting-room. Blanche and Devinne were alone. She turned anxious, enquiring eyes on him. He said: "It is very important and urgent, mademoiselle. It means life and death to Madame la Marquise up at the château and to Mademoiselle Cécile."

He noted with satisfaction that at mention of Cécile's name the young girl's figure appeared to stiffen, and that an expression almost of hostility crept into her eyes. She was silent for a moment or two. Then she turned and said coldly:

"Will you come in here, monsieur?" and led the way into the small dining-room, closing the door behind him. Chance, then, was bestowing her favours upon the traitor. He could talk to the girl undisturbed. Everything else would be easy. She offered him a chair by the table and sat down opposite him with a small oil-lamp between them, and Devinne, who studied her face closely, did not fail to see that the look of cold hostility still lingered in her eyes, and that her lips were tightly pressed together.

"I had best come at once to the point, mademoiselle," he began, "for my time is short. The question which I must put to you first of all is this: would you have sufficient courage to go up to La Rodière tonight? I would accompany you, but only as far as the gate, and you would then go on to the château and transmit Professeur d'Arblay's message to Mademoiselle Cécile."

Blanche hesitated a moment, then she said coldly: "That depends, monsieur."

"On what?"

"I must know something more about the message."

"You shall, mademoiselle, you shall. But first will you tell me this? Have you ever heard speak of the Scarlet Pimpernel?"

"Only vaguely."

"What have you heard?"

"That he is a dangerous English spy. The sworn enemy of our country. His activities, they say, chiefly consist in helping traitors to escape from justice."

"Would you be very surprised, then, to learn that Professeur d'Arblay is none other than the Scarlet Pimpernel himself?"

Once again Blanche paused before she answered. When she did, she spoke very slowly, almost as if she were searching her memory for facts which had been relegated up to now to the back of her mind.

"No, it would not surprise me. I always looked on Professeur d'Arblay as somewhat mysterious. Father liked him, and they often had long talks together, and *maman, pauvre maman*, looked upon him, I often thought, as a messenger of God. As a matter of fact, I never knew his name till quite lately, the day when the King was executed and the Abbé Edgeworth—"

"Yes? The Abbé Edgeworth? You knew about him and his escape from the mob who tried to murder him?"

"Yes. It was Professeur d'Arblay who brought him to this house."

"It was the Scarlet Pimpernel, mademoiselle."

"The Scarlet Pimpernel?" the girl murmured, "and you know him, monsieur?"

"I am English, mademoiselle, and we Englishmen all know him. We work together in the secret service of our country. I told him that I should be going past your house this evening, so he asked me to bring you the message which he desires you to convey to Mademoiselle de la Rodière."

"A verbal message?"

"No. I will write it if you will allow me. It would not have been over safe for a lonely wayfarer as I was to carry a compromising paper about his person. There are many spies and vagabonds about."

"But when we go up to La Rodière?"

"I am going down into Choisy first, and will hire a chaise. We will drive up to the château, with a couple of men on the box."

Blanche looked intently at the young man for a second or two, then she rose, fetched paper, ink and pen from a side table and placed them before him.

"Will you write your message, monsieur?" she said simply.

"Will you promise to take it?" he retorted.

"I will make no promise. It will depend on the message."

"Then I must take the chance that it meets with your approval," he decided, and with a smile he took up the pen and began to write. Blanche, her elbow resting on the table, her chin cupped in her hand, watched him while he wrote a dozen lines. In the end he made a rough drawing which looked like a device.

"What is that?" she asked.

"The Scarlet Pimpernel, mademoiselle, a small five-petalled flower. We always use it in our service."

"May I see what you have written?"

"Certainly."

He handed her the paper; she glanced down on it and frowned.

"It is in English," she remarked.

"Yes! my written French is very faulty. But Mademoiselle Cécile will understand."

"But I do not."

"Shall I translate?"

"If you please."

She handed him back the missive and he translated it as he

167

read:

> "MADEMOISELLE,
> Will you and your august family honour the League of the Scarlet Pimpernel by accepting its protection. Your arrest is only a question of hours. A coach waits for you outside your gate.
> It will convey you and Madame la Marquise with all possible speed to a place of safety and then return to fetch Monsieur le Marquis, your two servants and Docteur Simon Pradel."

The girl gave a violent start.

"Simon Pradel?"

"You know him, mademoiselle?"

"Yes . . . yes . . . I know him . . . but why?"

"He and Mademoiselle Cécile have arranged to get married as soon as they are in England."

"It's not true!" Blanche exclaimed vehemently. She then appeared to make an effort to control herself and went on more quietly: "I mean . . . Docteur Pradel has so many interests here . . . I cannot imagine that he would leave them and become an exile in England . . . even if his life were in danger, which I pray to God is not the case."

"I can reassure you as to that, mademoiselle," Devinne said with deep earnestness. "Only to-day did I hear that the charge of treason preferred against the doctor before the Chief Commissary has been dismissed as non-proven. He is held in high esteem in the commune, and like yourself, I cannot believe that he would leave his philanthropic work over here except under constraint."

"What do you mean by constraint?" the girl asked, frowning.

He gave a smile and a shrug.

"Well!" he rejoined, "we all know that when a woman is in love, and sees that her lover is not as ardent as she would wish, she will exercise pressure which a mere man cannot always resist."

"Then you do not think—" the girl cried impulsively, and quickly checked herself, realising that she was giving herself away before a stranger. A blush, that was almost one of shame, flooded her cheeks, and tears of mortification came to her eyes.

"I don't know what you will think of me, monsieur . . ." she murmured.

"Only that you are a wonderfully loyal friend, mademoiselle, and that you are grieved to see a man of Docteur Pradel's worth throw up his career for a futile reason. After all these troublous days will soon be over. Mademoiselle de la Rodière will then return from England, and if she and the doctor are still of the same mind, they could be affianced then."

Blanche's eager, enquiring eyes searched the young man's face, almost as if she tried to gather in its expression comfort and hope in this awful calamity which threatened to ruin her life.

There followed a few moments silence, while Devinne scrutinised the girl's face, aware though he was too young to be a serious psychologist, of the terrible battle which her better nature was waging against pride and jealousy. He had no cause now to doubt the issue of the conflict. Blanche Levet would be his ally in the act of treachery which he was about to commit. Ignorant and unsuspecting, she did not realise that she was on the point of sacrificing the man she loved, and depriving him of the protection of the one man who had resolved to save him. Jealousy won the day by letting her fall headlong into the trap which a traitor had so cunningly set for her. She was about to become the instrument which would deliver Simon Pradel into the hands of the revolutionary government.

"I will tell you what I can do, mademoiselle," Devinne resumed after a time, "and I hope my plan will meet your wishes. I am going straight into Choisy now, and will call on Docteur Pradel and use all the eloquence I possess to persuade him to put off his journey to England, at any rate for a few days. I shall be able to assure him that in his case it is not a matter of life and death, whilst, in any event, Mademoiselle de la Rodière and her family are perfectly safe under the aegis of the Scarlet Pimpernel. And then I hope to bring you news within the hour that your friend will do nothing rash until after he has seen you again."

Blanche listened to him with glowing eyes. In every line of her pretty face the speaker could trace the mastery of hope over the doubts and fears of a while ago.

"You really would do that for me, monsieur?" she exclaimed, and clasped her little hands together, while tears of emotion and gratitude gathered in her eyes.

"Of course I would, mademoiselle. I shall only be doing what our brave Scarlet Pimpernel himself would have suggested."

Blanche's heart now felt so warm, so full of joy that she broke into a happy litle laugh.

"It is my turn to write," she said almost gaily, and took up the pen and drew paper towards her. She only wrote a few lines:

"MY DEAR SIMON,
"The bearer of this note is a gallant English gentleman who was instrumental in saving the Abbé Edgeworth from being murdered by the mob. You know all about that, don't you? And cannot wonder therefore, that I beg you to trust him in everything he may tell you."

She signed the short missive with her name, strewed sand over the wet ink, folded the paper into a small compass and handed it to Devinne, who rose as he took it from her.

"I will fly on the wings of friendship, mademoiselle," he said, and picked up his hat. "On my return I will pay my respects to Monsieur Levet. Will you tell him everything, and prepare him for my visit of adieu? Au revoir, mademoiselle." She went to the door and opened it for him. "God guard you, monsieur!" she said fervently, "and send an angel from heaven to watch over you, on your errand of mercy."

She accompanied him to the front door. As he was passing out into the cold and the gloom, she asked naively:

"Your name, monsieur? You never told me your name."

"My name is Collin, mademoiselle," he replied with hardly a moment's hesitation, "a humble satellite of the brilliant Scarlet Pimpernel."

CHAPTER TWENTY-EIGHT

Check

Everything then had worked out to the entire satisfaction of this young traitor, who, unlike Judas, had no qualms of conscience for his shameful betrayal of his comrades and his chief. Not yet, at any rate. He had, of course, no intention of interviewing his enemy Pradel; in fact, he blotted the doctor entirely out from his scheme. It was good to think of him as remaining behind in Choisy while the girl whom he had planned to marry was safely on her way to England without any help from him.

A few minor details suggested themselves to him that would make his plan work more smoothly. He would stop the chaise at the smaller grille of La Rodière, the one opposite to the main gate, which gave on the narrow and less frequented cross-road to Alfort. Blanche Levet would take his message to Cécile, help her and Madame la Marquise to put a few things together, and accompany them to the chaise. She would have strict injunctions when going through the park with the two ladies to talk and move as if they were merely taking a stroll for the sake of fresh air. He certainly could reckon on Blanche to follow his instructions to the letter, she had as much at stake as he had himself, and jealousy, coupled with the desire to keep Simon Pradel in France, would be a powerful goad.

With the two ladies safely inside the chaise, he would then drive along to St. Gif as far as headquarters, where Galveston and Holte would be on the look-out for the chief and the refugees. This was a derelict house which had once been a wayside hostelry in the prosperous coaching days, but it had long fallen into disrepair, the landlord and his family having fled the country at the outbreak of the Revolution. It was now used as headquarters by the League whenever its activities required the presence of its members in this part of France. It had the great advantage of stables and barns which, though in the last stages of dilapidation, offered some sort of shelter for man and beast. Three or four horses were usually kept there in case they were wanted, and two members of the League took it in turns to remain in charge. There was always, of course, a certain element of risk in all that, but what were risks and dangers to these young madcaps but the very spice of their lives?

Luck had favoured St. John Devinne from the start, since it was he who had been deputed to seek out Galveston and Holte, who were in charge at St. Gif, and give them the chief's instructions for the provision of horses, of fresh disguises and above all of passports, some of them forged, others purchased from venal officials or merely stolen, of everything, in fact, that was required to ensure the success of the expedition that was contemplated for the rescue of the La Rodières and their servants and their ultimate flight to England. Mention had been made of the coach, but not of the likely number of its occupants nor of the size of the escort, and whether it would be headed by the chief himself or not. Galveston was to remain on the lookout at headquarters with horses ready saddled, and Holte was to make for Le Perrey with all speed and make provision there for relays.

And chance continued to favour the traitor's plans. He had no difficulty in hiring a coach in the town, giving himself out as an American merchant, a friend of General La Fayette, desirous to join a ship at St. Nazaire, and having no time to lose. The first halt would be made at Dreux. His manner, his well-cut clothes, his money of which he was not sparing, gave verisimilitude to his story and enabled him to secure what he wanted. He required, he said, an extra man on the box beside the driver, as his sister would be travelling with him; he understood that the road past Le Perrey was lonely, and she was inclined to be nervous. His papers were in order, as papers in the possession of members of the League always were, and forty minutes after his departure from the Levets' house he was back there again and ringing the bell at the front door.

Blanche was on the look-out for him. As soon as she had opened the door he stretched both his hands out to her, and in a quick whisper said: "Everything is well! I have seen Docteur Pradel. He laughed the idea to scorn that he was in any danger, and assured me that he had no intention of emigrating. Not just yet, at all events. I did not mention Mademoiselle de la Rodière's name, but he himself spoke of you and announced his intention of coming over to see you to-morrow."

The girl was dumb with emotion. All she could do was to allow her hand to respond to the pressure of his. He asked permission to pay his respects to Monsieur Levet. But father, it seems, was not in a mood to see anyone just now.

"I told him about the message which I was to take up to Mademoiselle," Blanche explained, "and he quite approved of my doing it. I told him that you were escorting me and that you were a friend of Professeur d'Arblay. This he already knew. He had also guessed, before I told him, that Professeur d'Arblay was in reality the Scarlet Pimpernel."

"Did you mention Docteur Pradel, also?"

"No, I did not. That is a matter which will remain between Simon and myself. I shall be eternally grateful to you for what you have done for him. But for you he would have made shipwreck of his life. Now he will, I know, take up its threads with his usual energy as soon as all this matter is past and forgotten."

"You are the best friend any man ever had," Devinne concluded as he escorted the girl to the coach; "Docteur Pradel is indeed a lucky man."

Devinne ordered the driver to pull up on the Alfort road at a couple of hundred metres from the small grille of La Rodière.

Grilles and gates were never bolted these days, by an order of the government which decreed that all parks and pleasure grounds were as much the property of the people as of those *aristos* who had stolen them, and that every citizen had the right to use them for pleasure or convenience. Devinne jumped out of the chaise and helped Blanche to alight. Together they walked up to the grille, and the girl passed through into the park. The young man remained standing by the low wall close to the gate in the shadow of tall bordering trees. He strained his ears to listen to Blanche's light footstep treading the frozen ground.

Nearly half an hour went by before his ear once more caught the sound of a light footstep treading the frozen garden path. One step only. He heard it a long way off, but tripping very quickly. Running now. It must, he thought, be Blanche returning for something she may have forgotten or, perhaps, with a message for him from the château. It was Blanche, of course. The clouds overhead rolled slowly away. The pale light of the moon revealed the dark figure of the young girl against the white background of frozen lawn. And she was running. Running. She was alone, and Devinne felt that his heart suddenly froze inside his breast. He held open the grille. Blanche almost fell into his arms.

"They have gone," she gasped.

"Gone? Who?"

"All of them. There is no one in the château. Not a soul. The doors are all left open. I ran upstairs, downstairs, everywhere. There is no one. Madame la Marquise, Monsieur, Mademoiselle Cécile, Paul, Marie. They have all gone. What does it mean?"

Aye! What did it mean, but the one thing? The one awful terrible thing, that it was his treachery that had been frustrated by the man whom he had betrayed. What had happened exactly, he could not conjecture. The plan was to effect the mock arrest of the La Rodières in the early dawn, and it was not yet midnight. Had suspicion of treachery lurked in the mind of the Scarlet Pimpernel? He was not the man to change his plans once he had mapped them out, for every phase of them fitted one into the other, like the pieces of those puzzles that children love to play with. Or had a real arrest been effected by soldiers of the Republic? Had Chauvelin contrived to escape? To liberate the men imprisoned in the stables?

As Devinne said nothing, Blanche began to cry.

"What are we going to do now?" she asked and tried to swallow her tears.

Devinne roused himself from his torpor. What chivalry there was left in him urged him first of all to see to the girl's safety.

"We'll drive back to your house, of course. Come."

He took hold of her arm and led her back to the chaise. She climbed in and he gave instructions to the driver.

"Straight back to Citizen Levet's house in the Rue Micheline."

Not a word was spoken between the two of them on the way home. Blanche's delicate form was trembling as if in a fit of ague. A name and eager questions were forming on her lips, but for some inexplicable reason she felt averse to uttering them. It was only when the chaise drew up outside her house, and Devinne, after he had escorted her to the front door, was taking his leave of her, that she spoke the name that was foremost in her thoughts.

"Docteur Pradel?" she murmured.

But apparently he didn't hear her, for he made no reply. The next moment the door was opened. Old Levet had been sitting up, waiting for his daughter. At sight of her he took hold of her hand and drew her into the house. She turned to say a last word to Devinne, but he had already crossed the short path that led to the gate. Blanche could hear his voice speaking to the driver, but it was dark and she could not see him. The next moment there was the crack of the driver's whip, the jingle of harness, the snorting of horses and, finally, the rumble of wheels. She was left with heart full of anxiety and fear for the man she loved. Many hours must go by before she could hope to glean information as to what had happened to him. And here was her father waiting to hear what had occurred at the château. She tried to tell him, but she knew so little. The family had gone, that was all she knew. Were they under arrest, awaiting trial, and, perhaps, death? Or was their mysterious departure connected in any way with that strange personage the Scarlet Pimpernel?

In either case, where was Simon now? In the cells of the Old Castle, awaiting the same fate as Cécile and the others? Or was he on his way to England and to safety, gone out of her life forever?

CHAPTER TWENTY-NINE

Checkmate

Devinne did not re-enter the chaise. He gave money to the two
men, the driver saluted with his whip, clicked his tongue,
whipped up his horses, and the vehicle went rattling down the
cobbled street, leaving the young man standing by the Levels'
gate. And here he remained for several minutes, until he heard
the clock in the tower of the Town Hall strike midnight. This
seemed to shake him out of his trance-like state. He started to
walk up the street in an aimless sort of way. The whole town
appeared deserted. Shutters tightly closed everywhere. Not a
soul in sight. Two cats, chasing one another, raced across his
path. But not a human sound to break the stillness of the night.

Devinne shivered. He was inured to cold weather as a rule;
considered himself hard as nails, and he had on a thick mantle,
but, somehow, he felt the cold tonight right in the marrow of
his bones, right into the depth of his heart. Still walking
aimlessly, he reached the Grand' Place. There on the right were
the Café Tison and the Restaurant, the scene of one of
Blakeney's maddest frolics. Blakeney! The leader, the comrade,
the friend whom he, St. John Devinne, was about to betray! His
plan, however, had failed. He had been forestalled. How? Why?
By what devilish agency, he did not know. But he was no longer
in doubt now. The more he thought about it all, the more
convinced he was that it was Blakeney who had forestalled him
as a counterblast to his insubordination. And a coach driven at
breakneck speed was even now outstripping the wind on the

road to St. Gif and Le Perrey.

An insensate rage took possession of Devinne's soul, for he had remembered Pradel. Pradel in that same carriage with Cécile, under the aegis of the Scarlet Pimpernel, who had never failed in a single one of his undertakings. Pradel and Cécile! The thought was maddening. It hammered in the young man's brain like blows from a weighted stick. Pradel and Cécile! Thrown together in England under the protection of Sir Percy Blakeney, the friend of the Prince of Wales, the arbiter of style and fashion. And then marriage. Of course, the marriage would follow. In England fellows like this Pradel, doctors, lawyers, and so on, were often held in high esteem, and if His Royal Highness approved, the marriage would come about as a matter of course.

He didn't know where Pradel lived or he would have gone there, rung the bell, asked to see the doctor. If he was in, he would kill him. That would be the best way out of this trouble. Kill him and get away. Nobody would know. But if Pradel was gone, that would mean that he was on his way to England with Cécile and the others, under the protection of the League, and he, Devinne, would have no longer any compunction in doing what he had already made up his mind to do. No compunction now, and no remorse in the future.

After a time he turned his back on the Town Hall, and on the Rue Haute, crossed the Grand' Place once more, and almost against his will his footsteps led him in the direction of the derelict cottage, the headquarters of the League, where he had first dreamt of mutiny, and Glynde and the others had been ready to knock him down. There it was, looming out of the darkness, a pale, moon mist covered, outlined its broken walls and tumbledown chimney. Devinne went in, groping his way about for the tinder-box, knowing where it was always kept. His fingers came in contact with it. It was in its usual place, so was the piece of tallow candle in its pewter sconce. He struck a light, put it to the wick and then looked about him. He picked up the guttering candle and holding it high above his head he wandered round the room. Seeking for what? He couldn't say. Unless it was for the broken fragments of an English gentleman's honour.

What he did come across was a pile of garments in one corner. Coats, hats, Phrygian caps, rags, tattered bits of uniforms and accoutrements, the whole paraphernalia so often used in the pursuit of those stirring adventures the like of which he would never witness again after he had accomplished his final purpose. He would have to make his way back to England unaided by his comrades, lacking the advice of his chief. Well, he had papers and money, both of which would help him on his route. He had gained experience, too, under the guidance of the Scarlet Pimpernel, of how to travel through a country seething with insurrection and suspicious of strangers. He spoke the language well. Oh, he would get on all right without help from anyone. His clothes, perhaps, were rather too tidy and too well-tailored for the adventurous journey. He turned over the pile of garments. Found what he wanted. Clothes, boots and hat such as a well-to-do farmer might wear going from market-place to market-place. He would hire a cabriolet when he could, or a cart; avoid big cities and frequented roads. Oh, yes! He had experience now, he would get on all right.

He dressed himself up in the clothes he had selected. In this too, he had experience, gained through the teaching of a veritable master in the art of disguise: he knew the importance of minor details, the discarding of a fine linen shirt, the use of mud and sand to hide the delicacy of the hands and face. By the time the tallow candle ceased to flicker and died out, he had become the well-to-do farmer right down to his skin. He was left in total darkness, his eyes were heavy with want of sleep and his head ached furiously. There were yet some hours to live through before the dawn when he could make his way back to Choisy and the Town Hall. So he threw himself down on the pile of garments and tried to woo sleep which refused to come. His brain was so alert that all through the night he heard the tower clock strike every hour. Sleep does not come when the mind is busy evolving a plan of treason and dishonour. Seven o'clock. Aching in every limb, half-perished with cold, my Lord St. John Devinne, Earl Welhaven, son and heir of the Duke of Rudford, went forth on an errand, which, for perfidy, was perhaps only rivalled once, nineteen hundred years ago. He had sworn to himself that he would have no compunction, if, on calling at Pradel's house, he was told that the doctor had gone away. He didn't know where Pradel lived, but it was morning now and he would find out.

His first objective was the Café Tison, for, besides being cold, he was also hungry. These sort of places, mostly new to provincial towns, usually opened their doors very early, and were frequented by men and women on their way to work: here for a few sous they could get a plate of hot soup, or, if they were more sophisticated, a cup of coffee. Devinne, in his rough clothes and with grimy hands and face, attracted no attention. There were a dozen or so workmen sitting at different tables noisily consuming their *croute-au-pôt*. The Englishman sat down and ordered coffee. This he sipped slowly and munched a piece of stale bread. The municipal offices in the Town Hall, he was told on enquiry, opened at eight o'clock. He then asked to be directed to the house of Docteur Pradel.

"Rue du Chemin Neuf, citizen," someone told him, "corner of the Rue Verte. You will find him at home for certain."

Devinne paid his account and went out. He found the house at the corner of the Rue du Chemin Neuf. A painted sign hung before the door stating that Citizen Docteur Pradel *de la Faculté de Paris* lived here and received callers between the hours of eight and ten in the morning, and two and three in the afternoon. Devinne rang the bell, a middle-aged woman opened the door.

"The citizen doctor?" he demanded.

"He is not in," the woman answered curtly.

"Not in?"

"As I have told you, citizen."

"Where can I find him? It is for an urgent case."

"I cannot tell you, citizen. The doctor was sent for late last night for an urgent case. He has not yet returned."

The woman was apparently becoming impatient and was on the point of closing the door in the visitor's face, when something in the expression of his eyes seemed to arouse her compassion, for she added, not unkindly: "It is probably a confinement, citizen. These cases often keep the doctor out all night. He was fetched away in a cabriolet. I expect him back every moment. Would you care to wait?"

While Devinne parleyed with her a few callers had assembled on the doctor's doorstep. He thanked the woman, but no, he would not wait. He would have liked to ask one more question, but thought better of it and, turning on his heel, went his way.

Why should he wait? What for? Pradel had gone and Percy had done his worst. It was up to him, Devinne, now to show that arrogant chief of a league of sycophants, who was the better man.

CHAPTER THIRTY

Dishonour

Although it was only a few minutes after eight, Devinne found the waiting-hall of the municipal building crowded with visitors waiting for an interview with the Chief Commissary. Men and women of all sorts, country bumpkins and townsfolk, ragamuffins scantily clothed, shivering with cold, business men in threadbare coats, women with a child in their arms and another clinging to their skirts.

When Devinne entered he was told to give in his name to a clerk who sat making entries at a desk. On the spur of the moment he gave his name as Collins and his nationality as Canadian.

"Your occupation?" the clerk asked him curtly.

"Farmer."

"What are you doing in Choisy?"

"I will explain it to the Citizen Commissary."

The clerk looked up at him and said peremptorily: "You will explain it to me, and state your business with the Citizen Commissary."

"My business is secret," Devinne retorted; "the Commissary himself will tell you so. Give me pen and paper," he demanded, "and I will write it down."

The clerk appeared to hesitate. He scrutinised the face of the visitor for a moment or two and seemed on the point of meeting the demand with a definite refusal, when something in the expression of this Canadian farmer's face caused him to change his mind. He pushed a paper towards Devinne and held out his own pen to him.

Pen in hand Devinne paused a moment, seeking for the right words wherewith to arrest the attention of the Chief Commissary. Finally he wrote:

> *"Citizen Chauvelin and a squad of Republican Guard are held in durance, the writer will tell you where. The aristos up at La Rodière have made good their escape. The writer will tell you how."*

He put down the pen, read the missive through, was satisfied that it was to the point, strewed sand over the wet ink, then demanded curtly: "Wax."

The clerk gave him the wax, he took his ring off his finger and sealed the note down. When handing it over to the clerk, he slipped a gold coin into the latter's hand. This settled the matter. The clerk became at once quite amenable, almost obsequious.

"One moment, citizen," he said; "I will see to it that the Chief Commissary receives you without delay."

A few minutes later St. John Devinne was sitting in the Chief Commissary's private office, opposite that important personage, once again giving his name, nationality and occupation, which the Commissary duly noted down.

"Mathieu Collin, Citizen Commissary. Of Canadian nationality and French parentage. Spent most of my life farming in Canada, hence my foreign intonation in speaking your language."

The Commissary was fingering Devinne's note, the seal of which he had broken. He read and re-read it two or three times over, gave the Canadian farmer a searching glance, then said: "And *you have come to give me certain information relating to Citizen Chauvelin, member of the* Committee *of* Public Safety?"

"Yes!"

"What is it?"

"As I have had the honour to inform you in my note, Citizen Chauvelin and a squad of Republican Guard are prisoners since yesterday afternoon."

"Where?"

"In the Château de la Rodière. Citizen Chauvelin and a sergeant of the Guard in the cellar, the men in the stables."

"But who dared to arrest Citizen Chauvelin?" the Commissary queried, almost beside himself with horror at this amazing statement.

"He was not arrested, citizen. He was just thrust into the cellar with the sergeant and locked in."

"But by whom?" the other insisted.

"By the Scarlet Pimpernel."

"The devil!" cried the Commissary, and gave a mighty jump, causing every article on his desk to rattle.

"No, citizen, not the devil, the Scarlet Pimpernel."

"One and the same."

"Not exactly. We do not believe in the devil in this free and enlightened country, but the Scarlet Pimpernel really does exist. He is just a spy in the pay of the English Government, and has set himself the task of aiding the enemies of the Republic to escape from justice. It was in order thus to aid the *aristos* up at La Rodière that he and his followers, among whom must be reckoned that abominable traitor Docteur Pradel, plied the soldiers with drugged wine, and when they were helpless locked them up in the stables, then proceeded to kidnap Citizen Chauvelin."

The Chief Commissary appeared almost ludicrous in the excess of his stupefaction; he puffed and he snorted like an old seal, took out his handkerchief and mopped his perspiring brow.

"And do you mean to tell me," he gasped, "that all this is true?"

"As I live, citizen."

"And . . . and . . . the citizen doctor—? You mentioned him just now. Surely—"

"I called Pradel an abominable traitor," Devinne asserted

firmly, "for I know him to be a follower of the Scarlet Pimpernel."

"But how do you know all that, Citizen . . . er . . . Collin? What proof have you—?"

"I will tell you, Citizen Commissary," Devinne replied, but got no further, because the clerk came in at the moment and announced that Citizen Maurin had just come into the building and desired to speak with the Chief Commissary. The latter gave a great sigh of relief. Lawyer Maurin was a man of resource. His advice in this terrible emergency would be invaluable. The harassed Commissary gave orders that Citizen Maurin be admitted at once, and no sooner had the lawyer entered the room and the door been closed behind him than he was put *au fait* of the appalling event. The whole story was retold by the Canadian farmer at command of the Commissary – the soldiers of the Guard drugged and locked up in the stables, a member of the Committee of Public Safety kidnapped and held in durance in the cellar, and finally the escape from justice of the *ci-devant* La Rodières when the order of their arrest had already been signed, and all through the agency of that limb of Satan, the English spy, the mysterious Scarlet Pimpernel, and his followers, including that abominable traitor, Docteur Pradel.

It was Maurin's turn to give a jump.

"Pradel?" He then added more soberly: "What makes you think that the citizen doctor is a member of the English gang of spies?"

"The simple fact," Devinne replied, "that he, too, has fled from justice, which he knew was about to overtake him and punish him for his crime."

"What do you mean?"

"Only this. All that I have told you I learned through listening to the talk of a group of vagabonds in the cabaret of the *Chien sans Queue* on the Corbeil road. They were the musicians who had scraped their catgut and blown their trumpets all afternoon up at La Rodière. I was one of the crowd who had gone up there to see the fun, and then adjourned to the *Chien sans Queue* for a mug of ale. The vagrants were talking in whispers. I caught a word or two. To my astonishment those ragamuffins were speaking English, which I, as a Canadian, know well. I edged closer to them and heard every word they said. That is how I know everything and how I knew all about their plans. And," he concluded, with slow emphasis, measuring every word, "they spoke of Pradel as being a member of their gang and of their resolve to take him along with the La Rodières to England."

After Devinne had finished speaking there fell a stillness over this banal office, in the centre of which, round the desk littered with papers and paraphernalia, three men sat pondering over what would follow the amazing events of the previous night. The Chief Commissary perspired more freely than ever and kept on muttering in tones almost of despair:

"What are we going to do? *Nom d'un nom*, what are we going to do?"

Maurin said nothing. He was thinking. Thinking very deeply indeed, and at the same time trying to keep a mask of indifference over his face, so as not to allow that fool of a Commissary to guess that he felt neither doubt nor bewilderment at this turn of events, but only satisfaction. Pradel, his enemy, was disarmed. No longer could he be a rival in the affections of Blanche Levet. Neither as an *emigré* flying to England to save his skin, nor standing at the bar of the Hall of Justice under an accusation of treasonable association with a gang of English spies, could he ever hope to capture the glamour which had dazzled an unsophisticated young girl. And when the Commissary reiterated his complaint for the third time: *"Nom d'un nom*, what am I to do?" the lawyer responded dryly: "It is too late to do anything now. That wily Scarlet Pimpernel with his drove of traitors and *aristos* will be half-way to the coast by now."

"Not so bad as that, citizen lawyer," Devinne put in. "They will have to make a forced halt at Le Perrey for relays. Of course, they will drive like Satan himself as far as there, but the coach with its heavy load will be slow of progress."

A ray of hope glistened in the eyes of the Commissary at this suggestion.

"You are certain about Le Perrey?" he asked.

"Quite certain. I heard the gang discuss the question of relays and the enforced halt there. At any rate, it might be worth your while, Citizen Commissary," he went on in an insinuating manner, "to send a squad of mounted men in pursuit. They could get fresh horses at Le Perrey and ride like the wind. They are bound to come up with the lumbering coach."

"Do you know which route they mean to take beyond Le Perrey?"

"Yes, I do. They will make straight for Dreux, Pont Audemer and Trouville. The Scarlet Pimpernel has established headquarters all along that route and it is the nearest way from here to the coast."

The Commissary brought his fist down with a crash upon the desk.

"*Par dieu!*" he said lustily. "Citizen Collin is right. There is time and to spare to be at the heels of those cursed spies. What say you, citizen lawyer?"

But the citizen lawyer really didn't care one way or the other. Whether Pradel was caught in the company of English spies, or was still in Choisy, when of a surety he would be arrested for treason on the evidence of this Canadian farmer, mattered nothing to Louis Maurin, the prospective husband of Blanche Levet. He gave a shrug of indifference and said casually: "You must do as you think best, Citizen Commissary."

The latter by way of an answer tinkled his hand-bell furiously. The clerk entered, looking scared.

"Send Citizen Captain Cabel to me at once," the Commissary commanded. He was feeling decidedly better. Much relieved. He mopped his still streaming forehead, picked up a pen and started tap-tapping it against the top of the desk. And while he did so a look of absolute beatitude crept slowly all over his face. He had just remembered that a reward of five hundred louis was offered by the government for the capture of the Scarlet

Pimpernel.

To Captain Cabel, who entered the office a few minutes later he gave quick orders: "A gang of English spies, probably in disguise, and escorting a coach in which are the *aristos* from La Rodière, are speeding towards the coast by way of Le Perrey, Dreux and Pont Audemer. They will probably make for Trouville. Take a mounted squad of sixteen picked men and ride like hell in pursuit. The leader of the gang is the famous Scarlet Pimpernel. There is a reward of five hundred louis for his apprehension. Fifty louis will be for you if you get him, and another twenty to be distributed among the men. Lose no time, citizen captain; your promotion and your whole future depend on your success."

Captain Cabel, dumb with emotion, gave the salute, and turning on his heel, marched out of the room. There was no mistaking the expression of his face as he did so. If it was humanly possible to accomplish such a thing, he would bring that audacious Scarlet Pimpernel back to Choisy in chains. The Commissary rubbed his hands together with glee. He had never done a better morning's work in all his life. Five hundred, or what would be left of it after he had shared it with the captain and the men, was a fortune in these days of penury. Yes, Chief Commissary Lacaune had reason to be elated. He rose and with an inviting gesture begged his distinguished visitors to join him in a *vin d'honneur* at the Café Tison.

Maurin accepted with pleasure. He liked to be on friendly terms with the Commissary, who was the most important personage in the Commune. But Devinne asked politely to be excused. He was heartily sick of all these people, the like of whom in his own country he would not have touched with a barge pole. He longed to be back in England, where rabble such as ruled France to-day would be sent to gaol for venality and corruption. He took his leave with as polite a bow as he could force himself to make. The Commissary tinkled his bell, the clerk re-entered and ushered Citizen Collin out of the place.

Maurin gazed thoughtfully on the door that had closed

189

behind the pseudo Canadian farmer.

"A strange person that," he remarked to his friend Lacaune. "Do you suppose he spoke the truth?"

The Commissary gave a gasp. He did not relish this sudden onslaught on his newly risen hopes.

"I'll soon ascertain," he replied tartly, "for I'll send up to La Rodière to liberate Citizen Chauvelin and the men from durance. If they are not there, it will give the lie to our Canadian; in which case—" he went on, and completed the sentence by drawing the edge of his hand across his throat.

"And, anyway, I am having him watched. You may be sure of that, my friend." After which he gave a short laugh and added lightly:

"But I am more than hopeful that my men will find the distinguished member of the Committee of Public Safety locked up in the cellar of the château, as our friend the Canadian has truly informed us."

With that the worthy Commissary took his friend the lawyer by the arm and together the two compeers adjourned for a *vin d'honneur* at the Cafe Tison.

BOOK V

THE CHIEF

CHAPTER THIRTY-ONE

The Dream

To Cécile de la Rodière that January day and night always seemed to her afterwards more like a dream than a reality. She certainly lived through those twenty-four hours more intensely than she had ever lived before. It seemed as if everything that the world could hold of emotion and excitement all came to her during that short space of time.

There was that awful rioting to begin with, the invasion of her stately home by that turbulent mob who shouted and sang and danced, and mocked and baited her in a manner that for years to come would always bring a rush of blood to her cheeks. And then the amazing, appalling and mysterious figure of that fiddler, who had suddenly grown in stature, and become a sort of giant, endowed with superhuman strength. She could see him at any time just by closing her eyes, stretching out his immense arms and picking up that small, sable-clad man as if he were a bale of goods, throwing him over his shoulder and carrying him away through the hall and down the grand staircase, followed by the yelling and cheering crowd. Cécile could see it all as a vision. Never would she forget it. She had by that time been worked up to such a pitch of excitement that the whole world appeared as if it tottered round her, and that at any moment she and all that awful rabble would be engulfed in the debris of the château.

After that intensely vivid picture, what followed was more dim and equally unreal. She remembered seeing poor François, who was nothing but a wreck of his former proud self, dragging himself out of the room and desiring her to come with him. But this she did not do. She remained in the great hall where a strange silence reigned after the din and hurly-burly of a while ago. The shades of evening were drawing in, and she was alone with Simon Pradel. He talked to her at great length in a quiet measured voice, and she listened. He told her of the danger in which she stood, she and all those she cared for. Strangely enough it never entered her head to doubt him. He said so, therefore it must be true. He then pointed out to her the way, the one and only way by which she could save *maman* and François and faithful old Paul and Marie from that awful, awful guillotine. Again she listened, and never doubted him for an instant. There was to be a mock marriage. She would have to bear his name, and nothing more, until such time as France and the people of France were granted a return to sanity. She and *maman* and François, and the two old servants, would have to live under his roof and accept his hospitality, for his name and his house would be a protection for them all against danger of death.

After that he went away and she was left alone to ponder over these matters. Since then so many more things had happened that she had no time to analyse her feelings. But now she was alone, and she could think things over, all those things that seemed so like a dream. One thing was certain. After Pradel had left her, she did not feel altogether unhappy. Very excited, yes, but not unhappy. She had gone back to *maman* and François. *Maman* was quite placid, doing her usual crochet-work, not the least bit interested in hearing what had happened during those two hours of nightmare when what she termed the lowest dregs of humanity had polluted the old château with their presence. François, tired out with emotion which he had been forced to suppress for so long, sat by sulky and taciturn, obviously pondering on what he could do to have his revenge.

All was quiet in the château then. After a time Paul and Marie gathered their old wits together and prepared and served supper for the family. It was taken almost in silence, all three of them being absorbed in thoughts they could not share one with the other. At nine o'clock they all assembled for prayers in the small boudoir, and at half-past nine came bedtime, and Paul was on the point of going downstairs to put out lights and bolt the front door, when the sound of heavy footsteps coming up the grand staircase caused terror to descend once again like a thundercloud upon these five unfortunates. François cursed under his breath as was his wont. Madame la Marquise raised aristocratic eyebrows, and, with a sigh of resignation, resumed her crochet-work. Marie shrank into a remote corner of the room, while Cécile strained her ears to listen to those footsteps which had halted on the threshold of the grand *salon* for a moment, only to resume their march in the direction of the concealed door of the boudoir.

What did it all mean? Pradel had, of course, warned her of danger, but had also declared that danger was not imminent. He was to call for her to-morrow morning at ten o'clock and go with her to the *mairie* where, if she consented, the formalities connected with the new form of civil marriage would immediately take place. She, Cécile de la Rodière, would after that become nominally Madame Simon Pradel, and *maman* and the others would be safe against such awful contingencies as those ominous footsteps now foreshadowed. Paul, with the instinct of the old retainer, set to guard the welfare of his masters, slipped out into the vestibule ready to face a whole crowd of miscreants, if they dared interfere with them. Before closing the door behind him he said to François in a half-audible whisper: "While I parley with them, Monsieur le Marquis, take the ladies down the back staircase to the *sous-sol*. I will say that

Marie and I are alone in the château, and that you all drove away an hour ago in the direction of Corbeil."

François saw the force of this advice. There were several good hiding places in the vast area below the ground. There was even an underground passage which led to a dependency of the château, where the laundry, the buttery and so on were situated. At any rate the advice was worth taking.

"Come, *maman*" he said curtly to his mother, and with scant ceremony took crochet-needle and wool out of her hands, even while from the grand *salon* there rang out the harsh word of command.

"Open in the name of the Republic!"

"How did those devils know where we were," François muttered between his teeth: "and how did they find the door behind the tapestry? There was no time, however, to speculate over that. Suddenly there was a terrific bang, a deal of cursing and swearing and an agonised cry of protest from Paul. The door had been broken open. Madame la Marquise, aided by her son and Cécile, was struggling to rise, but she was old and heavy. She got entangled in the wool and fell back in her chair dragging Cécile down with her.

Paul now slipped back into the room, but remained standing with his back to the door, holding it against the intruders.

"Quick, Madame la Marquise," he urged in a hoarse whisper, "the staircase."

It was too late. François wasted a few moments in fumbling in a drawer for a pistol and seeing that it was loaded, and he had just got the ladies as far as the opposite door, when Paul was violently thrown forward and sent sprawling right across the room.

Four men pushed their way in. They wore shabby military uniforms and each carried a pistol. François levelled his, but one of the men who appeared to be the sergeant in command said sharply in a tone of authority.

"Put that down or I give the order to fire."

By way of a retort François cocked his pistol. It was promptly knocked out of his hand, and he was left standing like an animal at bay, glaring at the soldiers, the ladies and the old servants crowding round him. Even his facility for cursing and swearing had deserted him. Madame la Marquise was speechless and dignified. She would not allow that rabble to think that she was afraid. Paul and Marie took refuge in murmuring their prayers. Cécile alone kept a level head.

When the sergeant rapped out the order: "Arrest these people in the name of the Republic," and all four men stepped forward, each to put a hand on her and those she cared for, she said, with as much pride as she could call to her aid: "I pray you not to put hands on us. We will follow you quietly."

And seeing that the sergeant then gave a sign to his men to step back again, she added: "I hope you will allow Madame la Marquise and myself, also our maid, to put a few things together which we may need."

"I regret citizeness," the sergeant replied firmly, but not unkindly; "time is short and my orders are strict. I have a coach waiting outside to convey you to Choisy without a moment's delay. Your requirements will be attended to to-morrow."

"But my man . . ." Madame la Marquise protested. They were the first words she had uttered since this unwarrantable incursion by these insolent plebeians into her privacy, but she did not get any farther with what she would have liked to say. She had a great deal of dignity, had this foolish old lady, and a goodly measure of sound French common sense. The fact that the sergeant stood by like a wooden dummy, obviously just a slave to his duty, with no feeling or humanity in him, helped her to realise that neither resistance, nor hauteur nor abuse, would be of the slightest use. The insolent plebeians stood now for Fate, inexorable Fate, and the decree of *le bon Dieu* who had chosen to inflict this calamity on her and her children, and against whose commandments there was no appeal.

Cécile did not speak again either. She picked up a shawl and wrapped it round her mother. She looked a pathetic little figure in her thin silk dress. The small room was warm with a wood fire burning in the grate, but it looked as if she would have to go and face a long drive with no protection against the cold save her lace fichu. She heard the sergeant say curtly: "There are shawls and wraps in plenty downstairs, citizeness."

That seemed a strange thing for a revolutionary soldier to say, for they had not the reputation of being considerate to state prisoners. Cécile glanced up at the sergeant, her lips framing a word or two of gratitude, but he stood back in the shadow and she could not see his face.

François had remained silent all this time, with still that look of a baffled tiger in his eyes. His teeth were tightly clenched, so were his fists. Cécile was thankful that he did not make matters worse by indulging in violent curses or loud abuse. At one moment he made a movement and raised his fist as if he meant to strike that insolent sergeant in the face first and then make a dash for freedom, but immediately four arms were raised and four pistols were levelled at him. Madame la Marquise said dryly: "No use, my son. You would, anyhow, have to leave me behind."

Each of the soldiers now took a prisoner by the arm. The sergeant leading the way with Madame la Marquise and poor old Marie left to follow on alone. The small procession then marched out of the room in close formation. They traversed the wide *salon* and descended the grand staircase. Staircase and hall were only dimly lighted by one oil-lamp placed in a convenient spot on a consol table. Cécile was walking immediately behind her mother. In the dim light she could vaguely see the tall sergeant walking in front of her. She could see his broad shoulders, one arm and the hand which held a pistol; the rest of him was in shadow.

Down in the hall, on the centre table a masterpiece of Italian art left untouched after two raids by riotous mobs, because of its size and weight – there was a pile of rugs and coats and shawls. Madame la Marquise and François took it as a matter of course that these things should have been provided for their comfort by the same men, police or military, who had chosen this late evening hour for the arrest of three women and two men against whom no accusation of treason had yet been formulated. Marie fussed round her old mistress with shawl and mantle, and Paul round his young master with a thick coat. Cécile saw the sergeant pick up a cloak and hood. He came behind her and put it round her shoulders. She looked up at him while he did this and met his eyes, kind, deep-set eyes they were, with heavy lids, and in their depths a gentle look of humour which for some unaccountable reason gave her a feeling of confidence.

But there was no time now to ponder over things, however strange they might appear. Within a very few moments all five of them, *maman*, François, the two servants and Cécile herself were bundled out of the front door and into a coach which was waiting at the bottom of the perron. A man, dressed like the others in military uniform, stood at the horses' heads. He stepped aside when all the prisoners were installed in the coach. Looking through the carriage window Cécile saw the sergeant talking for a moment to one of the men; he then climbed up to the box-seat and took the reins. It was very dark, and the carriage lanterns had not been lighted. One of the men led the horses all the way down the avenue and through the main gate. The others had evidently climbed up to the roof, for there was much heavy tramping overhead.

Surely all that had been a dream. It couldn't all have happened, not just like that and not in the space of a few hours. And the dream did not stop there. There were more happenings all through the night and the next day, all of which partook of the character of a dream. Outside the main gate of La Rodière the coach did not turn in the direction of Choisy, but to the right. It went on for a little while and then drew up. Someone lighted the carriage lanterns, and after that the horses went on at a trot. Cécile, whenever she looked out of the window, saw the snow-carpeted road gliding swiftly past. The moon had come out again and the road glistened like a narrow sheet of white crystals.

CHAPTER THIRTY-TWO

Stratagem

Cécile was wide awake for a long time. Her mother was asleep in the farther corner of the carriage, so was François, who sat between them, leaning against the back cushions. Paul and Marie had spent some time murmuring their prayers until they, too, fell asleep. She herself must have dozed off at one time, for presently she was roused with a jerk when the coach wheels went rattling over cobblestones. This must be St. Gif, she thought, for she could see houses and shuttered shops on either side and an occasional street lamp. At one time there was a peremptory call of "Halt!" followed by some parleying between the sergeant-driver and what was probably a police patrol. Cécile caught the words "citizen" and "papers" and "only my duty, citizen sergeant." And presently the call: "Right. Pass on."

And the wearying drive went on along the jolting road. Progress was slow, because the ground was slippery for the horses, and the night intermittently very dark when heavy snow-laden clouds, driven by the north-easterly wind, obscured the pale face of the moon. The coach went lumbering on for hours and hours, an eternity, so it seemed to the unfortunate inmates, until presently the first streak of a cold grey dawn came creeping in through the carriage windows. After which the pace became less slow. The ground was, of course, as slippery as before, but there was obviously a very firm hand on the reins, and nothing untoward occurred to interrupt progress.

It was not yet daylight when once again the carriage wheels

rattled over a cobbled street. There were gleams of light to be seen through shuttered windows on either side, and here and there a passer-by: men in blouses, women with shawls over their heads. Le Perrey in all probability, thought Cécile. The others were still asleep. Poor *maman*, she must be terribly stiff and tired, and François looked more dead than alive. Paul and Marie were muttering even in their sleep, words that were either prayers to God or protests against the cruel fate that befell their master and mistress. Cécile had no idea whether they were being driven, or whether this flight through the night would end in safety or disaster. Fortunately *maman* was obviously not thinking on the matter at all, whilst François effectually hid his own doubts and fears behind a mask of sullen indifference.

Le Perrey was soon left behind, and after a time the coach was again pulled up, this time in open country. There was a good deal of scrambling overhead, and a minute or two later the carriage door was opened and a pleasant cultured voice said:

"I am afraid there is a piece of rough ground to walk over. Can you do it, mademoiselle?"

This, of course, was still part of the dream. Cécile heard herself replying: "Yes, I can," and then adding tentatively: "But *maman*—"

And the pleasant voice responded: "I will carry Madame la Marquise if she will allow me. Will you and Monsieur le Marquis descend, mademoiselle?"

Whereupon Cécile obeyed without demur. It seemed quite natural that she should. François appeared too dazed to raise his voice. He got down, and was followed by Paul and Marie, still mumbling prayers to *le bon Dieu*. Madame la Marquise did not apparently care what happened to her. She allowed herself to be lifted out of the coach without protest and Cécile heard that same pleasant voice saying in English: "Cloaks and rugs, Tony, for the ladies, and, Hastings and Glynde, take the coach a couple of kilometres down that other road. Take out the horses and bring them along with you to headquarters."

She understood what was said, though not quite all. A man

put a shawl round her shoulders, over her cloak, whilst another busied himself by wrapping a rug round *maman*, who was lying snugly in the arms of the tall sergeant. After which the little procession was formed, the sergeant on ahead carrying *maman*, who was no light weight. Franfois came next with Paul and Marie, and finally she, Cécile, walked between two soldiers, one of whom had her by the elbow to guide her over the rough ground, while the other, after a minute or two, performed the same kindly office to poor old Marie.

And walking thus, in the rear of the little procession, the girl all at once understood what was happening. These soldiers had nothing to do with the Gendarmerie Nationale, the uniform of which they only wore as a disguise. They were friends who were helping them all to escape from death, the same friends who had saved the Abbé Edgeworth from that awful, awful guillotine. And the sergeant on ahead was none other than the fiddler who had carried that small sable-clad form of a man on his shoulder as if he were a bale of goods, and was carrying *maman* now as if she were a child. She gazed almost awestruck on the silhouette of that broad back ahead of her, for, if her conjectures were correct, then that pseudo-fiddler or pseudo-sergeant was none other than the legendary Scarlet Pimpernel himself.

After which surmises and reflections Cécile de la Rodière was entirely unconscious of the roughness of the road, of cold or hunger. She became like a sleep-walker, moving without consciousness. Presently a solid mass loomed out of the frosty mist. It was a house with trees clustered round it. Its aspect, as it gradually was revealed to her, appeared familiar to Cécile, but her brain was too tired to ponder over this. The place looked deserted, the house in a state of dilapidation. It had evidently been suddenly abandoned and left to the mercy of rust and decay. The time-worn façade and crumbling stonework told the usual pitiable tale of summary arrest and its awful corollary.

The way up to the front door was along a short drive, bordered by Lombardy poplars. There was a low perron of three or four steps. To Cécile's intense astonishment she presently perceived that the place was not deserted, as she thought, for two men were standing on the perron. At sight of the approaching party they came down the steps, and called out in English: "All well?" to which her own escort replied lustily: "Splendid!" They stood aside while the pseudo-sergeant carried Madame la Marquise into the house. The others, including herself, followed him. He crossed a narrow vestibule and went into what might have been a small *salon* at one time, but now presented a shocking spectacle of wreckage: windows broken, doors off their hinges, panelling stripped from the walls. There was no furniture in the room except a few chairs, a horsehair sofa and a kitchen table. The only cheerful thing about the place, and that was very cheerful indeed, was a log fire in the open hearth. In spite of the broken window the room was deliciously warm.

The sergeant deposited *maman* on the sofa, asked her in perfect French how she felt, and on receiving a grateful smile in response, he turned to Cécile.

"And now, mademoiselle," he said, "we will get you some hot wine, after which you can all have a short rest. But I am afraid we must make a fresh start within the hour, and I shall have to ask you and Madame la Marquise, as well as Monsieur le Marquis, to don the country clothes which you will find in the chest in the next room, together with all requirements to make yourselves look as like as possible to a company of worthy yokels and bumpkins on their way to the nearest market town. One of us will, with your permission, put the finishing touches on your disguise."

And the next moment he was gone, leaving behind him an atmosphere of cheerfulness and of security. Even François reacted to that. The ladies trooped into the next room, burning with curiosity to see the dresses which they were ordered to wear. *Maman* said quite seriously: "I think God has sent one of His angels to protect us." Marie-murmured a fervent: "Amen!"

But Cécile didn't speak. She was under the spell of the

marvellous discovery she had made, namely, that *maman*, she and François, and all of them, in fact, had been rescued from death by that marvel of God's creation, the Scarlet Pimpernel.

CHAPTER THIRTY-THREE

The Bald Pate of Chance

How surprised they would all have been could they have seen through the dilapidated walls of this ramshackle abode their rescuers sitting on the table in what was presumably the kitchen. They were sipping hot wine and talking over their impressions of this last glorious adventure. Their noses and hands were blue with the cold, and they were all going through the process of getting shaved. One of them had served the fugitives with the hot wine, and presently they were joined by Glynde and Hastings.

"Where did you leave the coach?" the chief asked them as soon as they appeared.

"Do you know Moulins?" Glynde responded.

"Quite well."

"Just the other side of it. Past the church. We rode back, of course, and Hastings was nearly thrown when his horse slipped on a sheet of ice."

"No other accident?"

"No."

"Good. Now, any news here?" He turned to my Lord Galveston.

"Yes. Rather strange. When Holte and I got here about an hour ago, we saw to our surprise smoke coming out of one of the chimneys. To make a long story short, we found that a vagabond had quartered himself in the place. We couldn't very well turn him out, and we felt that he was less dangerous here than at large. So we let him stay where he was."

"And where is he now?"

"In the room next to this with a fire, a chair and a bottle of wine."

"Let's have a look at him."

Blakeney and Galveston went into the room to have a look at the intruder. He was just a miserable wreck of humanity, of the type found, alas, all too frequently on the high roads these days. There were a few dying embers in the hearth and three empty bottles on the floor beside it.

"The miserable muckworm," my Lord Galveston muttered and swore lustily; "he has ferreted out our stores and stolen two bottles of our best."

The "miserable muckworm", however, was impervious to his lordship's curses. He was squatting on the floor, his head resting precariously on the hard seat of the chair, fast asleep.

Galveston was for shaking the fellow up and throwing him out of the place. But Blakeney took his friend by the arm and dragged him back forcibly into the kitchen.

"You lay a hand on that gossoon at your peril," he said, with his infectious laugh. "Do you know what he really is?"

"No, I do not."

"He is the one hair on the bald pate of Chance which you and Holte have enabled me to seize."

"I don't understand."

"No, but you will by and by. Is there a key to that door?"

"Yes, on the inside."

"Get it, my dear fellow, will you? Then lock the door and give me the key."

"Everything all right here?" he asked, turning to Holte (Viscount Holte of Frogham, familiarly known as "Froggie").

"I think everything."

"Horses?"

"With the two out of the coach we have six. Those here are quite fresh."

"And vehicles?"

"Two light carts. Covered."

"Good. Tony, you must take charge. You and Hastings on one cart. Glynde and Galveston on the other. I want Froggie to remain here with four horses which we shall want later. You fellows must drive by way of Dreux to that little village we all know they call Trouville. Avoid the main road and you will find the side tracks quite safe. Tony has all the necessary papers. I bought them of a poor caitiff in Choisy who works in the commissariat, and, as a matter of fact, the country on this side of the Loire is not yet infested by that murdering Gendarmerie Nationale. When you get to Trouville make straight for the Cabaret Le Paradis, a filthy hole, but the landlord is my friend to the death. He is noted in the district as a rabid revolutionary, but, as a matter of fact, he battens on me and is exceedingly rich. He is grimy and stinks of garlic like the devil, but he'll look after you till I come, which won't be long. Of course, there are risks. You all know them and are prepared to face them. Bless you all."

There was silence amongst them after that for a moment or two. Four of them there had one name on their lips which they were loth to utter – Devinne. But Jimmy Holte and Tom Galveston, knowing nothing of the young's traitor's mutiny, asked where he was.

"Back in Choisy," the chief replied simply.

There were one or two more details of the expedition to discuss. The present military uniforms must be discarded and simple country clothes donned.

"I have already told the ladies about that," Blakeney explained, "and I imagine you will find the whole party quite excited to play their role of country bumpkins. Froggie, who is such a dandy, will see that they have not forgotten any important detail. Madame la Marquise is quite capable of playing the part of a labourer's wife with a dainty patch under her left eye and her finger-nails carefully tended."

"But what are *you* going to do, Percy?"

"Ffoulkes and I have a little piece of business to transact here.

205

He doesn't know it yet – that is why he looks such an ass, ain't it, Ffoulkes? But he'll know presently. As a matter of fact, we are going back to Choisy to get hold of Pradel. He must be in a tight corner by now, poor fellow. But that one hair on the bald pate of Chance is going to work miracles for us. I have all sorts of plans in my head and Ffoulkes and I are going to have a rattling day, eh, Ffoulkes?"

"I am sure we are if you say so," Sir Andrew replied simply.

After which the party broke up on a note of gaiety and excitement. The refugees were found to have donned the required disguises. Madame la Marquise looked an old market woman to the life, Cécile was a very presentable cinder-wench, and even François had taken pains to enter into the spirit of the adventure and was as grimy and as unkempt as any vagabond might be. A few small details here and there suggested by my Lord Holte and the transformation from *aristos* to out-at-elbows patriots was complete, which does not by any means tend to suggest that elegance of mien is entirely a matter of clothes and cleanliness, but that it goes very near it.

The start was made at nine o'clock. Two covered carts had been got ready and their drivers were waiting in the road. Madame la Marquise was again carried over the rough ground by the pseudo-sergeant, who to her mind was more than ever a messenger from God. The whole party was bundled in the two carts, the drivers cracked their whips and away they went.

The last picture that Cécile saw when she ventured to peep round the hood of the cart remained engraved in her memory for the rest of her life. This was the tall figure of the pseudo-sergeant standing by the roadside, his slender hand up to the salute, looking for all the world like one of those representations of the heroes of old which she had admired in the museums of Paris – tall, erect, a leader of men, the mysterious and elusive Scarlet Pimpernel.

206

CHAPTER THIRTY-FOUR

The English Spy

Long before midday the whole of Choisy was seething with excitement. All sorts of rumours had been flying about for the past two hours and now they had received confirmation, and the most amazing happenings ever known even in these revolutionary times were freely discussed in the open streets, in every home and more especially in the cafes and restaurants of the commune.

It seems that no less a personage than Citizen Chauvelin, who, it appears, was an influential member of the Committee of Public Safety, had been discovered in the Château de la Rodière, locked up with a sergeant of the Gendarmerie Nationale in the cellar, and that thirty men of the same military corps were found to have been locked up in the adjoining stables. And the person who had single-handed perpetrated this abominable outrage was none other than that legendary English spy, that messenger of the devil known as the Scarlet Pimpernel. And would you believe it, he was the fiddler who with his band of musicians had played the *rigaudon* all the afternoon at the cMteau! Of course everybody remembered how he had shouted: "A spy! A spy!" and "We shall all be massacred. Remember Paris!" and how he had picked a little man up as if he were a bale of goods and had carried him on his shoulder down the stairs and locked him up in the cellar. Well, that little man was no spy at all, but a very important personage indeed, member of the Committee of Public Safety, Citizen Chauvelin.

207

The men of the Gendarmerie Nationale, when they were liberated from the stables, had hardly recovered from a drugged sleep. A large jorum of wine and a number of empty mugs all containing the dregs of some potent drug were scattered about the floor. The men knew nothing of what had happened to them. They understood that Citizen Chauvelin, under whose orders they were, had sent them some wine to keep them warm. They were not fully in their senses yet when presently they were marched back to Choisy, there to give an account of how they came to have neglected their duty in such a flagrant manner by drinking and falling asleep.

These remarkable events, however, were not by any means the only ones that excited the population of Choisy almost to frenzy. There was the rumour, now amounting to a certainty, of what had happened to the citizen Dr. Simon Pradel. It appears that he had been out all night, having been called to a serious maternity case in the late evening. By the time he was free it was past nine o'clock and he went straight to the hospital situated about three kilometres outside Choisy in the little village of Manderieu. His regular time for attending there was seven o'clock, so he went straight there without going home first. But, mark what happened – and this was authentic – Docteur Pradel, founder and chief supporter of this hospital for sick children, was refused admission into the building. The gates were held by armed sentinels who crossed their bayonets in front of him. On his demanding an explanation an officer came across the forecourt and coolly informed him that the government had taken over the hospital, that no doctor, save those nominated by the National Convention, would be allowed to practise there, and that if there were any reclamations to be made, these must be addressed directly to them.

Of course, no one could say exactly what Citizen Pradel thought of this insult to the dignity of his profession. What was known, however, was that he went straight back to Choisy and lodged a formal protest with the Chief Commissary at the Town Hall against what he called this outrageous action on the part of the government. It was also known that he was there and then put under arrest and conveyed under escort back to Manderieu, there to remain in charge of the Commissary of the Commune, until such time as it was decided what course should be taken with regard to conduct that was nothing short of an insult directed against the Republic. As a matter of fact, those in the know asserted with a wink that the Chief Commissary of the district desired to hand over the responsibility of dealing with Citizen Pradel to his subordinate at Manderieu. The young doctor was so well known in Choisy that there was no knowing what the populace, already in ebullition over the incidents at La Rodière, might not do when it heard of the arrest of their popular townsman.

But even this extraordinary event paled before what really and truly was the most astonishing, the most marvellous, the most miraculous and most unexpected of all. The English spy, the mysterious and elusive Scarlet Pimpernel, who for over two years had led the police of France by the nose, who was the greatest and most dangerous enemy the Republic had yet known, was captured, caught on his way to the coast. Yes, captured, laid by the heels, trussed and manacled, and was now under lock and key in the dungeons of the old castle. And there was a big reward to come from the government for his apprehension. Five hundred louis to be divided between the Chief Commissary, who had ordered the pursuit, Captain Cabel, who had effected the arrest, and the men who had co-operated in it with unexampled valour. What had actually happened was this: Captain Cabel at the head of a squad of Gendarmerie Nationale was in hot pursuit of the spy and the *aristos* from La Rodière who were fleeing from justice. Half-way between St. Gif and Le Perrey, they spied coming towards them, two horsemen who were riding like the wind. Captain Cabel, seized with suspicion, drew his men across the road, and was on the point of crying "Halt", when the two horsemen suddenly drew rein at a distance of not more than three metres, throwing their horses on their haunches. They, too, wore the uniform of the Gendarmerie Nationale, and one of them had a man riding on the pillion behind him.

"We've got him!" this man cried in a stentorian voice.

"Got whom?" the captain countered.

"The English spy! The Scarlet Pimpernel!"

"No!"

"Yes!"

"Where is he?"

"On the pad of my saddle."

The captain raised himself on his stirrups and beheld a kind of vagabond with head hanging down on his chest and blood streaming from his forehead. His legs were firmly secured together under the horse's belly and his arms were tied with a rope round the soldier's waist.

"What?" he cried in amazement, "that beggarly tramp, the Scarlet Pimpernel?"

"Beggarly tramp forsooth? He and his gang fought like ten thousand devils. There were eight of us. Six are now in hospital at Le Perrey with battered heads and broken bones. I downed him at last by giving him a crack on the head with the butt end of my pistol. When the others saw him fall, they turned and fled taking their wounded with them."

"Wasn't there a coach?"

"Yes. Stuffed full of *aristos*. We saw that first and ordered them to halt, when we were suddenly attacked from the rear, and while we fought for our lives, the coach was driven away. But," the man concluded with a shout of triumph, "we have got the leader of the gang, and we are taking him to Choisy to get the reward. Do not bar the way, citizen captain."

He set spurs to his horse, but Cabel and his squad did not move.

"One moment," the captain commanded. "Where do you come from?"

"From Dreux, of course," the other responded, and pointed to his regimental number on his collar. "And we are going to Choisy."

"By whose orders?" Cabel asked.

"The Citizen Commissary at Dreux."

"What orders did he give you?"

"To keep a sharp look out for a gang of English spies, disguised, of course, who are known to be in the neighbourhood, and, if we find them, to convey them under arrest to Choisy."

"And do you know who I am?"

"Yes! The captain commanding the second division of the Gendarmerie Nationale."

"Very well then, listen to my orders. You will immediately transfer your prisoner to the saddle of my sergeant here, and you and your comrade can go back to Dreux and report."

For a moment it seemed as if the other would refuse to obey. He and his comrade even turned their horses as if ready to gallop back the way they came, but at a word of command from the captain, the squad closed in round them and no doubt they realised the futility of rebellion. Within a very short time "the English spy" was transferred to the sergeant's saddle. The captain watched the operation with a grin of satisfaction. Here was luck indeed! He recalled the words wherewith the Chief Commissary had finally dismissed him: "Lose no time, citizen captain, your promotion and your whole future depend on your success."

And here were promotion, reward, success, all within his grasp and without striking a blow. His name would ring throughout the length and breadth of the land as the saviour of the Republic, the man who had captured the Scarlet Pimpernel.

The squad was reformed, and soon the horses were put to a trot, leaving those two others in apparent discomfort in the middle of the road. Not a head was turned to see or an ear strained to hear what they said. If it had, a strange sound would have come wafted over the frosty air, a prolonged and ringing laugh, and a resonant voice calling gaily in a language not often heard in these parts: "That's done it, eh, Ffoulkes? Gad! I never spent such a pleasant half-hour in my life. Now, hell for leather, dear lad. I know a short cut across those fields, which will save us at least four miles."

But Captain Cabel and the men of his squad heard nothing of that ringing laughter and resonant voice. They were trotting merrily along the hard road back to Choisy, bearing in triumph, on the pillion of the sergeant's saddle, the unconscious form of a beggarly vagabond who was none other than the daring English spy, the Scarlet Pimpernel.

CHAPTER THIRTY-FIVE

An Unwelcome Guest

To say that the news of the arrest of Docteur Pradel caused agitation in Choisy would be to understate the true facts. The whole commune had been seething with excitement all day, and by the time the street lamps were lighted and the munition workers had trooped out of the factories, excitement had turned to frenzy. A frenzy fostered partly by indignation but mostly by fear. If the citizen doctor, as good a young man as anyone could wish to see, as straight, as loyal, as generous, could without any warning see the bread taken out of his mouth, could be cast into prison without as much as an accusation being brought against him, could *nom d'un nom* be brought to trial and perhaps to death, then what chance had any respectable citizen, father of a family perhaps, of escaping out of the clutches of such a relentless government? Guillotine to the right of them, guillotine to the left, guillotine and threat of guillotine all the time. life would soon not be worth an hour's purchase. As for liberty, was there such a thing as liberty these days? Liberty to starve, yes, to send your sons to be slaughtered in wars against the foreigners, but slavery in everything else, and one trembled more fearfully these days before the Chief Commissary or the Committee of Public Safety, than one did in the past before those arrogant *aristos*.

Of course, none of these mutterings and grumblings reached the ears of the powers that be. They were all done in a whisper, for one never knew where government spies plied their dirty trade, nor in what disguise, witness the citizen doctor who was obviously a victim to one of that *canaille*. So everything that was said was said in a whisper, whilst furtive glances of contempt were cast oh the inscriptions that decorated the portals of every public building: *Liberté, Fraternité, Égalité*.

Liberty, I ask you!

As usual the Restaurant and Café Tison were the chief centre of grumblings and discontent. Pradel! The doctor! The man who looked after one when one was ill and after the children! What was going to happen to the children when Pradel was no longer there? Oh, if one only dared—!

But one didn't dare, that was the trouble. All one could do was to troop down to Manderieu and there learn for certain what was happening to Pradel. It was evening now, nearly six o'clock. But no matter. It was dark, but everyone knew the road to Manderieu. And so the company trooped out in a body from the Restaurant Tison. As they all emerged out into the Grand' Place, they called to their friends, and to casual passers-by to join them. "Art coming, Jean? And thou, Pierre?"

"Whither are you going?"

"To Manderieu. The hospital is closed."

"I know."

"And Docteur Pradel a prisoner in the commissariat."

"I know, but what can we do?"

"Let's go and see, anyway."

The three kilometres to Manderieu were soon got over. The little village, usually so tranquil, had also caught the excitement which was raging in the town. In the market-place where stood the hospital and the Commissariat of Police, a small knot of country folk had assembled, some by the gates of the hospital, where sentinels stood on the watch, and others in front of the Commissariat. It was a silent crowd. Only now and again was a voice raised to murmur or to curse. The place was only dimly lighted by a couple of oil-lamps at the hospital gates and one over the portal of the Commissariat. The crowd from Choisy joined in now with the villagers of Manderieu. After this fusion, silence was broken more frequently, but the attitude of Pradel's sympathisers remained subdued. They were sorry enough for him, and they were indignant, but they were also very much afraid. None of them quite knew what it was that had brought them out in a body to Manderieu, except perhaps the desire to ascertain just what was happening to the citizen doctor and to the children's hospital. A man down in the Restaurant Tison, they didn't know who he was, had urged them to it. "After all," he had said, "things might not be so bad as they seem. Docteur Pradel may not have been arrested and the hospital may not be closed." But the hospital was closed and the country folk of Manderieu declared that the doctor was a prisoner in the Commissariat.

"Let us ask and make sure," someone in the crowd suggested to his neighbour. And, as is the way with crowds, the suggestion was taken up. It travelled from mouth to mouth until there were quite two hundred malcontents who kept on reiterating: "Let us make sure," while others just muttered: "Doc Pradel. Doc Pradel. Where is Doc Pradel?"

The Commissary was beginning to feel worried. Manderieu was a quiet little hole where such things as turbulent crowds and rioters were unknown. The holding of the popular doctor in durance pending further instructions had been thrust upon him and he had been promised by his superior that he would be relieved of responsibility by nightfall, when the prisoner would be conveyed, under escort, back to Choisy. But here was six o'clock and Docteur Pradel was still the unwelcome guest of Citizen Delorme, Commissary of Manderieu. The latter in his distress sent a mounted messenger over to Choisy with a hurriedly written note to his chief, demanding that the prisoner be removed from the village as quickly as possible. But half an hour, at least, must elapse before the return of the messenger, and in the meanwhile the crowd had concentrated in front of the commissariat and was striking terror in the heart of Citizen Delorme by its persistent parrot-cry of "Doc Pradel! Doc Pradel! We want to see Doc Pradel!" After a time the cry was accompanied by boos and hisses and banging of lists and sabots against the door of the Commissariat.

Delorme now was like Bluebeard's wife of the fairy tale. He had posted two of his gendarmes at the entrance of the village, at a point where a narrow side street led to the back of the Commissariat, with orders to intercept any messenger or escort from Choisy, take them round to the back gate of the building, then fetch the prisoner from the lock-up and hand him over to the escort for conveyance to the city. And like Bluebeard's wife, the unfortunate Commissary might have called in his agony of mind: "Sister Anne, Sister Anne, is no one coming down the road?"

His sergeant of the guard suggested his going to the door and talking to the people. Delorme demurred. He did not relish facing the crowd. There were a lot of loose stones lying about, one of them might be hurled at his head.

"Sister Anne! Sister Anne!" He didn't use those words exactly, but the sentiment that prompted the words he did use were the same as those that caused Bluebeard's wife to call to her sister in the depths of her terror and distress. In the end he had to come to a decision. Some kind of risk had to be taken, flying stones or the certain disapprobation of his superiors, if things went wrong with the prisoner or the crowd got beyond control. The thought of such disapprobation gave the unfortunate Commissary an unpleasant feeling round the neck.

"Sister Anne! Sister Anne! Is no one coming down the road?"

CHAPTER THIRTY-SIX

Duped

At about this same hour in the late afternoon of this cold January day, Citizen Lacaune, Chief Commissary of Choisy, was going through a far more lamentable experience than that which befell his subordinate at Manderieu. He had had two hours of absolute bliss when Captain Cabel presented himself at the Town Hall with the marvellous, the miraculous, the amazing news that he had really and truly succeeded in capturing that damnable English spy, the Scarlet Pimpernel, and had brought him into Choisy strapped to the pillion of the sergeant's saddle, wounded and nearly dead, after a terrific fight wherein he, Cbela, and his squad had displayed prodigies of valour. The worthy Commissary nearly had a fit of apoplexy when he heard this wonderful news. He gave the order that the notorious spy, safely bound and gagged, be brought into his office and thrown down like a bale of refuse in a corner of the room. He gazed with awe not unmixed with astonishment at the helpless form of what seemed at first sight to be that of a drunken vagabond. Like Cabel himself, his first feeling was one of doubt that this miserable wreck of humanity could be the daring adventurer whose name was dreaded throughout the whole country and who had led the entire police force of the Republic for three years by the nose. It was only after he had learned from the captain the whole story of the amazing capture, the coach crammed full of escaping *aristos*, of the attack and desperate fighting, that his doubts were finally set at rest. Everyone knew, of course, that spies are the scum of the earth, and English spies more ignoble than those of any other land. He ordered two of his gendarmes to stand guard over the prisoner, and then sent word of the joyful news to Citizen Chauvelin, Member of the Committee of Public Safety.

The latter was at the moment nursing his wrath and humiliation in the house of Citizen Maurin, the lawyer, who had offered him hospitality after his liberation from the cellar of La Rodière.

Chauvelin had not only suffered humiliation for close on four- and-twenty hours, but also bodily pain, lying on damp straw in an atmosphere of stale alcohol and decaying corpses of rats and mice. He had spent a few hours in bed, nursed devotedly by the lawyer, always on the look-out for a chance to secure for himself influential friends. The news of the capture of the Scarlet Pimpernel was real balm for his mental and bodily ills.

"I pray you, citizen, come at once," the Chief Commissary had written in his hurried message. "I am keeping the prisoner here under guard so that you may have the satisfaction of seeing him yourself. I must say he is not attractive to look at, nor does he inspire one with awe. A big hulking fellow who looks like an unwashed mudlark. I had no thought that a reputable government would employ such *canaille* even as a spy."

A big hulking fellow who looks like an unwashed mudlark? How well did that description fit in with Chauvelin's recollections of the several disguises so cleverly assumed by that prince of dandies, Sir Percy Blakeney, Bart. He could have laughed aloud, as that reckless Scarlet Pimpernel was ever wont to do, when he remembered Mantes and Limours and Levallois-Peret, the trial of Henri Chanel and Mariette Joly, the coal-heaver, the drunken lout of the Cabaret de la Liberté, the fiddler at La Rodière and the countless other times when he had been baffled by that past-master in the art of disguise. A big hulking fellow who looks like an unwashed mudlark may have raised doubts in the mind of the Chief Commissary of Choisy, but not in his. He sent word to Citizen Lacaune that he would be round at the Town Hall within half an hour, and while he rose and dressed himself, he forced his mind not to dwell on the triumph which awaited him there, for he felt that if he thought on it too much he would surely go mad with joy.

Then, of course, came the catastrophe. As soon as Citizen Chauvelin arrived at the Town Hall he was ushered with every mark of respect into the office of the Chief Commissary. It was a large room, lighted by an oil-lamp which hung from the ceiling and a couple of wax candles on the centre desk. In a far corner, to which the light did not penetrate, Chauvelin perceived the vague outline of a human form lying prone behind two men in uniform with fixed bayonets. His enemy! A deep sigh of contentment, of joy and of triumph escaped his breast. The excitement of the moment was almost more than he could bear. His hands were cold as ice and his temples throbbed with heat. He tried to appear calm, to show dignity and aloofness while receiving the deferential greeting of the Chief Commissary, and a brief report of the circumstances under which the amazing capture was effected. Then at last he felt free, free to gaze on the humiliation and the helplessness of the man who had so often brought him to shame. He picked up a candle and walked with a firm step across the room. The prisoner lay on his side, his head turned to the wall. He was bound round and round his whole body with a rope. Chauvelin stooped, holding the candle high, and with his thin, claw-like hand turned the man's head towards the light.

He gave one cry, like that of a man-eating tiger when robbed of its prey, and the heavy candlestick fell with a loud clatter on the floor. Then he turned like a fury on the Chief Commissary, who was standing by his desk, rubbing his hands complacently together, a smile of beatitude on his face.

"You oaf!" he cried out hoarsely. "You fool! You . . . you . . ."

Words failed him. Lacaune's face was a picture of complete bewilderment, until Citizen Chauvelin finally almost spat out the words at him: "This lout is not the Scarlet Pimpernel."

There followed a dead silence. The Commissary felt that his senses were reeling. He trembled as if suddenly stricken with ague and sank into a chair to save himself from falling. The candle sent a stream of wax on the carpet; Chauvelin stamped on it viciously with his foot.

"Not the Scarlet Pimpernel?" Lacaune contrived to murmur at last.

"Any idiot would have known that," the other retorted savagely.

"But . . . but," the Commissary stuttered, "the captain—"

"I don't know what lies the captain told you, but they were deliberate lies, and he and you and the whole pack of you will suffer for this blunder."

With that he strode out of the room, thrusting aside the obsequious clerk, whilst Citizen Lacaune, Chief Commissary of Choisy, remained sunk in his chair in a state of collapse.

When presently the messenger from Manderieu was ushered into his presence, he was not in a fit state to give instructions to anyone. What he needed was first a tonic for his shattered nerves and then guidance as to what in the world he was to do now to save his own neck. The clerk who had introduced the messenger casually mentioned the name of Pradel, whereupon the Chief Commissary contrived to pull himself somewhat together. Pradel!

Yes, something might be done with regard to Pradel, now in durance at Manderieu, a man of distinction who was both noted and popular. If a charge of treason could be proved against him, and he was brought to justice, the credit of it would be ascribed to the zeal of the Chief Commissary, and it would effectively counterbalance such accusations as Citizen Chauvelin would in his wrath formulate against all those connected with this unfortunate affair. The risk of rioting in the city, following an unpopular arrest, appeared as nothing compared with this new terrible eventuality.

Lacaune remembered the talk he had earlier in the day with Louis Maurin, the lawyer, and the Canadian farmer. The latter had certainly denounced Pradel as being in league with the Scarlet Pimpernel, and Maurin had confirmed the charge. With a little luck, then, all might yet be well. Chief Commissaries in outlying districts had before now received important promotion through indicting notable personages in their district and bringing them to justice. Then why not he? His first move, then, was to send Delorme's messenger back to Manderieu with written orders to send Docteur Pradel at once under escort to Choisy; he then gave instructions to his clerk to seek out first Citizen Maurin, the lawyer, and tell him that his presence at the Town Hall was urgently required, and then the Canadian farmer named Collin, who had sent in a request for a special travelling permit and would probably be waiting at the Café Tison till summoned to come and get them.

CHAPTER THIRTY-SEVEN

Accusing Spectres

It was close on midday before the rumour of the arrest of Docteur Pradel reached the ears of St. John Devinne. He had spent the morning in planning and making active preparations for his journey first to Paris and thence to England. Although he, like every member of the League, was well provided by his chief with papers requisite for travelling across France, he, Devinne, had never done that journey by himself, nor had he done it since France and England were actually in a state of war, when difficulties that usually confronted travellers of foreign nationality would be considerably increased. Against that he flattered himself that he had made friends with the Chief Commissary and the staff at the Town Hall, and that he could apply there for special permits and papers that would greatly facilitate his movements across country, and this he did. The clerk received him most affably, took his petition in to the Chief Commissary and came back with the reply from his chief that Citizen Collin's request would be complied with as soon as the papers could be got ready. But, as in all official matters in France these days, the getting the papers ready took a considerable amount of time. Devinne had no fixed abode in Choisy. He did not feel that he could go again to the derelict cottage, so full of memories, and was compelled in consequence to kill time as best he could in one of the smaller cafes of the town. And here it was that he first heard the rumour of the closing of the hospital at Manderieu and of the arrest of Docteur Pradel.

He heard it with unmixed satisfaction. Blakeney's plans, then, had been brought to naught. Pradel was not being conveyed to England in the company of Cécile de la Rodière and the almighty Scarlet Pimpernel had failed in his purpose. Failed lamentably, despite his arrogance and belief in himself. Devinne could have stood up on a table and shouted for joy. As to what would be the ultimate fate of that upstart Pradel, he cared not one jot. Anyway, he would be parted from Cécile forever. Time after that did not seem to hang quite so heavily on the young traitor's hands. He went two or three times over to the Town Hall to see about his papers, but he was still put off with vague assurances that they were being got ready. All in good time.

Then, in the early part of the evening, he heard the great news, the wonderful, miraculous news which spread through the little city like wildfire. The English spy, the daring and mysterious Scarlet Pimpernel, had been captured by Citizen Captain Cabel of the Gendarmerie Nationale, captured and brought to Choisy, wounded and bound with cords, and was even now in the Town Hall pending his incarceration in the Old Castle. It must be said with truth that Devinne did not receive this news with the same satisfaction as he had that of Pradel's arrest. Something stirred within the depths of his soul which he could not have defined. He certainly could not have shouted for joy. It was not joy that he felt. Not elation. Not triumph. Was it the first stirring of remorse or of shame? He, St. John Devinne, Earl Welhaven, son and heir of the Duke of Rudford, the greatest gentleman, the finest sportsman that ever sat a horse, had done a deed of darkness which for infamy had not had a parallel for close on two thousand years. And as he sat there in this squalid café, he fell to wondering whether if, amongst that rag-tag and bobtail round him, there was one man base enough to have done what he did. He saw before his eyes a vision of the friend he had betrayed, light-hearted, debonair, the perfect type of an English gentleman, now lying bound with cords at the mercy of a proletarian government that knew no compunction.

So insistent was the vision and so harrowing, that he felt he could bear it no longer. He tried to visualise Cécile, the woman for whose sake he had committed this vilest of crimes, but her picture evaded him, and when his mind's eye caught sight of her fleeting image, she was looking down on him with horror and contempt. There rose in him the desire to obliterate these phantasma, to saturate his brain with a narcotic that would rid him of their obsession. He ordered *eau de vie*, and drank till he felt a warm glow coursing through his veins, and his sight became so blurred that he could no longer see those accusing spectres. Soon he felt hilarious. Avaunt ye ghosts! Ye vengeful apparitions with your flaming swords! Come pride, come triumph! The arrogant schoolmaster, the tyrannical dictator has been effectually downed. Let us laugh and sing and dance, enjoy every moment of life as this half-starved rabble was doing, pending the inevitable day when that all-embracing guillotine would hold them in her arms.

St. John Devinne was not quite sober, nor was he very drunk when a couple of hours later he became aware of a certain agitation among the customers of the café. Words which at first had no meaning for him were bandied to and fro. Men rose from the tables at which they had been sitting and joined others, and remained with them in compact groups talking in whispers, gesticulating: "Impossible!" or "Who told thee?" together with plenty of cursing and mutterings. Excitement became more intense when Andre the street-cleaner came running in, brandishing his broom and shouting: "It is true. True. The man they have got is not the English spy." And those last words: "not the English spy," were taken up by others, until the low-raftered room seemed to ring from corner to corner with them. Devinne sat up and pricked up his ears, demanded a glass of cold water and drank it down at a gulp. Yes! Someone was just saying: "Where didst hear all this, André?"

And the street-cleaner explained with volubility:

"I have it from the clerk of the Town Hall himself. He was talking to the citizen captain and telling him, as he valued his neck, to go into hiding somewhere, anywhere, at once, if he could. It seems that the Member of the Committee of Public Safety who was locked up in the cellar of La Rodière has sworn that every man connected: with the affair would be sent to the guillotine within twenty-four hours."

Devinne never could have said afterwards what exactly were his feelings when he heard this news. It must have been relief, of course, to a certain extent. His crime was none the less heinous, of course, but, at any rate, the spectral vision of his friend, Percy Blakeney, lying at the mercy of a crowd of savage brutes thirsting for his blood, would no longer haunt him. He rose, paid for his drinks and with somewhat uncertain steps made for the door and the open. Here he paused a moment, leaning against the wall. His temples were throbbing, and at the back of his mind there stirred the recollection of those papers and the travelling permit which were to be delivered to him at the Town Hall. As soon as the cold, frosty air had revived him, he made his way to the commissariat, hoping to get speech with the Chief Commissary or, at any rate, with the clerk.

But to his chagrin he found the gates closed and sentinels posted to warn off all visitors. Impossible to gain access even to the courtyard. An amiable passer-by, noting his distress, volunteered the information that the Citizen Commissary had given orders that no one was to be admitted inside the Town Hall under any circumstances whatever.

"I suppose you have heard the news, citizen," the passer-by continued affably. "It will be a regular cataclysm for all the officials in Choisy when the Committee of Public Safety gets hold of the affair . . ."

But Devinne listened no further. He suddenly had the feeling as if a trap was closing in upon him. Not that he was actually frightened, for he had not yet realised that his position after this might become serious, but he did suddenly remember that when he applied for the special travelling permit he had been made to deposit his existing passport at the Commissariat, but he had done it under a promise from his friend the Chief

Commissary that all his papers and the special permit would be delivered to him in due course. But there was the question now, would this friend be in a position to keep his word with this awful cataclysm hanging over his head?

Anyway, there was nothing that could be done tonight. It was close on nine o'clock, and the various cafés did not of a certainty offer any attraction, with their squalour, their abominable coffee and their jabbering crowds. But there was always the derelict cottage which, though not very attractive either, did, at any rate, offer shelter for the night, and Devinne turned his footsteps thither, hoping that he might get a few hours' sleep, free from the nightmare that had haunted him for the past four-and-twenty hours. The place looked very much the same as it had done when he left it in the morning, the candle and tinder were in their usual place, but as soon as he had struck a light he got the impression that someone had been in the place during the day—was it Blakeney, by any chance?—surely not, for he must be half-way to Trouville by now with the refugees. There had always been the possibility of the cottage being invaded by vagabonds or even by the police. Certain it was that someone had been here, for the pile of garments in the corner had been disturbed, and on looking round Devinne spied on the floor near the empty hearth, a bottle of wine, half empty, and beside it a mug with dregs in the bottom. The place as a night-shelter would obviously not be safe. Devinne blew out the candle and made his way out once more, and then turned his steps back in the direction of Choisy.

There was a fairly decent inn in the Rue Verte. Devinne secured a room there. He was quite thankful now that he had been obliged to seek night quarters elsewhere than in the cottage, for he was badly in need of what the derelict cottage could not offer him, namely, a good wash.

CHAPTER THIRTY-EIGHT

Sister Anne

And all this time the tumult in the neighbouring little village of Manderieu had been growing in intensity, and Citizen Delorme, Commissary, was at his wits' end and in a state bordering on despair. Then suddenly, when the crowd was on the point of storming the Commissariat, "Sister Anne", in the form of one of the gendarmes whom Delorme had posted at the entrance to the village, came running in with the welcome news that Chief Commissary Lacaune had sent an escort round with written orders to convey Docteur Pradel immediately to Choisy. Even Bluebeard's wife could not have felt greater relief than did the harassed Commissary.

"Where," he asked, "is the escort now?"

"At the back, citizen," came the quick answer. "Waiting at the gate."

"On horseback?"

"Yes, citizen."

"How many men?"

"Only two, but they are stalwarts. The Chief Commissary sent word that they would be sufficient. They have a third horse on the lead."

"Quite right. Quite right. Let the prisoner be smuggled out very quietly by the back way – he'll make no trouble, I'll warrant – and let him be handed over to the Chief Commissary's men. After that, we shall have peace in Manderieu, please God—"

He checked himself abruptly. On the spur of the moment, much relieved at the conclusion of this tense situation, he had forgotten that the Government had decreed by law that God no longer existed. Delorme, a loyal servant of the Republic, hoped that the gendarme had not heard his pious ejaculation.

Five minutes later, satisfied that his unwelcome guest had been duly handed over to the men from Choisy, and was well on the way to the city, he made up his mind to face the noisy crowd outside. No sooner had he commanded the door of the commissariat to be opened than he was greeted with hoots and boos, and a first shower of loose stones, which, fortunately, failed to hit him. The gendarmes then charged into the crowd and thrust it back some way down the place, whilst Commissary Delorme's voice went ringing across the market square.

"Citizens all," he bellowed at the top of his voice, "you are mistaken in thinking that Docteur Pradel is in my charge. By order of my superior he was conveyed to Choisy some time ago."

As was to be expected, this assertion was received with incredulity. There were more boos and hisses, and one stone flung by a practiced hand hit and broke a window. The crowd then stormed the commissariat, and made their way down to the lock-up, where they found the door wide open and the captive bird very obviously flown. They also wandered in and out of the offices and the private rooms of the Commissary, but, not finding the man they sought, they went away again in a subdued mood, some to their own homes in Manderieu, others to more distant Choisy. They all shook their heads thoughtfully when they went past the hospital and past the two sentinels at its gate.

It was some time later, when the small village had re-assumed its air of tranquillity and one by one windows and shutters had been closed for the night, that the watchman asked leave to say a word to the Citizen Commissary. The clock in the market-place had not long before struck ten. The Commissary was in his nightshirt, about to get into bed, but he ordered the watchman to come up.

"Well? What is it?"

"Only this, Citizen Commissary," the man said, and held up a grimy piece of paper.

"What's that?"

"I don't know, citizen. A letter, I think. I was doing my round and had got as far as the cross-road, when a man of the Gendarmerie Nationale gave me the paper and said: 'Take this to the Citizen Commissary; he will reward you for your pains, and here is something for your trouble.' And he gave me a silver franc."

Delorme took the paper and turned it round and round between his fingers. There was something queer, almost eerie about this missive, sent at this hour of the night.

"How long ago was this?" he asked.

"About half an hour, I should say. I finished my round and then came on here. Is it all right, citizen?"

"Yes," the Commissary replied curtly. "You may go."

Only when the watchman had gone did Delorme unroll the mysterious missive. It turned out to be nothing, but a hoax. There were four lines of what looked like verse, but as these were written in a foreign language which he, Delorme, did not understand, the joke, if joke there was, failed to amuse him. The only thing that interested him was a rough device at the end, by way of a signature possibly. It represented a small five-petalled flower and had been lined in red chalk.

The worthy Commissary put the note on one side, thinking that, perhaps, on the morrow he might meet a learned man who was conversant with foreign tongues. He would show the funny message to him.

After that he got into bed, snuffed out the candle, and went peacefully to sleep.

CHAPTER THIRTY-NINE

The Canadian

Chief Commissary Lacaune had spent a restless night. His mind was not altogether at ease when he thought over the happenings of the past eventful day. The tragic farce of the pseudo Scarlet Pimpernel, and his capture by that dolt Cabel, weighed heavily on his soul. As for the wrath of Citizen Chauvelin, whenever Lacaune thought of that a cold shiver would course down the length of his spine. Somehow he had a presentiment which drove away sleep from his weary lids, a prevision of worse calamities yet to come.

And when they came, which they did early in the morning, they proved to be more dire than he had anticipated. No sooner had he settled down to work in his office than his clerk brought in the staggering news that the two men of the Gendarmerie Nationale whom he, Lacaune, had despatched in the course of the evening to Manderieu in response to an urgent request from his subordinate, had been discovered half an hour ago, lying bound and gagged in a field a hundred or so metres from the roadside, half-way between Choisy and Manderieu. The third man, who belonged to the village gendarmerie and had been Delorme's messenger, was found a couple of hundred metres farther on in a field the opposite side of the road. He had started from Choisy a quarter of an hour before the other two. All three men, when freed from their bonds, told the same pitiable tale. They were attacked in the dark by what they supposed were common footpads, when there were no passers-by on the road. The rogues had suddenly jumped out from behind a clump of trees and were on them before they had a chance of defending themselves. Commissary Delorme's messenger had been quickly knocked out. He was alone. The other two vowed that they had put up a good fight, but the miscreants were armed with pistols, while they only had their cutlasses, which they never had a chance of drawing. They were dragged out of their saddles by a man who was a veritable giant for strength, and knocked on the head so that they lost consciousness and remembered nothing more till they found themselves in the field, trussed like fowls and frozen stiff. Their horses were nowhere to be seen.

The three men were ushered into the presence of the Chief Commissary, but they could only reiterate their story. They supposed that robbery was the object of the attack, but none of them carried anything of value. One certainly had the written order of the Chief Commissary tucked in his belt, but that would be of no use to highway robbers; at any rate, it had disappeared, supposedly been lost in the scuffle.

At first the incident, grave as it seemed, could not be called staggering. Three valuable horses were lost, and there were two desperate footpads at large, but that was all. On the other hand, Commissary Delorme over at Manderieu was doubtless fretting and fuming, waiting for the orders which had not come, and Chief Commissary Lacaune now set to at once to re-indite the order to his subordinate that the prisoner Pradel be at once sent under escort to Choisy. He had just finished writing this out when another messenger from Manderieu came riding in with the report from the Commissary of the happenings of the evening before. After a graphic account of the riots which had disturbed the peace of the little village and had only been quelled by his, Delorme's, presence of mind and courage in facing the irate mob, the Commissary went on to say:

"You may imagine, citizen, how thankful I was when your men arrived on the scene with your orders to deliver the

prisoner to them. I am glad to be rid of him, as the people here
would never have quietened down while they knew that
Pradel was held in durance in the Commissariat. I presume
you have him locked up in the Old Castle and can but hope
that the citizens of Choisy will prove less choleric over the
incarceration of their favourite leech than the country-folk of
Manderieu."

Chief Commissary Lacaune had to read these last lines over and
over again before their full significance entered his brain. When
it did he was on the verge of an attack of apoplexy. What in the
devil's name did it all mean, and where in h— was Pradel? The
escort whom he, Lacaune, had sent to fetch him, had been put
out of action before they ever got to Manderieu. Then what
happened? Where did it happen? And what had become of
Simon Pradel? Ah! if he ever put hands on that stormy petrel
again, the guillotine would not be robbed of its prey. But in the
meanwhile, what was to be done? He sent a mounted courier in
haste to Manderieu to ask for fuller details. The courier returned
in less than half an hour with a further report from the
Commissary, stating that the prisoner, Docteur Simon Pradel,
was duly handed over to the two men of the Gendarmerie
Nationale on a written order from the Chief Commissary
himself. To prove his assertion, Citizen Delorme enclosed the
order which one of the soldiers had handed over to him.
Moreover, he respectfully would ask his chief why his own
messenger had been detained in Choisy; he wanted all his men
in Manderieu, as the temper of the village folk was far from
reassuring.

This second report, on the face of it, only made matters
worse. Chief Commissary Lacaune thought that both he and his
subordinate were going mad. Who were the two men of the
Gendarmerie Nationale who had come to fetch away the
prisoner? How did the written order come into their hands?
What had they done with Pradel once they had got him? Was
he, Lacaune, awake or dreaming?

Luckily for him, his friend Louis Maurin presented himself just then. At any rate, here was a sane man with whom one could talk things over fearlessly. But the lawyer was in an unhelpful mood. He appeared entirely indifferent as to the whereabouts of Simon Pradel.

"My good friend," he said with a shrug, "your stormy petrel, as you rightly call him, is on his way to England by now, you may be sure, and a good thing to. Let him be, I say. Once he is in that land of fogs and savages, he can do no more mischief. If you start running after him you will only get yourself into more trouble . . . like you did yesterday. Let him be."

"But why should you say that he is on his way to England?"

"I am sure he is."

"But two of my men fetched him away from Manderieu."

"They were not your men at all."

"Who were they?"

"The English spies."

"You don't mean—?"

"The Scarlet Pimpernel whom that fool Cabel failed to lay by the heels, and who has tricked you, my friend, as he has tricked our police and our spies all over the country for nigh on two years. Yes! That's the man I mean, and if I were you I would make the best of what has happened and leave others to fish in those turbid waters."

At mention of the Scarlet Pimpernel, Chief Commissary Lacaune felt thoroughly uncomfortable. Since the establishment of a free-thinking and enlightened government, one had to be rational, what? Had to be a man and not a weakling with a mind full of superstitious nonsense such as the *calotins* used to put into one in past days. But *nom de nom!* There was something unpleasantly mysterious about this elusive English spy. Here one day, across country the next. A regular will-o'-the-wisp. He slipped through one's fingers when one thought one had him and trouble awaited any man who ever came across him. Lacaune drew a deep sigh.

"You may be right, my friend," he said, "but it goes against the grain and against my duty to let things be. I have always been a faithful servant of the Republic, and I will not rest till I get to the bottom of this extraordinary occurrence. I am already in bad odour with the Committee of Public Safety over that unfortunate affair yesterday, and I feel that nothing but zeal will save me from disaster."

"Well, you will act as you think best," the lawyer said, and rose to take his leave, "but, believe me—"

He was interrupted by the entrance of the clerk who handed him a letter which had just come from the Committee of Public Safety, sitting in special session at Sceaux, the capital of the department. He asked at the same time if the Citizen Commissary would receive Citizen Collin, who had come to enquire about his papers.

"Collin? Collin?" the jaded Commissary exclaimed, and fingered with obvious apprehension the letter from the Commitee of Public Safety. Did it contain good or bad news for him? A threat? A warning? Or what? To the clerk he said: "Tell Citizen Collin to wait." And when the clerk had gone he turned to his friend. "It was that Canadian, or whatever he is, who led me into sending Cabel after that cursed English spy. I believe that it was all a conspiracy to lead me off the scent, and that this man Collin is the prime mover in it all. But I'll have him under lock and key at once. I'll send him to join that ruffian who impersonated the Scarlet Pimpernel and led us all by the nose."

After which piece of oratory, delivered with all the spite which he felt against everything and everybody, he at last made up his mind to read the letter which had been sent to him from Sceaux. First he looked at the superscription. The letter was signed "Armand Chauvelin, Member of the Committee of Public Safety," and its contents were the following:

"Citizen Commissary,
We, the Committee of Public Safety, sitting in extraqrdinary session at Sceaux, desire you to send over to us for special enquiry the man who impersonated the English spy and was

brought a prisoner to you in the course of yesterday. Our sittings are held in the Maine. If you have any other prisoner or suspect of note in your district, send him also. The bearer of this note is in our employ. He knows just what to do. Your responsibility ceases with the handing over of the prisoner or prisoners to him."

Lacaune held the missive out to his friend, the lawyer. His hand was shaking with excitement. His face was beaming both with joy and with triumph. There was not a word of threat or warning in the letter. It was quite simple, official, almost friendly; it showed, in fact, that he had not forfeited the confidence of his superiors since it left it to his discretion to send along "any other prisoner or suspect in his district." Here was relief indeed after the torturing fears of the past twelve hours.

"My friend! My friend!" he cried, and rubbed his hands gleefully together. "I feel a new man for all is well."

He took pen and paper and wrote a few words rapidly.

"What are you going to do?" Maurin asked.

"Send that damned Canadian too before the Committee of Public Safety for special enquiry."

He tinkled his bell, and on the entrance of the clerk, handed him the paper he had just written.

"Here," he said, "is an order for the arrest of the man, Collin. See it carried out, then send the messenger from Sceaux in to me."

The lawyer now finally took his leave. The matter of the Canadian and the pseudo Scarlet Pimpernel did not interest him in the least. With Pradel out of the way he cared about nothing else. Left to himself, Commissary Lacaune strode up and down the room, unable for sheer excitement to sit still. At one moment he pricked up his ears when he heard a tumult and some shouting outside his door. "The Canadian is giving trouble," he muttered complacently to himself.

Presently the messenger was ushered in. He was a sober, fine-looking official dressed in dark clothes. He wore a hat of the new sugar-loaf shape which he took off when he entered. He also turned back the lapel of his coat to show the badge which he wore indicative of his status as representative or employee of the government. Lacaune addressed him curtly: "Who gave you this letter?"

"Citizen Chauvelin."

"You know its contents."

"Yes, citizen."

"Your orders are to convey a certain prisoner to Sceaux."

"That is so."

"Are you riding or driving?"

"Driving, Citizen Commissary. I have requisitioned a cart with a hood and a couple of good horses from a yard just outside this city. Citizen Chauvelin said he did not wish the prisoner to be seen."

"A very wise precaution. Now listen. One prisoner will be handed over to you here. Keep a special eye on him, he is dangerous. There is another whom you will go and fetch at the Old Castle. One of my men will accompany you as far as there with an order from me that the prisoner be delivered over to you."

"I understand, citizen."

"Would you like an escort as far as Sceaux?"

"Not unless you desire to send one, Citizen Commissary. But it is not necessary. I am well armed and so is the driver."

"Very good, then. You can go."

The man saluted, turned on his heel and went out. The Commissary wrote out the order to be taken to the Old Castle, gave it to his clerk and then went to the window from which he had a view of the street. He saw a cart with hood up, standing outside the gates. A pair of horses were harnessed to the cart, they looked strong and fresh. After a moment or two he saw the Canadian being brought across the courtyard by two soldiers. He was in chains, wrist to ankle both sides of him, and was apparently only just able to walk. Obviously he had given trouble. His clothes were torn, his hair dishevelled, and his knuckles stained with blood. The soldiers did not deal any too gently with him, and bundled him like a bale of goods into the cart. The government representative watched the proceedings with an official eye. When he had satisfied himself that the prisoner was safely out of mischief, he beckoned to one of the soldiers to sit on the tail-board of the cart while he himself took his seat beside the driver. The latter flicked his whip and away they went down the Rue Haute.

Chief Commissary Lacaune watched all these doings with utmost satisfaction. He strode back to his desk, turned a few papers over, but he felt too excited to settle down to business. He thought a glass of wine would do him good; he picked up his hat and coat and went out, telling his clerk that he would be back in an hour.

He didn't go straight to Tison's for his glass of wine, being tempted to stroll down as far as the Old Castle and see that miserable ruffian who had hoodwinked him take his place, also in chains, by the side of that cursed Canadian. He was just in time to see this pleasing spectacle; there is always something very soothing to the nerves to witness the discomfiture of one's enemies. Citizen Lacaune exchanged a few affable words with the government official, gave orders that the two prisoners be chained one to the other for additional safety, and when this was done, he went with a light, springy step to enjoy a quiet half-hour with a glass of wine in the Café Tison.

CHAPTER FORTY

Remorse

Under the hood of the cart, St. John Devinne gradually came to
the consciousness that this was in very truth the end of his
inglorious life. Shame and remorse both held him in their grip,
and not only because he had staked his honour on a despicable
gamble and lost, but also because he had at last realised the
utter baseness of what he had done. Visions of happy days
under the leadership of a man who was the bravest of the brave,
who sacrificed his comfort, his happiness, even his love, in order
to succour the helpless and the innocent, to follow whom was
in itself a glory, tortured him with the knowledge that they
could never come again. They were past for ever because of his
own black treachery and there was nothing now ahead of him
save darkness, and in the end a shameful death.

It was not of death itself that he was afraid, but of the awful,
awful shame of it all, and of this racking remorse which might
unnerve him when the end came. That Chief Commissary had
played him false, trapped him like a noxious feline, and here he
was now lying like a captive beast driven to the slaughter-house,
chained to a malodorous mudlark – he, St. John Devinne, Earl
Welhaven, son and heir of the Duke of Rudford! Oh, the shame,
the shame of it all! He ached in every limb, his ankles and wrists
were bleeding under the weight of the irons. The close
proximity of his grimy companion made him feel sick. The cold
was intense. Devinne trembled under a thick cloak that had
been thrown over him at one time, he did not recollect when.

The day wore on with agonising slowness. At first Devinne had wondered whether he was being driven, but soon he knew that he really didn't care. The ultimate end of his journey would anyhow be the guillotine, so what did the halts on the way matter? There were one or two halts, probably in order to give the horses a drink and a rest. Several villages were passed on the way, and at one time the cart rattled over what obviously was a cobbled street, at the end of which the driver pulled up. There was a good deal of talking and shouting. Apparently fresh horses were being put to. Presently Devinne heard subdued voices quite close to him in a rapid colloquy: "You know the way, citizen?"

"Quite well. I thank you."

"You will find good accommodation there for the night. Tell Landlord Freson I sent you. Henri Gros, that's my name. He will do the best for you."

"And what do I owe you, Citizen Gros?"

"Twenty gold louis, citizen. That will be for the two horses and the cart. And if you ever bring them back this way and the horses are in good condition, I will buy the lot back from you."

There followed obsequious thanks, from which Devinne gathered that the bargain had been concluded. Vaguely he wondered why it had been made. A change of driver apparently as well as of horses, but what did it all matter to him? Somewhere in the town a clock struck three. The shades of evening were beginning to draw in and through a chink in the hood Devinne saw that snow was falling.

After many hearty "Good-byes" and "*Bon voyages*" a fresh start was made. Soon the road became very rough and the jolting of the cart added greatly to Devinne's discomfort. He felt terribly tired and drowsy, but too ill to get any sleep. Everything around him now seemed to be very still; the only sounds that reached his ears were the clap-clap of the horse's hoofs over the snow-covered road and the stertorous breathing of his fellow-captive. Weary almost to death, Devinne fell into a trance-like somnolence. What roused him was the presence of someone bending over him and the sound of the grating of a steel file near his ankle. The cart was at a standstill and it was getting dark; only the feeble glow of a small storm-lantern threw a narrow circle of light round where his foot was. The pain of it was almost intolerable, even when after a few minutes he felt those heavy irons lifted away from his ankle. Through half-closed eyes he saw a dark form bending to the task. As soon as his ankles were free, dexterous fingers, armed with the file, started working on the irons on his wrists.

Devinne thought that he was either delirious or dreaming. A sense of well-being spread right through him when those horrible irons were removed, and presently an arm was passed under his shoulders and the neck of a bottle was pushed into his mouth. He took a great gulp, a fiery liquid flowed down his throat, he coughed and spluttered and then fell back in a real state of unconsciousness.

Again he woke, this time feeling a different man. His ankles and wrists were free and he was not nearly so cold. He sat up and looked about him. The vehicle was still at a dead stop, and the night was fast drawing in. All that Devinne could perceive through the gloom was the body of his fellow-captive being lifted out of the cart by a pair of powerful arms; the head was just vanishing beyond the tail-board. Then he heard footsteps, heavy measured footsteps receding into the distance. For a long time he was alone in semi-darkness, sitting up with his legs drawn up and his arms encircling his knees. He wanted to think, but couldn't. His mind was at a standstill, as it is in a dream.

All was silence around him, save for those footsteps treading the snow-covered earth, receding at first, then a pause while he heard nothing at all, and then the same footsteps returning. His heart was beating furiously. He tried to call out, but the one word which he longed to utter was smothered in his throat. It was the name of the friend whom he had betrayed and who had risked his life to save him. He could vaguely discern through the gloom the familiar tall form mounting the driver's seat and picking up the reins, and after that just the broad back, a solid mass hardly distinguishable now. He had never felt quite so alone in his life, not even during that night in the derelict cottage when he had planned his abominable treachery. He had the company of his thoughts then, black, ugly thoughts and torturing visions of past joys and future ignominious triumphs. Now he had nothing, just that indistinct shadow in front of him which seemed to be fading, fading into the gloom like his hopes, like his honour and his joy of life.

There was still a faint pale light in the sky when the cart turned abruptly to the left and then went plodding over very rough ground. Devinne crept on hands and knees to the tail-board, and squatting on his heels, he peeped out under the hood. Even in the gathering darkness the place looked familiar. Away on his right he could see the dim lights of what appeared to be a small city, but the cart was driven round it, always over very rough ground, gradually leaving those city lights behind. And suddenly Devinne realised where he was. The small city was Le Perrey, and he was being driven to the lonely house which was the headquarters of the League of the Scarlet Pimpernel.

The cart drew up, and he heard a distant shout: "Hallo!" immediately followed by an eager question: "All well?" It was the voice of Jimmy Holte, familiarly known as Froggie. He was over at the house and came running along, swinging a lantern.

Whereupon there came the answer in a voice which Devinne thought he would never hear again.

"All well!"

The next moment he saw Blakeney through the gloom standing by the side of the cart.

"Can you get down?" he asked, "or shall I give you a hand?" Devinne was still squatting on his heels, but he couldn't move. Not at first. His eyes peered through the darkness, trying to see Blakeney's face.

"Percy . . ." he murmured, but could say no more, for an aching sob had risen to his throat.

"Easy, lad," Blakeney responded; "pull yourself together.

241

Froggie knows nothing."

Froggie was within earshot now. He began to talk. Devinne did not at once catch what he said, for all his senses were numb. But he did make an effort to pull himself out of the cart . . .

fellow, Froggie, but you talk too much. Suppose you get us something to eat. Devinne is famished and so am I."

"All right! All right!" Holte retorted good-humouredly and turned to go. But at the door he halted.

"I'll tell you all about it, Johnnie," he said, "just as I had it from Ffoulkes. I tell you it was nothing short of—"

He was interrupted by his own hat being hurled at his head, and his chief's voice saying peremptorily: "And if you don't go and get that luxurious supper, I'll put you in irons for insubordination."

Holte went and the two men were alone. He who had done to his friend the greatest possible injury any man could do to another, was now face to face with the chief whom he had betrayed. Blakeney went over to the window and gazed out into the darkness and the thickly falling snow. Devinne rose and went across the room. He put out his hand. Tentatively. It was moist and shaking. He took Percy's hand, which was hanging by his side, that slender hand which had so often grasped his in friendship, and with a heartrending sob laid his hot forehead against it.

"Percy!" he murmured, "for God's sake, say something."

"What shall I say, dear lad?" Blakeney responded, and gently disengaged his hand. "That I could not bear to see an English gentleman, the son of my old friend, thrown to those hyenas."

"How you must despise me!"

"I despise no one, Johnnie. I have seen too much of sorrow, misguided enthusiasm, even of crime, not to understand many, many things I had not even dreamed of before."

"Crime? There is no worse crime in the world than mine."

"And no worse punishment, lad, than what you will endure."

"God, yes!" Devinne said fervently. "Then why did you risk

your precious life to save my miserable one?"

Blakeney broke into his infectious laugh.

"Why? Why? I don't know, Johnnie. Ask Ffoulkes – he will give you a sentimental reason. Ask Tony and he will say it is for the love of sport, and I am not sure that good old Tony wouldn't be right after all. Thanks to you, lad, I have had one of the most exhilarating runs across country I have ever had in my life."

Devinne sank into a chair and buried his face in his hands.

"How they will all loathe the sight of me," he murmured.

"Well, you will have to put up with that, my good fellow, and with other things as well. Anyway, your father knows nothing and never will. After that . . . well! England is at war with France, so you will know what to do."

"Percy . . ."

"Easy now. Here's Holte coming with his banquet."

And the three of them sat down to a sumptuous meal of pig's meat and stale bread and drank hot wine, which put warmth into them. Blakeney was at his merriest.

"You should have seen," he said to Holte, "that miserable caitiff who, much against his will, impersonated the Scarlet Pimpernel. The one thing I shall regret to my dying day is that I was not present when my dear Monsieur Chambertin first gazed on his beautiful countenance and saw that it was not that of his friend, Sir Percy Blakeney."

Holte did a great deal of talking, and asked numberless questions, but Devinne, with aching soul and aching body, soon made his way to one of the other rooms in the house where there was a truckle bed on which he had slept more than once in the happy olden days.

He sat down on the edge of it, and burying his head in his hands, he sobbed like a child.

CHAPTER FORTY-ONE

Epilogue

Often, after the curtain has been rung down on the last act of a play, comedy or drama, one would wish to peep through and see what is going on on the darkened stage. A moment ago it was full of light, of animation, of that tense atmosphere which pervades the closing scene of a moving story, and now there are only the scene-shifters moving about like ghosts through the dimmed light, the stage-manager talking to the carpenter or the electricians, the minor roles still chattering in the wings, or the principals hurrying to their dressing-rooms.

In the same way it seems to me that one would wish to see just once more those actors who each in their individual way have played their part in that strange drama which had for its chief characters a young traitor and a light-hearted adventurer, reckless of his life, a true sportsman who in a spirit of sublime devilry achieved one of the noblest exploits it has ever been the good fortune of an historian to relate.

Thus it is possible to have a peep at the minor roles, to see Monsieur le Docteur Pradel and Cécile, his pretty young wife, in their humble home in the village of Kensington. They are supremely happy, but are as poor as the proverbial church mice, as poor as all those unfortunate French men and women whom a lucky chance has enabled to find a refuge in hospitable England – chance or the devotion of a man whose real identity they will never discover. Sometimes one among them who is over-sensitive, perhaps, will feel a thrill when meeting a pair of lazy, good-natured blue eyes, the true expression of which is veiled behind heavy lids. Such a one is Cécile Pradel, who, when she meets those eyes, or hears the timbre of a quaint rather inane laugh, will suddenly recall a day of torment in the old château of La Rodière, a dance, the music of the *rigaudon*, a fiddler with grimy face and ringing voice and strange compelling eyes. The same voice? The same eyes? No! No! It couldn't be! And she would look up almost with apology for those foolish thoughts on the magnificent figure of Sir Percy Blakeney, Bart., the friend of the Prince of Wales, the most exquisite dandy that ever graced a ballroom, the most inane fop that ever caused society to laugh.

And she would see the greatest ladies in the land crowd round him, smirk and flirt their fans, entreating him to repeat the silly doggrel which he vowed had come to him as an inspiration while tying his cravat:

"We seek him here, we seek him there,
Those Frenchies seek him everywhere.
Is he in heaven! Is he in h—?
That demmed elusive Pimpernel."

He would recite this for the entertainment of his admirers with many airs and graces which of a certainty could only belong to a man who had no thought save of vanity and pleasure.

More often than not the talk in ballrooms would be of the Scarlet Pimpernel and his exploits, and Sir Percy Blakeney, who usually was half asleep in a chair whenever the subject cropped up, was dragged out of his slumbers by the ladies and asked with many a jest what he thought of the national hero. Whereupon he would endeavour to be polite and to smother a yawn, whilst he gave reply: "Excuse me, ladies, but on my honour I would prefer not to think of that demmed fellow."

And he would turn to a group of friends and call to them: "Come Froggie, Ffoulkes, you too, Tony, a manly game of hazard, what, while the ladies sit around and worship a cursed shadow."

No, no, a thousand times no! This empty-headed dandy, this

fool, this sybarite, could never have been the grimy out-at-elbows fiddler who slung a man over his shoulder as if he were a bundle of shavings, or the sergeant who carried *maman* in his arms over rough ground from the coach to the lonely house by the roadside. But the next moment, as Sir Percy Blakeney strode out of the room, Cécile would catch a quick glance which flew to him from the deep violet eyes of Lady Blakeney, his exquisite wife, and another which that perfect *grande dame* exchanged with His Royal Highness, and Cécile Pradel, who owed her life to the Scarlet Pimpernel, was left wondering. Wondering!

Still peeping through the curtain which has fallen on the last act of the drama, one likes to see little Blanche Levet as a young matron now, married to a well-to-do and kindly fellow who stands well with the authorities that are in power after the terrible days of the Terror and the fall of Robespierre. There are times when memories and regrets become over-poignant, and she sheds tears over the bundle of tiny garments which she has fashioned in view of a happy eventuality, just as there are times when Docteur Pradel would gladly exchange the life of peace in England for one of activity in Choisy and in his beloved hospital in Manderieu. But with him regrets soon vanish, whereas with Blanche they will always abide.

And one last peep at St. John Devinne, home on leave after the English victory over the French at Valenciennes, and kneeling by the death-bed of his father. Percy Blakeney stands beside him. Some of the last words the old man spoke were: "Percy, you will look after the boy, won't you? He is headstrong, but his heart is in the right place, and, thank God, his honour is intact."

BARONESS ORCZY

THE ELUSIVE PIMPERNEL

In this, the sequel to *The Scarlet Pimpernel*, French agent and chief spycatcher Chauvelin is as crafty as ever, but Sir Percy Blakeney is more than a match for his arch-enemy. Meanwhile the beautiful Marguerite remains wholly devoted to Sir Percy, her husband. Cue more swashbuckling adventures as Sir Percy attempts to smuggle French aristocrats out of the country to safety.

THE LAUGHING CAVALIER

The year is 1623, the place Haarlem in the Netherlands. Diogenes – the first Sir Percy Blakeney, the Scarlet Pimpernel's ancestor – and his friends Pythagoras and Socrates defend justice and the royalist cause. The famous artist Frans Hals also makes an appearance in this historical adventure: Orczy maintains that Hals' celebrated portrait *The Laughing Cavalier* is actually a portrayal of the Scarlet Pimpernel's ancestor.

Baroness Orczy

The League of the Scarlet Pimpernel

More adventures amongst the terrors of revolutionary France. No one has uncovered the identity of the famous Scarlet Pimpernel – no one except his wife Marguerite and his arch-enemy, citizen Chauvelin. Sir Percy Blakeney is still at large, however, evading capture…

Leatherface

The Prince saw a 'figure of a man, clad in dark, shapeless woollen clothes wearing a hood of the same dark stuff over his head and a leather mask over his face'. The year is 1572 and the Prince of Orange is at Mons under night attack from the Spaniards. However Leatherface raises the alarm in the nick of time. The mysterious masked man has vowed to reappear – when His Highness' life is in danger. Who is Leatherface? And when will he next be needed?

Baroness Orczy

The Triumph of the Scarlet Pimpernel

It is Paris, 1794, and Robespierre's revolution is inflicting its reign of terror. The elusive Scarlet Pimpernel is still at large – so far. But the sinister agent Chauvelin has taken prisoner his darling Marguerite. Will she act as a decoy and draw the Scarlet Pimpernel to the enemy? And will our dashing hero evade capture and live to enjoy a day 'when tyranny was crushed and men dared to be men again'?

The Way of the Scarlet Pimpernel

The year is 1793, the darkest days of the French Revolution, and little Charles-Léon is ill. The delicate son of Louise and Bastien de Croissy is recommended country air, but travel permits are needed – and impossible to come by. Louise's friend, Josette, believes she knows a way out. For Josette is convinced that her hero, the Scarlet Pimpernel, will come to their rescue. She refuses to believe that he only exists in her imagination. 'I say that the Scarlet Pimpernel can do anything! And I mean to get in touch with him,' she vows, and sets forth into the streets of Paris…

Made in the USA
Lexington, KY
21 December 2013